The firestorm continued

Bolan was out of frags, and tear gas wasn't going to stop a helicopter. There was a chimney directly behind the cement stairwell. He ran for it.

He dived behind the chimney and ducked as the chopper fired a barrage of tracers into his former position. Bolan rose and emptied his entire magazine into the cockpit. Slugs whined and the nose of the chopper spun to track him. The M-16 couldn't penetrate the Russian crash-proof aircraft glass.

Bolan dropped and the chimney began to come apart under the onslaught. He reached for the Desert Eagle. Its heavy .44 Magnum rounds were likely to smash through the cockpit of the helicopter, but he would have to stand in front of the machine guns to do it.

He was ready.

D0018028

MACK BOLAN ®
The Executioner

DON PENDLETON'S
THE EXECUTIONER®
SKYSNIPER

A GOLD EAGLE BOOK FROM
WORLDWIDE®

TORONTO • NEW YORK • LONDON
AMSTERDAM • PARIS • SYDNEY • HAMBURG
STOCKHOLM • ATHENS • TOKYO • MILAN
MADRID • WARSAW • BUDAPEST • AUCKLAND

If you purchased this book without a cover you should be aware that this book is stolen property. It was reported as "unsold and destroyed" to the publisher, and neither the author nor the publisher has received any payment for this "stripped book."

For my Muse, Valerie Jane Swartz

First edition October 2000
ISBN 0-373-64263-6

Special thanks and acknowledgment to
Chuck Rogers for his contribution to this work.

SKYSNIPER

Copyright © 2000 by Worldwide Library.

All rights reserved. Except for use in any review, the reproduction or utilization of this work in whole or in part in any form by any electronic, mechanical or other means, now known or hereafter invented, including xerography, photocopying and recording, or in any information storage or retrieval system, is forbidden without the written permission of the publisher, Worldwide Library, 225 Duncan Mill Road, Don Mills, Ontario, Canada M3B 3K9.

All characters in this book have no existence outside the imagination of the author and have no relation whatsoever to anyone bearing the same name or names. They are not even distantly inspired by any individual known or unknown to the author, and all incidents are pure invention.

® and TM are trademarks of the publisher. Trademarks indicated with ® are registered in the United States Patent and Trademark Office, the Canadian Trade Marks Office and in other countries.

Printed in U.S.A.

When were the good and the brave ever in the majority?

—Henry David Thoreau

I once read that there is no evil in the world. That there is only weakness, temptation, hardship and pain. That's true, and these are the places where the monsters are born.

—Mack Bolan

THE
MACK BOLAN®
LEGEND

Nothing less than a war could have fashioned the destiny of the man called Mack Bolan. Bolan earned the Executioner title in the jungle hell of Vietnam.

But this soldier also wore another name—Sergeant Mercy. He was so tagged because of the compassion he showed to wounded comrades-in-arms and Vietnamese civilians.

Mack Bolan's second tour of duty ended prematurely when he was given emergency leave to return home and bury his family, victims of the Mob. Then he declared a one-man war against the Mafia.

He confronted the Families head-on from coast to coast, and soon a hope of victory began to appear. But Bolan had broken society's every rule. That same society started gunning for this elusive warrior—to no avail.

So Bolan was offered amnesty to work within the system against terrorism. This time, as an employee of Uncle Sam, Bolan became Colonel John Phoenix. With a command center at Stony Man Farm in Virginia, he and his new allies—Able Team and Phoenix Force—waged relentless war on a new adversary: the KGB.

But when his one true love, April Rose, died at the hands of the Soviet terror machine, Bolan severed all ties with Establishment authority.

Now, after a lengthy lone-wolf struggle and much soul-searching, the Executioner has agreed to enter an "arm's-length" alliance with his government once more, reserving the right to pursue personal missions in his Everlasting War.

1

Kosovo

"Control, has there been any movement around the hostages?"

Barbara Price's voice came across the satellite link from Stony Man Farm in Virginia. "Negative, Striker," the mission controller said. "No movement. We believe the hostels remain unaware of our operation."

"What's my window?"

"We have thirty minutes of satellite time before we have to switch. You're on schedule. Satellite triangulation has you on course, three miles out from objective."

The man known as the Executioner made his decision. "Affirmative. Proceeding as scheduled."

Mack Bolan moved through the predawn darkness. The subdued splinter pattern of his raid suit was nearly invisible to the naked eye, but it also disrupted the pattern of his body to light-amplification devices. The fibers of the suit were woven of several layers of chemically treated fabrics that broke up and reduced his heat signature to infrared viewing. Bolan was a shadow moving among shadows.

The terrorists had made a major mistake. They thought they were well hidden up in the woods, outside the spectrum of United States Intelligence.

The terrorists should have kept their hostages in the city. Bolan would have kept them downtown, in a fortified town block. Such a stronghold would prevent a counteroperation from being mounted. A major firefight within the city would create international attention from the many news crews there. The terrorists could have filled the area with their own friendlies, as well as forced the rescue team to risk killing innocent civilians. Instead, they had gone up into the hills outside the city and hidden in a farmhouse. It was a terrible blunder to go hide in the trees, and a classic blunder many urban terrorists made. It was one of the great advantages the good guys had.

"Any movement?" Bolan asked.

"None, Striker. We have four hostiles on sentry duty in the woods. Intelligence tells us at least three more are in the house. All armed with automatic rifles. No heavier weapons are suspected. We see no lights."

"Affirmative," Bolan answered as he moved on through the purple of predawn.

There were two hostages, both American journalists. Andy Reed was well-known for his work for the cable news networks in trouble spots around the world. Sarah Hedner's work was much less publicized. Her face had never appeared on the evening news. She had never been nominated for a Pulitzer Prize. Her journalism consisted of support work for stories that broke across the wire services. Even less publicized than her journalistic work was the fact that she was also a CIA field operative and a highly valued information resource. She had been invaluable in Baghdad during the Gulf War and in the ongoing crises in Sarajevo. Her base of operations had been moved to Kosovo. She had been doing both of her jobs with her usual élan when the kidnapping had occurred.

The CIA believed the terrorists had no idea who she really was. They didn't intend to lose such a highly valued resource. Both she and Reed were American citizens. However, the city of Pristina, in the area of Kosovo, wasn't a place the administration in Washington felt comfortable sending in Delta Force or a team of Navy SEALs. It was a delicate situation in the extreme, both politically and militarily, and the last message from the kidnappers had been that the hostages would be killed if their demands weren't been met in the next twenty-four hours. That had been twenty-three hours ago.

Mack Bolan moved through the trees, skirting the patches of snow on the ground.

He cradled a Colt 9 mm submachine gun. It looked like a stunted version of a U.S. Army M-16 rifle. The telescoping stock was collapsible, the barrel was shortened to eleven inches and its entire length shrouded by the hand guard. The hand guard surrounded the perforated barrel with a series of baffles that reduced the muzzle-blast and firing signature of the weapon to a whispering chuff as the 9 mm subsonic rounds found their target. A laser sighting device was mounted over the barrel and projected a laser dot on the target up to two hundred meters. The laser's frequency was invisible to the human eye, but not to the light amplifiers in Bolan's night-vision goggles. No target would know when it had been designated, or hear the shot that terminated it. The weapon's express purpose was stealth, an invisible attack and a silent kill.

Beneath the barrel of the weapon was an M-203 40 mm grenade launcher for when it was time to break the silence.

Bolan closed on his objective. The snow was thin on the ground and the rolling mountainside and thin pine forest made for easy going. At half a mile he stopped and examined the objective. The house was a typical Slavic mountain dwelling. Half stone, half wood, the house could easily have been a hundred years old. The door was thick wood bound with iron. Deeper in a thicket of trees Bolan could see two Yugo compact cars underneath camouflage netting, boughs and shrubs. Beside them was a pair of Russian-made jeeps. He examined the house more closely. The windows were covered by heavy wooden shutters. No light came out through any cracks in the windows or the door. Bolan suspected they had been covered with blankets from the inside. No smoke came out from the chimney. The night was overcast, and without night-vision equipment, the darkened house would have been invisible under the trees.

Bolan closed in to 150 yards and turned his attention to the sentries.

The closest was fifty yards away. An AK-74 rifle was slung over his shoulder and Russian-made night-vision binoculars were slung around his neck. A radio receiver was buckled under the epaulet of his field jacket. He leaned against a tree, and his breath misted in the green-and-gray landscape of Bolan's night-vision. The man was the epitome of a bored sentry. Each of the other guards was similarly armed and equipped, and each was approximately a hundred yards away from the house, forming a loose diamond pattern. Three were visible, and Bolan assumed the fourth was behind the house to complete the formation.

"Is the fourth sentry behind the house?"

"Affirmative, Striker. The house should be directly between the two of you."

Bolan closed to one hundred yards.

The sentries were obviously not expecting company. Informants in the villages lower down the mountain would have alerted them to any strangers operating in the area. Anyone coming up the road would be easily spotted by day or night.

Bolan had jumped from a B-2 Stealth bomber to a tiny plateau four miles across the mountain ridge and made his way cross-country to his objective.

Bolan made his decision. "Keep Jack hot. I'm going in."

The big man hurled himself to the ground as his night-vision goggles solarized under the sudden glare of spotlights. An automatic weapon tore into the trees ahead. There had been a ditch in the ground to his right, and Bolan continued his roll until he fell a foot and then rolled into the cold mud of a rivulet. He flipped up his goggles.

"Striker! The objective is lit up like a Christmas tree! Get out of there!" Barbara Price shouted in his ear.

"Roger that." Bolan looked up, squinting. The glare was blinding. Spotlights were sweeping the trees. The light was constant, which told him that the source was floodlights mounted in the trees. Somehow he had tripped an alarm. But he was nearly invisible to infrared scanners. His night-vision goggles were sensitive to the range of light used in laser trip wires, and he would have seen the ghostly glow of the security beams that would have been woven like a web through the trees. Motion sensors in the ground wouldn't be an ideal choice in a forest that was experiencing a spring thaw and snowfall. The most likely method would have been magnetometers set in a perimeter around the house to form a very low frequency magnetic field. That field would be interrupted by someone carrying metallic objects like rifles, pistols, handguns, grenades and knives. Setting up a perimeter defence with magnetometers would be an expensive proposition, and would require someone who knew a great deal about security measures. Bolan's instincts had been right. This wasn't a rescue operation.

This was a trap.

Bolan looked up again.

The telltale green tracers of Russian-based weapons hissed through the trees. Most of them were flying high and wide, which told him the enemy didn't know exactly where he was. The door to the house flew open with a bang.

Dobermans came streaming out of the house. Even if the enemy couldn't pinpoint his position, the coursing canines didn't have any such problem. Their range of hearing was three to four times as good as a human's. Their sense of smell was incredible.

Bolan wore Kevlar body armor and camouflage greasepaint on his face. With his chemically-treated raid suit, Bolan smelled nothing like the sentries guarding the house. He was an intruder.

The six-pack of attack dogs changed course and arrowed directly toward Bolan.

For all their superior senses, Dobermans weren't search dogs or trackers. Search dogs were adept at picking up air scents and went over an area of ground yard by yard. Tracker dogs ran on a leash and followed ground scents. Dobermans were adept at neither task. They had but one function, and that was to find and kill intruders at close range. At ninety-plus pounds of muscle and bone, there was no beast raised by man that was more efficient for the task.

There was no way to outrun them, but Bolan was unwilling to reveal his position by firing on the dogs. Bolan sank back down into his culvert and pulled a grenade from his bandolier. He could hear the rapid pattering of the dogs' feet hitting the snow as they homed in on him. The soldier pulled the pin and one of the dogs barked as it heard the tiny scrape of metal on metal. He counted to two. The dogs were nearly on top of him. Bolan tossed the grenade up and over the edge of his cover.

White light, brighter than the glare of the floodlights, pulsed over the culvert and thunder rolled through the trees. Even in daylight the intensity of the burning magnesium flare of the flash-bang stun grenade was blinding. To an animal with a sense of hearing several times greater than a human's, the supersonic crack and concussion wave was the end of the world. The brimstone scent of burned magnesium would degrade their sense of smell for hours.

Bolan rose.

Five of the dogs lay on their sides panting and twitching with all of their major sense organs overwhelmed. The pack leader tottered drunkenly, and then fell over in abject surrender.

The grenade launcher beneath his carbine was loaded with a similar munition. Bolan aimed at a cluster of floodlights up in the trees and fired. He turned his head as the weapon boomed and flared and the blast wave shattered the lights. A welcome cloak of darkness fell. Tracers streamed through the trees to his previous position as he ran and reloaded his grenade launcher. Bolan kneeled behind a tree and took aim at one of the sentries. He squeezed the Colt carbine's trigger, and a short burst walked up the sentry's chest and toppled him into the snow.

"Striker, what is your situation?"

Armed men were pouring out of the house.

"Numerous hostiles! Far more than predicted. Situation going out of control." Bolan chose another group of lights and squeezed two bursts from his sound-suppressed weapon into them. Glass shattered and sparks flew as more darkness fell over the forest.

"What is the hostage situation?"

"I suspect no hostages present. This is a trap to suck in the rescue force for capture or kill. Request immediate extraction!"

"Affirmative, Striker. Break contact. Head due—"

Bolan's earpiece went dead.

"This is Striker. Come back."

There was no sound in the earpiece. Not even static. Bolan switched to his emergency frequency. "This is Striker. Come back."

Silence answered. Bolan opened a flap on his vest, and the little green light told him he was transmitting. He ripped out his earpiece as he moved and pulled his spare from his pack. He plugged it in and twisted it into his ear. "This is Striker. Come back."

The second receiver was as dead as the first.

Bolan smothered a curse as he moved. It seemed that a platoon was boiling out of the mountain house. He took a second to reconnoiter. The men coming out were still in the glare of the lights. Each man had night-vision goggles pushed up on his forehead, ready to be deployed once he hit the forest.

Things were going from bad to worse.

The killers weren't going to get a free shot at him. Bolan picked a lane through the trees. He squeezed the M-203's trigger, and a white-phosphorus grenade detonated in the midst of the charging men. Molten metal and superheated smoke exploded in streamers like a lethal Fourth of July display. Men screamed. Tracers reached out for Bolan as men outside of the grenade's radius fired at his muzzle-flash.

For a moment Bolan considered going to his tactical radio. His satellite transmission was almost impossible to pinpoint. A radio transmission could be easily triangulated on by even limited equipment.

Bolan assumed his adversaries had limited equipment at the very least. Bolan tore across the mountainside toward his primary extraction point.

A voice spoke in his ear. "Striker! Come back."

"This is Striker! What happened?"

"We lost satellite transmission. The second satellite has crossed your position horizon. We have your signal."

Bolan gave this fleeting consideration. It was difficult to interfere with a satellite transmission. It would require equipment that only a major power like the United States, the former Soviet Union or NATO could field, and it would have to be in place locally. It was just about out of the realm of possibility, and it was just as unlikely that a Pentagon top secret security satellite could suffer a major systems malfunction.

The Executioner gave it no more thought. ''What do you see?''

''We have major movement. Vehicles are deploying. Two are heading south down the road. Two are deploying through the trees.''

Bolan grimaced. The Yugos would be taking the road back down the mountain. It was within the realm of possibility that the hostages had indeed been in the house, and he was running for his life in the opposite direction of the people he had been sent to save. That was speculation. He had no doubt about the other two vehicles. Those were the all-terrain vehicles. They coming for him.

Bolan considered the situation. The clearing he was running for was the most obvious place for an extraction. If the enemy had gone to all this trouble to set a trap for a rescue or reconnaissance mission, it was highly likely they had considered this themselves.

''This is Striker. I am heading for secondary extraction site. Advise Jack that—''

''Striker! We have lost observation. Repeat, we have lost observation. We are blind. Recommend you—'' Bolan's earpiece went dead. A snarl ripped out of his throat. This was well beyond the purview of Murphy's law. A well-worn saying in British Intelligence rang in his mind: Once was happenstance. Twice was coincidence. Three times was enemy action.

Bolan loaded an armor-piercing projectile into the breech of his grenade launcher as he ran. He didn't know whether Barbara Price approved of his switching extraction sites or whether it was even safe. He no longer had a good path toward it, but it now had one advantage. His path would take him where even jeeps would have problems. Bolan broke his easterly course. He checked the compass in the bezel of his watch and headed due west. At one hundred yards the rolling mountainside fell away steeply. The soldier leaned back and began chatter stepping down the mountain.

A sound rose over the sound of Bolan's own breathing and his hammering heart. His teeth flashed in the dark in rage. The sound was the baying of dogs. It occurred to Bolan that there had to be a good-sized bunker beneath that hundred-year-old stone-and-timber mountain house. The dogs were a more immediate problem. Dobermans rarely barked, much less bayed. These would be tracker dogs.

He was outnumbered and outgunned. He had lost his eye in the sky and communication with the outside world. He stood a good chance of losing the jeeps, but he had no chance of losing the dogs. He also suspected that the enemy wouldn't make the same mistake and release the dogs as they had before. They would run them on leads and keep them close to the gunmen. Only when the humans had sighted Bolan would they then release the dogs to pull him down or distract his fire as gunmen closed in for the kill.

That was his only chance. He would have to beat the men handling the dogs. He had only one card left to play, and that was sheer athletic ability. The words of his drill sergeant reached out to Bolan across time and space and barked in his brain. "Running downhill is easy, ladies! Just lean forward and raise your knees!"

Bolan leaned forward. His feet left the ground and then fell in great hammer strikes as he lifted his knees. His stride became great bounds. Tree branches whipped at him as he practically fell down the mountainside at a dead run. Empty space yawed ahead of him as he bounded over a bush. He had fifteen yards of mountainside left, and then it dropped away.

There was no way to stop.

There were trees that rose beyond the drop-off. Bolan aimed at one of them and accelerated.

Both of his feet left the earth. He tossed away his carbine. His legs still ran in midair as his arms windmilled. He wasn't going to reach the branch he had aimed at. His soaring turned into falling almost immediately. Branches smashed at him as he fell. His hands clawed as limbs broke and pine needles pulled and slipped sappily through his fingers. Pine trees were like ladders with their branches almost always laid out horizontally from the trunk. Bolan's boot caught and he was twisted in midfall. The air smashed out of his lungs as a bough rammed into his chest. Only the ceramic trauma plate of his body armor kept his rib cage from cracking.

His body slid off the bough. He instinctively reached out and his arms hooked over the next branch as he slid past it. Bolan hung by his armpits and tried to suck air into his burning lungs.

Remarkably, his night-vision goggles were still on his head. However, only his left eye was showing him anything. He looked back up toward the top of the mountain. He couldn't see anyone, but he heard voices and the barking of the dogs. They knew he had gone down the mountainside. The question was, would they try to follow him, or did they know of ways to flank him?

Bolan climbed down the tree. The branches formed a convenient ladder, but they stopped twenty feet off of the ground. Bolan hung by his hands from the lowest branch and dropped. His heels hit the soft snow and he bent his knees and rolled as he hit. The force of it still rattled his bones and clacked his jaws together.

Bolan slid the Beretta Model 93-R machine pistol out of its holster and flipped the selector lever to burst mode. Above the treetops a searchlight swept through. The sound of engines grinding in low gear echoed, and Bolan knew that somehow the enemy jeeps were finding a way down the mountain. The soldier checked his compass and broke back into a run.

He switched on his tactical radio. With the satellites out, he would have to hope that if he was indeed going to be rescued, someone would try to reach him.

The supersonic crack of a bullet passed over Bolan's head. The enemy had sniper rifles with night-vision scopes. The setup had been a trap from the get-go. Someone wanted to bring down a United States rescue team, and they had wanted it bad enough to expend an immense amount of effort.

"Striker." Bolan's earpiece crackled. Jack Grimaldi's voice came through over the sound of rotor noise. "Striker, come in."

"This is Striker."

"Where are you? I'm inbound. ETA ten minutes," the pilot stated.

"I'm heading for secondary extraction site. I had to make a detour. Estimate you'll beat me to landing zone. LZ may be hot. Might have to Willie-Pete."

"Affirmative."

Bolan ran on. His LZ was a clearing he estimated was five klicks from his present position. He wove through the trees. He heard the sound of a vehicle several hundred yards off to his right. The jeep was trying to get ahead of him. The extraction sites had been picked so that a Black Hawk helicopter could land and pick up hostages. The enemy must have had the most likely extraction sites already picked out. Off to his left Bolan could hear the grinding of gears as the other jeep moved parallel in a pincer movement. Behind him the baying of the dogs had renewed in vigor.

He was being flanked.

"This is Striker. I'm cut off. Cannot make LZ."

"Affirmative. We have one moving vehicle in sight. Pick your spot and pop smoke."

"Affirmative."

Bolan could begin to hear the thunder of rotors up in the predawn sky. Orange fire suddenly lit up against the low clouds. For a scant second the swollen dragonfly shape of a Black Hawk helicopter was silhouetted in black. A streak of fire and white smoke hissed down from the helicopter and flew down into the trees. The forest lit up as the Hellfire missile detonated.

"One vehicle down. Be advised, Striker, men dismounted before detonation. You have hostiles ahead of you."

"Affirmative."

The trees ahead lit up with stuttering orange fire. Bolan recognized the hammering of a heavy machine gun. Tracers reached up into the sky for the helicopter. Bolan ran on. With his one working lens on his field glasses, he saw a creek cutting through the pines. A large moss-covered boulder astride it was the best strong point available. He splashed across the creek and folded himself into a crevasse in the rock. He took out a white-phosphorus grenade and pulled the pin. The cotter lever pinged away, and Bolan hurled it across the creek. Streamers of molten metal and white-hot smoke shot up into the sky. The rescue team now knew where he was.

So did everyone else within ten miles.

Bullets began smashing into the rocks around him.

Bolan pulled his last two white-phosohorus grenades and hurled them. The grenades detonated and acrid clouds of molten metal and superheated gas and smoke now formed a triangle around his position. The clouds of white-hot smoke would destroy the acuity of night-vision devices, and the thick white smoke would obscure Bolan, as well. But it wouldn't prevent people from lobbing fragmentation grenades into his position.

It was time to get out of Dodge.

"This is Striker. Am abandoning EZ. Look for light fifty yards north of the willie petes. Downstream."

"Affirmative."

The soldier leaped out of the rocks.

Bolan slid down the moss and splashed into the creek. The fact that the frigid water constricted his lungs and made him gasp told him his armor had held. Bolan took a deep breath and submerged himself. The spring thaw had swelled the creek. Bolan's fingers touched the mud four feet below. His fingers almost felt as if they were burning with the intense cold. The creek was barely melted snow and he immediately felt his limbs slow. His blood was leaving his extremities in a desperate attempt to keep his internal organs working.

Bolan stayed submerged and forced his failing limbs to drag him downstream. The light of the burning phosphorus quickly faded to black. The burning in his own lungs fought with the numbness in his arms and legs. Bolan gave in and surfaced. His shuddering legs pushed toward shore. He could no longer feel his hands and feet and he had to walk himself out of the freezing water on his knees and elbows.

The Serbian night wasn't much better. He would quickly succumb to hypothermia without help.

Bolan reached down to his web gear where he kept a miniflashlight. He couldn't feel his hands, much less fumble open the pouch in his webbing and work the flashlight.

"Striker! Where are you? We're taking ground fire! We don't see you!"

Bolan's teeth chattered in his skull. The wind was sucking every bit of heat out of his body. "This...is...Striker."

"Are you hit?"

"No."

"We can't see you!"

"Wait." Bolan's clouding mind sought an option. He could bite the pin out of a grenade but he couldn't throw it or crawl out of its lethal radius before it detonated. The Beretta 93-R was a lump in his thigh holster. Bolan clasped deadened palms against the grips and dragged the pistol free.

"Striker!"

He managed to jam the butt against his stomach and hook his thumb through the trigger guard. He couldn't feel it, but his thumb had to be against the trigger. "R-red tracers."

"Repeat, Striker! Repeat!"

Bolan had to drag his whole arm backward to move his hand. The gun against his stomach squirmed in his numb fingers and rattled off a 3-round burst into the sky.

"Striker! Where are you?"

Bolan sucked in a shuddering breath. "Red tracers." He yanked off two more bursts.

"Roger, Striker! Repeat signal!"

Bolan dragged his thumb against the trigger and the pistol twisted out of his hands. He squinted as rotor wash whipped the trees overhead. The night lit up. There was a sound like ripping canvas as the Black Hawk's .50-caliber gatling guns began tearing into the trees at over a hundred rounds per second.

A black shape detached from the helicopter and plunged down toward Bolan like a spider.

Carl Lyons roared in Bolan's ear. "Are you hit?"

A harness was hooked under his arms before he could respond. There was a yank and Bolan felt himself leave the ground. The Gatling tore into the outlying forest and stalked each tracer that reached up toward the helicopter. Hands seized Bolan and his boots clattered numbly on the metal floor of the helicopter's cabin.

Lyons looked carefully into his face as he patted him down for wounds. "You look cold."

Bolan couldn't tell whether this was an attempt at humor or careful observation. With Lyons you could never be sure.

2

American Embassy, Macedonia

"Well, that was a total goat f—"

Carl Lyons censored himself at the last second as he remembered Barbara Price and Aaron Kurtzman were linked on the secure intercom. Lyons was as close to being a human juggernaut as one could come, but he had remarkably good manners around people he considered civilized.

Bolan shook his head. "I'm sorry, Carl. Our intelligence was good. This wasn't a botched rescue effort. Someone wanted to suck in some SEALs or Special Operations Group boys and lead them into a massacre. It was a trap someone had laid months in advance. But that doesn't bother me," Bolan said as he wrapped both hands around his coffee and shivered slightly under the blanket wrapped over his shoulders. "What intrigues the hell out of me is how they managed to block communications between me and two of our best satellites. Much less blind our dedicated observation platform. It couldn't have been a malfunction."

Price's voice was crystal clear across the link. "Oh, it wasn't."

"How did they make them malfunction? The only thing I can imagine would be a computer virus, but how some Serbian terrorists could uplink a virus into our military intelligence satellites is beyond me."

"It wasn't a virus."

Lyons frowned as he took a sip of coffee. "What's the status of the three satellites?"

"They're gone."

Bolan straightened in his chair. "Gone?"

"Gone. As in they are no longer transmitting or receiving. Their radar profiles have been altered, which implies they have taken severe structural damage. We're assuming they have purposefully been destroyed."

Bolan and Lyons exchanged glances.

Jack Grimaldi set down his espresso. "The last time I heard, the only people with antisatellite capability were us and the Russians."

Bolan nodded. "That's true. We have some prototype anti-satellite missiles that can be launched from jets at high altitude. But I find it hard to believe that Serbian terrorists could have broken into Langley Air Force Base and stolen one of our most technologically advanced missile systems."

"Well, it's even more difficult than that. Our ASAT missile is designed to be launched from a specially modified F-15. Even then, that F-15 has to be vectored from the ground by a tracking station capable of monitoring satellites. There's no way our system can be deployed by anyone except us. We ran a check with Air Force intelligence. All of our missiles are accounted for. Neither of the specially modified F-15s were airborne during your operation."

Lyons grimaced before taking a sip of his coffee. "That leaves the Russians."

Kurtzman sighed over the link. "Well, the problem with that is the only operational ASAT capability the Russians have are some antisatellite satellites. The system is still in place, but it's pretty damn crude. Their ASAT satellites are really just giant shotgun shells parked in orbit over the earth. They have to use maneuvering jets to creep up close to another satellite, and then blast it to pieces with a pattern of unguided projectiles, and by close, I mean within several hundred yards. In space, that literally means eyeball-to-eyeball.

"This was marginally effective against some of our earlier intelligence platforms. They didn't have tactical warning systems or any real maneuvering capability of their own. That's all changed. The Russian system was first fielded in the early 1980s.

Since then our technology had grown by light-years. If a strange Russian satellite began creeping into the orbit of one of our intelligence satellites, our ground tracking would detect it hours before it got into range. The onboard tactical warning systems on our newer satellites would detect an intruder almost as fast.''

Bolan leaned back in his chair. ''I suppose neither ground tracking or the onboard tacticals detected any suspicious objects sidling up close before our three satellites went missing.''

''No. Not a thing. According to both NORAD and the Pentagon, it was clear skies and then all three of our platforms went dead. Even then, why in God's name would the Russians take out three of our satellites? We know they are the only people with the capability. It would be equivalent to an act of war.''

''Bear, what about X-ray lasers?'' Jack Grimaldi asked, using Kurtzman's nickname. ''I know some shuttle jocks over at the Cape who said there were rumors that the Russians had deployed some satellites with that capability. They said an X-ray laser deployed in space could cut a shuttle in half even through its heat-reflecting reentry tiles.''

''I had considered that. An X-ray-laser-armed satellite would have fit the bill very nicely. They are highly accurate. They can engage multiple targets simultaneously. They have nearly infinite range. If your math was good, you could hit a target on the moon from an earth orbit. There's only one problem with that scenario.''

''What's that?''

''With current technology, there is no way to pump enough energy into an X-ray laser to make it work unless you use a nuclear weapon as the power source, and we're talking about a weapon of at least ten kilotons. If someone had used an X-ray laser last night, it would have lit up every early-warning system on earth. Millions of people would have seen the flash. I know you guys have been incommunicado, but I assure you, no such event made the papers this morning.

''Another problem is the timing. An X-ray laser can take out as many targets as you have laser rods on the satellite, but the nuclear explosion that powers the satellite also destroys it. It's a one-shot deal. The satellite has to take out all of its targets at the same time. It only has a few milliseconds before it's vaporized. Last night our satellites were taken out one by one, with a interval of two to ten minutes between each hit. This just isn't within an X-ray weapon's profile.''

Any conversation with Kurtzman was bound to be highly educational, Bolan thought. ''I suppose we've contacted the Russians?''

''The President spoke with their president a little more than an hour ago. The Russians deny having anything to do with it,'' Barbara Price answered.

Lyons spoke in a low growl. ''They always do.''

''I know how you feel, Carl, but the President believes them, and in this situation, so do I. They would have had nothing to gain by last night's action, except severe degeneration of relations with the United States. The former Soviet Union is in such desperate straits these days, they would be very circumspect in doing anything to get on our bad side. They would have to have a hell of a lot to gain to do this, and no one in the know can think of a thing.''

Neither could Bolan. ''I agree. I don't think the Russians had anything to do with this, at least not their government, but I'm not buying last night's rescue mission and the loss of the satellites being a coincidence. They're connected. There has to be another player involved.''

Bolan could almost hear the wheels turning in Kurtzman's mind.

''So one would think,'' Kurtzman responded.

Lyons didn't look happy. ''So we're back to square one. The mission remains the same. We've still got two American hostages missing. One's an innocent civilian, and the other is a valuable CIA asset. Their time is running short.''

Kurtzman's voice brightened. ''Well, now there we have something.''

Bolan perked an eyebrow. ''Oh.''

''Well, it's obvious the setup was a trap. The opposition was clearly expecting some kind of rescue attempt. What the opposition didn't expect, however, was Striker dropping in on them out of the belly of a B-2 Stealth bomber. Our observation satellite detected vehicles moving down the mountain by road, while the jeeps went after you cross-country. We had the B-2 turn back and loiter when we lost communication with you and the satellites. It couldn't get any kind of bead on you, Striker, but its infrared image picked up the fleeing vehicles with ease. We had the B-2 track them from high altitude.''

Bolan, Lyons and Grimaldi sat up in their seats as one. "I suppose the boys up in the *Spirit of Texas* managed to find out where our friends went," Bolan stated.

"Oh, they did, and they took high-resolution photos, as well."

"I'm faxing them to you right now," Barbara Price said. "You have presidential authorization to resume the rescue operation. We don't believe your playmates will expect to get hit again so soon."

"IT WAS a total disaster!"

Commander Branko Nemanja sat in the tin shack and sweltered in the tropical heat. He took a sip from the sweating bottle of beer and spoke into the Russian-made secure communications link. "On the contrary, Viktor. I would call the exercise an unmitigated success."

"What? The rescue team escaped. Many of our men are dead. The location has been compromised. You call this unmitigated success?"

"Oh, indeed. We have destroyed three of their most powerful military communication and observation satellites. They have no idea who did it or how it was done."

"But we wanted bodies, prisoners."

Nemanja sighed. That would have, indeed, been preferable, but it was a minor setback at best. One that wouldn't have occurred had he been in command. However, he had seen the plans and had found them fairly well thought out. That the tactical aspect of the operation had failed was troubling, and he couldn't easily chalk it up to the incompetence of others.

The commander didn't let himself get distracted. "The fact

that we took no prisoners is of little consequence. It's a secondary objective. If the leaders really want the heads of some American Special Forces operatives, that can be arranged. In the meantime we have struck a great blow, and what's more, the Americans have failed. We still have the hostages. Indeed, with little planning, we can run almost the same operation, and this time we can ensure its success."

These last words weren't lost on Viktor Stasny. The commander had come up with the initial strategy, but he had been excluded from the planning of the trap itself. It was clear that next time the tactical situation should be left to a man with military experience. It galled him, but Stasney had to admit Nemanja was right. "I understand what you are saying. I'll forward my own personal recommendation to this effect."

The commander actually smiled. For a political toad, Stasny actually seemed to have a brain. "Thank you. Our strategic success had much to do with your efforts."

The line was silent for a moment. "Thank you. I appreciate that."

The commander snorted to himself. Politicians were utterly predictable. They were ruled by their egos. It cost nothing to stroke them, and in this case, the flattery was actually true. "What's the situation with the hostages?"

"Ah, they have been safely transported to a village we control. They'll be safe there until we move them into the city. Once there, they will be beyond the help of anyone."

"I recommend you move them as quickly as possible," Nemanja stated.

"It will be done in a few hours," Stasny replied.

3

Serbia

Mack Bolan watched the endless hills roll by. The country was rugged but green and fertile. Off on a hillside the remains of a fallen MIG-29 rusted in a crumpled heap. One wing tip stood out of the wreckage like a tombstone beneath the leaden sky where it had fallen victim to a NATO jet. The morning sun was hidden behind clouds that almost seemed to reach the ground and drizzled and misted incessantly. The thick wool sweater he wore resisted the morning cold, but Bolan still shivered.

The seat of his overalls were soaked through, and he had nearly gone into hypothermia less than four hours ago. Sitting in the back of a hay wagon in the rain wasn't doing him any good. Lyons handed him a thermos of hot coffee without being asked. They rumbled toward their objective.

The tractor-drawn hay wagon wasn't an ideal assault vehicle, but it didn't earn a second glance on the muddy one-lane road, either. The size of the men on the wagon couldn't be hidden, but their bulky sweaters and overalls hid the weapons they carried. Within the haystack itself was a small arsenal of heavier equipment. With their muddy boots, knit caps pulled down low and their shoulders hunched against the weather, they could easily be mistaken for hearty Serbian farmers working the land.

As long as no one had to speak.

Twice they had been hailed by trucks carrying workers that could have been clones of themselves. Bolan and his team had grunted, waved and kept on going. There had been a moment of tension as they pulled over to let a pickup truck carrying men in camouflage uniforms pass. The men in the truck bed had been bristling with AK-74 rifles. Bolan couldn't be sure whether they were police, paramilitary or Serbian regulars. The lines between those organizations were becoming extremely blurred. A big man in the back of the truck had hoisted his automatic rifle in salute. Bolan had recognized the words "good morning" and waved back. The armed men had all smiled.

Hay wagons were inherently a nonthreatening mode of transportation.

Carl Lyons lowered his gaze from the cloud cover he had been examining all morning. "It's going to break up fairly soon."

"What's our ETA, Ironman?"

Lyons carefully examined the surrounding hills and pointed a thick finger. "I'd say another ten minutes. I think the village is right on the other side of that hill."

Bolan nodded. He and Lyons were thinking along the same lines, which was always a good sign. There were few better measuring sticks of mission effectiveness than Lyons.

Jack Grimaldi drove the tractor. They had liberated it from a farm a few miles down the road. It was slow going. The tractor could make fifteen miles per hour with the pedal down. The open hay wagon offered no cover, and the flat little valley they trundled down offered even less.

Two bewildered United States Marines from the brigade in Macedonia sat in the hay wagon with them. Bolan would have preferred men from Able Team or Phoenix Force, or some Navy SEALs for that matter, but time had been of the essence. The two Marine sergeants were the closest and fastest assets he could lay his hands on, and both of them were Force Recon. Bolan had to admit he could have done much worse.

Sergeant Waikem chewed a piece of hay meditatively. He spoke with a thick Texas drawl. "Sir, what kind of opposition are we expecting?"

Bolan passed the thermos of coffee to the Marine. "Last night we met with heavy resistance, but we were expected. This time I believe we're going to achieve surprise."

Sergeant Judd's right hand never left the hay covering his M-16 rifle. "Are the hostages those news correspondents we heard about on CNN?"

"That's correct. You're both clear on the plan?"

"Crystal clear, sir."

Lyons's voice rumbled low as they passed between some low hills. "Here we go."

A little village appeared in a small depression of land between the hills. A creek ran through it and was spanned by a small stone bridge large enough to allow motor vehicles one at a time. Grimaldi drove the tractor straight for it.

Bolan consulted his map. "According to intelligence, most of the inhabitants actually live on farms in the surrounding hills. Most of them come into the village to go to church and do business. The population in the village is no more than 150. Two cars, both Yugo compacts, left the mountainside earlier. Counting the two hostages, that means that there are six hostiles from the mountain. The number of accomplices they have in the village is unknown. However, all Serbian men between the ages of twenty and fifty have had military training. They're probably not very good, but we have to assume every adult male in the village knows which end of an AK-47 is which, and over the past year the government has been passing out rifles like candy. The locals are more than likely to take the side of the opposition in any altercation we get into.

"The vehicles stopped at a barn at the edge of town. The B-2 was forced to cut and run at dawn. So if the vehicles are no longer there, then we're going to have to play it by ear."

Waikem looked at Bolan. "It kind of sounds like we're playing by ear already."

"Sergeant, we're playing this one by the skin of our teeth."

Grimaldi kept the tractor trundling toward the village. Some sheep were grazing on the hillsides. There were chickens behind wire in the outlying houses. The tractor crossed the bridge and went down the single road that formed the main street of the village. Few people were about. It was Sunday morning, and that was to the team's advantage. Most Serbs, particularly in the rural areas, were devout Greek Orthodox. The shadow of the steeple crossed them as they passed the little church. Most of the village's inhabitants were probably inside and unarmed.

An old man sat on his stoop smoking a cigarette. He waved cheerfully, and Sergeant Judd waved back as they passed. He muttered out of the corner of his mouth. "This is too easy—we're just walking right in."

"Don't worry, it'll—" Bolan smothered an impulse to draw a weapon and spoke low. "Heads up. Here we go."

Up ahead was an armed man. He sat leaning his chair against a wall. An AK-47 with the stock folded was resting across his knees. He smoked a cigarette and seemed bored. The hay wagon was the focus of his attention. His chair fell forward onto its front legs as he leisurely stood. The automatic rifle hung casually from his hand by the pistol grip. The man held up his left hand in a halting motion, and his lips moved his cigarette to the corner of his mouth.

Bolan kept his eyes on the man and kept his voice below the sound of the tractor's engine. "Judd, anyone behind us?"

"The old man is still outside. He may be asleep. He's not eyeballing us."

The tractor ground to a halt, but Grimaldi kept the engine running. The sentry spoke to Grimaldi, but the pilot knew no Serbian. Bolan knew only a few words, and whatever the sentry said was little more than a stream of vowels and consonants. "Lyons, you take him out. I'll screen. Judd, keep a lookout behind us."

The sentry spoke something at Grimaldi again. The pilot put his finger to his ear as if he couldn't hear over the engine. The sentry waved his hand to cut the motor. His rifle was still hung at his side by one hand. Bolan observed the safety was still on as he and Lyons hopped off the wagon. They walked forward with smiles on their faces. They both said good-morning in the stock Serbian phrases they knew.

The sentry waved his hand to cut the motor again. Unconsciously his rifle rose to fill his other hand. Bolan threw the coffee thermos underhand. It wasn't a powerful throw, but the thermos was heavy glass-lined aluminum. It flew end over end and hit the sentry square in the face. Lyons stepped forward and ripped the AK out of the man's hand and rammed the pistol grip up under his jaw, rendering the guard unconscious.

Lyons threw the rifle into the hay wagon and bodily tossed the sentry in behind it. Bolan took a quick look behind them. Judd gave him the thumbs-up. The old man down the lane was sleeping with his chin on his chest. Bolan scooped up the thermos and he and Lyons jumped back up in the wagon. It lurched as Grimaldi ground the gears and they continued on. Their objective lay straight ahead. A large barn stood on a slight rise just outside of the village.

Bolan poured some coffee on the sentry's head. He spluttered and jerked. Judd sat on him and pressed a .45 automatic with an attached sound suppressor against his temple. Bolan flexed one of the few phrases he had memorized during the morning. "In the barn, how many?"

The man blinked up at him. He was still dazed from the shot to the jaw Lyons had given him. Judd pressed the muzzle into the man's temple and leaned into it. Bolan repeated himself. Lyons leaned in close and slid a combat knife out of his sleeve. The man's eyes widened as he answered, "Eight."

Bolan decided this sounded reasonable. "Tie and gag him."

Lyons rapidly trussed the sentry and piled some hay over him. Bolan kept his eye on the barn. There were no cars outside, but they were probably inside. If the barn ran to form it would have a large main floor and a loft. Of course, there was always the possibility the enemy had dug a bunker beneath it and filled it with a platoon of Serbian paramilitaries. There was a shuttered window with a hay hoist above it. The shutter was open but Bolan couldn't see anyone inside. They closed within fifty yards.

"All right. Lyons, you give us our diversion and then cover us. Waikem and I take the front. Judd, you and Grimaldi go around the sides and take down anyone who bolts out the back."

Lyons began shoving hay bales aside. Judd and Waikem both pulled M-16 rifles out from under the hay. Grimaldi was steering the tractor with one hand. His sound-suppressed MAC-10 submachine gun filled the other. Lyons wrestled his own seventy-five-pound weapon onto its tripod and locked it into place. The Mk-19 belt-fed 40 mm automatic grenade launcher was a fearsome weapon. It looked like a machine gun on steroids, with a short stubby barrel that was a thick as a man's wrist. Lyons laid out three belts of ammo and then locked and loaded a fourth into the breech. He took the firing grips in both hands and nodded his readiness.

Bolan had his Colt submachine gun from the night before. Only now the laser sight had been removed and a daylight scope sat in its place. Bolan kept his carbine at his shoulder and his eye on the window of the loft.

The Executioner brought the scope to his eye.

A man appeared. He held a rifle in one hand and he used the other to lean out of the loft and peer at the oncoming tractor. His eyes flew wide at the sight of Lyons's heavy weapon mounted on the hay wagon. Bolan put his crosshairs on the man's chest and fired three times in rapid succession.

The 9 mm carbine was nearly silent by itself. Over the sound of the tractor's engine it was felt rather than heard. The subsonic bullets weren't man-stoppers, nor did they have the power to drive the man back into the loft. That was in Bolan's favor. Using the scope, his bullet placement was lethal. The man's grip on the loft window broke. To anyone inside, it would have appeared as if the man had just fallen out the window.

Bolan heard a yell and kept his scope on target. A second man appeared in the loft. He looked down to where his comrade had fallen. He never got the chance to look up as Bolan walked three rounds up his torso.

Bolan shouted at Lyons. "Do it!" He reached down into the hay. "Masks!"

Waikem, Judd and Bolan leaped from the hay wagon. Grimaldi was already moving at a run.

Lyons cut loose.

The Mk-19 fired the same kind of 40 mm grenade as the launcher mounted beneath Bolan's carbine, only the massive Mk-19 fired them like a belt-fed machine gun. The weapon shuddered in Lyons's hands as he fired it on full auto. It was a weapon of terrible destruction.

Of course, they had to assume that the two hostages, Andy Reed and Sarah Hedner, were still inside the barn.

Lyons punched thirty nonlethal flash-bang grenades into the main barn. His next twenty went through the window into the loft. The plank walls of the barn vibrated as four hundred submunitions detonated nearly simultaneously. Strobes flashed between the boards and out of knotholes like camera flashes. The open window of the loft was too bright to look at.

The Mk-19 racked open on a smoking empty chamber. Lyons opened the breech and fed in a fresh 50-round belt and racked the action.

Bolan pulled his gas mask down over his face.

Lyons cut loose again.

The Mk-19 thundered like a sledgehammer, and tear gas grenades spewed out in a steady stream and tore into the barn. Lyons kept his bursts short. The closed barn would keep the tear gas concentration high, but not high enough to kill anyone inside.

Bolan brought his weapon up to his shoulder. The barn's wide double doors were closed, and Bolan put his front sight on the heavy wooden pegs in the center that marked where the door would be barred from the inside. He fired his own 40 mm grenade launcher at point-blank range. The munition was a flat pancake of high explosive that detonated on contact. The door shattered inward with a crack, and the splintered bar fell in two halves to the floor.

The Executioner flicked his selector lever to burst mode and entered.

Tear gas spilled from the interior in a thick cloud. A man with a pistol staggered with one hand over his tear-streaming face. He fired blindly toward the open door. Bolan hammered him down with a burst.

There were three vehicles in the barn. Two were the Yugo compacts, while a third was a Volkswagen bus. Two more men came staggering through the choking gas with rifles in their hands. Bolan took down one, and Waikem's M-16 snarled into life and took out the other.

Bolan spoke into the transmitter in his mask as he checked the vehicles. "I count five hostiles down. There should be three more."

Waikem had moved to the back of the barn. "Affirmative."

The Mk-19 fired once outside. Bolan turned as a man outside was smashed off of his feet. Lyons's voice came across the receiver in the mask. "One jumper, Striker. He is down."

"Affirmative. Jack, what have you got?"

"No motion out back. No entry to the loft."

"Affirmative. Hold position."

"Roger."

Bolan turned to Waikem and jerked a thumb toward the loft. There was a hole in the roof above, and the Executioner moved to the ladder that led up to it. He scooped up a shovel and threw it up at the entryway. Bullets spanged off of it as someone upstairs fired along burst. Bolan could see the muzzle-flashes through the boards of the floor. He pointed his own muzzle up at the floor of the loft and fired three quick bursts.

"Lyons! Give me another spread of flash-bangs. Into the loft."

"Affirmative." The Mk-19 hammered out a 10-round string. Bolan closed his eyes as the entry to the loft filled with pulses of white light and sawdust filtered down from the concussions.

Bolan slung his rifle and drew his Beretta 93-R pistol as he moved to the ladder. He scrambled up. He fired a burst upward before sticking up his head when no answering fire came back. There was a sudden sound of a scuffle and a burst of automatic fire. Bolan could see tracers tear into the roof above his position. The floorboards thudded with the sound of bodies. Bolan thrust himself into the loft.

The gas was thick inside. A man lay to one side. Two figures struggled in the straw. A man was getting the upper hand on a redheaded woman. Bolan strode forward and jammed the steel toe of his boot into the man's temple as he rolled on top. He dropped on top of the woman as if he had been shot. Bolan seized his shoulder and heaved him off. He pulled the woman to her feet.

"Sarah Hedner? We're here to rescue you."

The woman coughed and nodded blindly through streaming tears. "Check on Andy. He's shot."

Bolan herded the woman to the open window where she could get air. He pulled in the rope from the straw hoist and thrust it into her hands. "Can you hold on?"

She clutched the rope and nodded.

Bolan swung her out and quickly lowered her down. She collapsed at the bottom. The soldier moved to Andy Reed. The white-haired correspondent was a small wiry man. He was also covered with blood. Bolan slung him into a fireman's carry and took him to the window. He grabbed the ropes and his palms burned as he maneuvered both their weights down the rope.

"Waikem, find the keys to the van," Bolan ordered.

"I'm on it."

Bolan pulled off his mask and examined Andy Reed. The journalist didn't look good. He was gasping and choking for air. His lips were blue and the left side of his dress shirt was soaked with blood. Bolan pulled open his shirt and looked at the rifle wound in his chest.

"Reed! Can you hear me?"

Andy Reed gasped and brought up blood. The wound in his chest bubbled as he struggled to pull air into his lungs.

Jack Grimaldi knelt at Bolan's side. "The rear of the barn is secure. People are starting to come out of the church. Carl has them under observation. He doesn't see any guns, and no one is coming this way yet."

"That won't last long. Have Waikem pull the van out. Get Judd to help Ironman mount the Mk-19 through the sliding door. Hold it down with some hay bales. Get me the medical kit from the wagon and toss down the rest of the bags."

"You got it."

Sarah Hedner crawled over and looked at Reed. "How is he?"

"He has a serious chest wound, and all that tear gas he's

breathed hasn't helped matters," Bolan said as he tore a field dressing from his pack.

"He's a brave man. There were three men upstairs with us. When one was shot and the other jumped, Andy tackled the third. He took a bullet as I piled on."

Bolan taped a flutter dressing in place. One half of the dressing was loose so that when Reed exhaled air could escape from the wound, but it would clamp down and seal when he breathed in so his lungs could inflate. Reed groaned as Bolan rolled him and dressed the exit wound in his back.

The van pulled out in a cloud of dispersing tear gas. Waikem and Lyons were already moving the Mk-19 off of the hay wagon. Judd tossed Bolan a saddle blanket from the barn, and they wrapped Reed as warmly as they could. They eased him onto a second blanket and carried him to the van.

"Striker, I see rifles. I think we're in for some company," Grimaldi warned.

Bolan pulled out his field glasses and scanned the village. There were men with automatic rifles in the crowd. The faces in the village looked angry. They would be sitting ducks if they tried to go back through the village, and even if they tried to skirt it, riflemen could still chew them to pieces.

"Ironman, how much more CS do we have?"

"One belt of fifty," Lyons answered.

"I want that village socked in. ASAP!"

Waikem set down the tripod and Lyons climbed beside it. Within seconds the Mk-19 was hammering out short bursts of CS grenades. People in the village began screaming. Rifle shots answered and bullets shrieked off the tractor. Clouds of gas quickly began to bloom between the village and the barn. More gas began to billow up in the narrow lanes of the village itself.

The Mk-19 clacked open empty. "We're out! All we've got left are frags and armor piercing."

The gas would disperse quickly out in the open. They didn't have long. "Hedner, how's your Slavic?"

"I speak a little," she answered.

Bolan looked over at their prisoner. He had been laid down in the dirt to keep under cover behind the tractor. "See if he knows how they intended to take you out of here."

Hedner wrinkled her nose in confusion. "In the van, I'd suspect."

"You and Mr. Reed are high-profile hostages, I'm not so sure they would want to transport you in daylight on open one-lane roads in the country. They must know we're looking for you and that you are being moved. They must have had another plan."

"Well, I'll ask him."

Bolan reached into a kit bag. "Here." He pulled out a Walther PPK .22 autopistol. "It will make your argument more persuasive."

The CIA agent checked the load with practiced ease and smiled. "You've read my file."

The agent went over to the captive and screwed the muzzle of her pistol between his eyebrows. Bolan looked over at the van. The roads would be suicide once the opposition knew they were fleeing, and the van would be a poor cross-country vehicle. Bolan had faith in his ability to get them over the border on foot, since it wasn't far, but Reed's condition had blown that option. He needed medevac and he needed it now.

"What have you got, Sarah?"

"He says a helicopter is coming to pick us up."

"When?"

"Ten-thirty."

Bolan checked his watch. It was 10:10. "Where?"

"Right here."

Bolan quickly calculated. "Are there any radios in the village?"

Hedner asked the sentry. "He says no, the only radio is in the barn upstairs. I can confirm that, I saw it."

Bolan decided. "Waikem! Judd! Burn the barn!"

The Marines didn't have to be told twice. Both sergeants pulled white-phosphorus grenades from under their bulky sweaters. Grimaldi looked at Bolan and grinned. "You're thinking about hijacking a helicopter?"

"The idea has crossed my mind."

"The village is full of gas. You're setting fire to their LZ. They won't be able to establish radio contact. What on earth makes you think they'll land?"

"I'm going to ask them nicely," Bolan said as he pulled a pen and notepad out of the kit bag. "Sarah, ask our friend to spell out the following words in Slav. 'We are under attack. Radio out. Need immediate extraction.'"

"We don't know what frequency the chopper will be on."

"Doesn't matter, just do it. Judd, take the van to the top of the knoll behind the barn. Jack, get the tractor and the hay wagon up there, as well. We may need some cover."

Within minutes both vehicles were pulling up the hill. Bolan scanned the village behind them. The tear gas was dispersing, and smoke rose from the burning barn. Bolan loaded his grenade launcher and fired a white-phosphorus grenade between the barn and the village. Fire and smoke erupted.

The tractor ground to the top of the knoll. The van was already there ahead of them.

Grimaldi stared up into the sky. The misting had let up, and the sun was shining through in patches. "Here she comes."

Bolan looked up. The thumping of helicopter blades was becoming audible. The chopper came into view as it flew low over the hills. It popped up suddenly and Bolan knew they had spotted the smoke from the burning barn. They disembarked from the hay wagon. Bolan took a signal mirror from his kit bag and the piece of paper Sarah Hedner had given him. He looked down at the phrases in Slavic. The CIA agent had written the words in capital letters with a space between each one. Bolan couldn't read the words, but he didn't have to. Virtually all pilots who had been military trained knew Morse code.

Bolan checked the angle of the sun and began slowly and methodically flashing the three phrases of code. The helicopter hovered and Bolan repeated it. The helicopter swooped forward.

"Miss Hedner?"

The CIA agent looked up at Bolan. "Yes?"

"I need you to struggle."

"What?"

Bolan seized her by the hair and began dragging her away from the tractor. The agent fell of her own accord and kicked at him. Bolan yanked her to her feet and kept moving. Waikem and Judd kept their faces down as they carried Andy Reed on the makeshift stretcher.

The helicopter orbited the knoll and then dropped down. Its skids crushed the grass as it settled. It was an Italian-made Augusta, and its cabin would have plenty of room for all of them. Since it was an Italian clone of an American Huey, Grimaldi would have no trouble flying it.

The door slid open and two men with rifles stood in the open cabin. Bolan shoved Hedner forward, and when the men reached out to pull her in, Bolan shot one and Lyons shot the other.

The Executioner leaped into the cabin as the motors whined into higher gear. He lunged into the cockpit as the pilot started to yank on the stick and he shoved the muzzle of his carbine into his face. The pilot eased the stick back down.

Waikem and Judd loaded Reed aboard. Grimaldi eased into the copilot's seat and grinned at the Serb.

Bolan slapped him on the shoulder. "Jack, take the controls. Keep the radio on the intercom. Sarah, you're going to be our translator. Make sure our Serbian friend here behaves when he answers them. Keep him talking. See if you can get anything interesting, like who he needs to contact. Contact them if you can, and learn anything you can. If our friend here screws up, shoot him. Make sure he knows we only need him for a mouthpiece, and that he knows we consider him expendable."

"Not a problem."

"Good, call if you need me. I'll be in back."

"What are you going to do?"

"I'm going to try and keep Mr. Reed alive." Bolan shouted. "Jack!"

"What?"

"Get us the hell out of here!"

4

"This is intolerable!" Stasny declared.

Commander Branko Nemanja was forced to agree. The attack on the mountain had been bad, but when facing resistance from United States Special Forces troops, one had to accept casualties and possible failure. That the hostages had apparently been snatched from their hands little more than a couple of hours later seemed like a tremendous breach of security. Nemanja found that very interesting. "What do we know of the attack itself? How many attackers were there? How did they insert? It was daylight. Unless our men are totally incompetent, they should have seen parachutes or heard the helicopters."

"They didn't come in by air," Stasny answered.

"Well, then how did they insert their team? By sailboat?"

"According to witnesses, they came into the village in a hay wagon."

There were several long moments of silence. "They made their assault in a hay wagon?"

"So I'm told," Stasny said as he cleared his throat. "The hay wagon was being pulled by a tractor."

Nemanja was furious. "How many were there?"

"I am told five."

"You're telling me five men just rolled into the village and took the hostages in a hay wagon?"

"Five men in a hay wagon don't attract much attention on a Sunday morning. They were dressed like farmers. Apparently one sentry in the village hailed them. He was subdued silently, then they were through the village and assaulting the barn before any-one knew anything was amiss.''

"Five men?" Nemanja repeated.

"They all had automatic weapons, and some kind of automatic cannon was hidden in the hay bales. They also had tear gas and explosives. Our men in the barn were overcome before they knew what hit them."

"We must have had at least a dozen armed men in the village. Our men should have been able to call on many of the villagers for assistance, as well. How did they take out the hostages?"

"In a helicopter," Stasny answered.

"Did it have any kind of markings?"

"It was our helicopter."

"They hijacked *our* helicopter?" Nemanja's tone grew even more incredulous.

"So it seems. There is a knoll up behind the barn—"

"I know the area," the commander interrupted.

"They took the hostages up onto the knoll with the tractor and one of the vehicles from the barn. The radio in the barn had been destroyed. The pilot came in as he was scheduled. People on the ground said they saw flashes of light up on the knoll. The heli-copter came in, and then they took it."

Nemanja scratched his chin in thought. "They must have used signal mirrors. That explains how the pilot was fooled. Do we know the status of the pilot?"

"He's in custody. My guess is that he is in Macedonia."

The commander frowned. "What can he tell them?"

"More than we can afford. Also the pilot communicated with some of our elements in the surrounding countryside. He also made a radio call to Belgrade. He was making somewhat strange requests for an emergency landing and needing to be picked up and having the hostages. During transmissions we received word that the village had been attacked. We believe he made the com-munications under coercion. Nothing was revealed."

"Fool! Everything may have been revealed!" the commander fumed. "The Americans currently have many intelligence assets in the Balkans. If they were in contact with CIA or military intelligence assets, it is possible they had them triangulate the radio transmissions. Anyone who was contacted must move. Now!''

"My God!"

"My God is right. We need a full evacuation now," Nemanja ordered.

"I will see to it at once."

Nemanja came to a decision. It was a remarkable set of circumstances, and remarkably bad ones. However, it didn't change the plan of operation or the timetable. "It is my recommendation that we go forward with the plan. Immediately."

"You believe it is a safe option?"

"I believe it's our only option. Now, tell me. Do we have capable men in Macedonia?"

"Yes."

"Men willing to die?"

"We do," Stasny confirmed.

"Silence the pilot, then kill the Americans if possible. Do it now."

American Embassy, Macedonia

MACK BOLAN RELENTLESSLY assaulted the rifle bag. The Marine guards had hung it in an empty room along with some barbells and dumbbells to fill time. The bag was filled with sand and wrapped with silver duct tape. He drove his left fist into the bag and then stepped in and whipped his right elbow around in a hook. He rammed his knee upward and then leaped backward. His right foot snapped out. As it recoiled, the inside edge of his right hand scythed around and chopped into the bag like an axe.

Sweat poured down his chest and shoulders as he repeated the drill for the forty-eighth time. Bolan was a master of close-quarters combat. At Stony Man Farm there were men who were experts in the deadly fighting skills of nearly every continent. Bolan sparred with them relentlessly to hone his skills. All techniques were burned into his muscles until the memory of them were second nature to his unconscious. Any improper technique or faulty movement was beaten out of him gleefully and without remorse by his team members.

"Very impressive."

Bolan smiled as he savaged the bag with his reverse knife hand again. "Thank you."

Sarah Hedner ran her eyes up and down Bolan with extreme frankness. "I wanted to thank you for rescuing us. I hope I didn't startle you."

Bolan mopped his face with a towel. "No. You've been standing there for a couple of minutes. I'm sorry I didn't say anything, but I promised the bag fifty drills without stopping."

The CIA agent raised an eyebrow. "The door was open. I'm wearing tennis shoes. What did you do, smell me? Or do you have ESP?"

"You've changed clothes, but you're still wearing the same shoes we rescued you in. They smell like tear gas."

She eyed Bolan long and hard. "You're pretty good."

"Thank you."

"Who do you work for?"

"The American people. Same as you."

"Okay, so that was a stupid question." Her face grew serious. "I want to thank you. When I was taken to that mountain house, I thought we were just being kept for some kind of demand. I saw all those men with rifles down in the bunker just laughing and waiting, and I knew something was up with all those dogs and ordnance. Then when they deployed and we were moved...I thought for sure that Andy and I were about to become expendable."

"What did you learn during your captivity? Was there anything you could glean from what you heard? Anything about the satellites or their organization?"

"Not too much. I knew nothing about the satellites being hit until you told me about it on the ride back. I know they were waiting for a rescue attempt. They seemed very confident."

"Any clues at all as to who they might be or what they represent?"

"Well, they were definitely Serbs. I don't think they were Serbian army regulars. There wasn't a lot of saluting or use of titles. I think they must be paramilitary or militia."

Bolan already had it figured that way, but Hedner confirmed his thinking. "Any names? Anyone who seemed in charge whom you could describe?"

"No, I think they were being careful about that. We were kept down in the bunker in a small room. The only people we saw were the same three guards who brought us food."

"Did they say anything of note?"

Hedner frowned. "No, not much. Andy has mild asthma. He had one coughing fit. The guards asked if he was sick. I pretended I didn't speak any Slavic. Andy waved them away and said he was okay in English." The agent sighed. "They brought him a glass of water. Other than that, they never really spoke directly to me. They questioned Andy once, but I wasn't allowed in with them during the questioning. You should talk to him when he wakes up."

A crease ran down Bolan's brow. Andy Reed had been taken off the critical list, but at the moment he was still unconscious. Time was trickling through Bolan's fingers, and he could feel what few leads he had growing cold.

"How did the radio triangulation work?"

"Well, it worked to a degree. We know the pilot was communicating with someone in southern Belgrade. That doesn't give us much to go on. The other radio transmission was to someone out in the countryside. Three villages lay along the path of triangulation—we have them under observation, but there are also dozens of farms and homesteads in the area, and that's not even taking into account our friends being in some underground bunker or a cave."

"What do you—? Down!"

Bolan dropped at the sound of gunfire and dragged Hedner to the floor with him. His 9 mm Beretta 93-R appeared in his hand like a magic trick. Bolan recognized the high-pitched cracking of an M-16 rifle. "The guards are firing on someone."

Hedner drew her Walther automatic. "There weren't any protests today—"

The entire embassy shuddered. Bolan hurled himself on top of the agent as windows shattered with a massive clap of thunder. The soldier yawned wide to clear his ringing ears. Sporadic gunfire broke out on several fronts outside the building. Bolan pulled Hedner to her feet. "Are you all right?"

"Jesus, what was...?"

"A car bomb. The embassy has been breached. Our enemy is hitting back. We have to move. Now!"

Hedner nodded and got her legs underneath her. "I'm right behind you."

Bolan snatched up his phone and hit the predial. Carl Lyons answered on the first ring. "Where are you?"

The sounds of screaming began to ring out throughout the embassy.

"Agent Hedner and I are in the gym. Where are you?"

"Second floor. Are you armed?"

"Yeah, but we could use more. We'll rendezvous at the staircase."

"Affirmative," Lyons said.

Bolan moved out of the gym and into the hallway. The gym was in the back of the embassy, so that gave them precious seconds. They moved swiftly past screaming diplomats. The gunfire had begun in earnest. They came to the landing of the staircase.

The opposition was already there.

Several dead Marines lay on the floor. Two men in khaki coveralls and ski masks lay dead on the floor. Two more who were alive were headed for the stairs with automatic rifles in their hands.

The Executioner raised his machine pistol on the man in back and squeezed the trigger twice. The man twisted around, and Bolan's third shot put him down.

Hedner's pistol snapped in rapid succession as she dumped nearly the entire 10-round magazine into the other man. The killer wasn't going down. He ripped off a burst that went just high and wide of the CIA agent. Bolan put his last two rounds into him and he fell.

Three more armed intruders spilled into the room.

A shotgun roared from the stairs, then roared again. Two khaki-clad men twisted and fell under the hail of buckshot. The third fired a burst in return and ducked back behind the door.

"Striker!" Lyons tossed his shotgun from the top of the stairs, and Bolan caught it.

The shotgun was a Marine-issue Mossberg 12-gauge with rifle sights and an 8-round magazine. Spare shells were thrust through loops in a nylon sleeve on the stock, and Bolan pushed fresh shells into the pump shotgun's action. Hedner scooped up the fallen Marine's M-16 rifle. Lyons came down the stairs with a second shotgun in hand.

"They've breached the wall with a car bomb," Lyons explained.

Bolan nodded. The foyer was filled with broken glass and debris. Armed men were moving out in the courtyard. The Executioner moved toward the shattered front door. An armed man burst in, and Bolan put his front sight on the gunner and fired. The buckshot smashed the man down. Tracers streamed in through the door as the men outside responded.

Jack Grimaldi ran in with two Marines behind him. "There's at least a squad out there."

Bolan thought fast as he fired a round out the door. "Hold the doorway as long as you can."

Lyons fired his shotgun as Hedner popped off several rounds from her rifle. "What are you going to do?" she asked.

"I think they intend to take out the embassy. The car bomb breached the wall, but they don't have time to take the whole building in a room-to-room firefight, and they know there is a detachment of Marines."

"What do you mean?"

"I think they intend to blow us up. Now hold the door if you can, fall back if you can't." Bolan turned to one of the Marines. "Trade me," he ordered.

Bolan tossed him the shotgun and took the private's M-16 rifle. He rose and ran for the stairs.

For the half second he was in view through the doorway, at least half a dozen rifles outside ripped off bursts as he ghosted across their vision. Splinters flew from the staircase as Bolan took the steps three at a time.

He rounded the landing and ran down a hallway. The sounds of screaming and shouting came from the upstairs rooms. Bolan ignored it and went for his objective. He found the door to the roof was locked, but his foot smashed it backward. He slung his shotgun and went up the ladder.

Another door at the top opened, and Bolan was on the roof. He ran to the eaves of the embassy roof and peered over the edge. Eight men took turns shooting into the front of the embassy with automatic rifles. Two of the men had belt-fed Russian RPK light machine guns and they were burning out the barrels pouring in fire. They weren't trying to take the embassy. They were just pinning down the people inside.

The embassy wall had a ten-foot gap blown into it, and shattered brick and smoking rubble were strewed all over the courtyard. The riflemen and machine gunners had taken embassy cars as cover. An old jeep was crawling through the breach over the rubble. A machine gun was mounted on the hood on the passenger side. Another machine gun was mounted on a pedestal in the back. Both weapons tore into the front of the embassy as the jeep approached.

Bolan's eyes widened. The back of the jeep was loaded with olive-drab cases the size of footlockers.

Bolan spoke quickly into his phone. "Lyons, get everyone to the back of the building. Do it now!"

The jeep was going to drive right through the shattered doors and then detonate. The men down below wouldn't evacuate. They would stay and be killed to make sure the jeep and its lethal target got inside.

Bolan popped up with his M-16 shouldered.

The machine gunner in the back of the jeep saw Bolan. He shouted a warning to his comrades and desperately swiveled his weapon up. The Executioner put the front sight of his rifle on the cases behind him, and squeezed the trigger. The M-16 rattled in his hands, and tracers streaked down into the jeep. Answering fire tore up into the eaves, but Bolan had already dropped and was rolling.

Searing heat and pressure washed over the roof of the embassy.

A column of orange smoke and fire rose like a mushroom cloud. White streamers of burning phosphorus twisted and shrieked upward through the inferno. Bolan rose and ran for his life. Sparkling yellow elements of the white phosphorus twinkled down like falling fireworks. If he was caught in the open, the molten metal particles would burn right through him.

Bolan leaped through the doorway of the roof access and slammed the door behind him. He slid down the ladder and snapped open his phone. "Lyons, are you all right?"

"We're all right. One of the Marines took some debris in the face but he's mobile. The entire front of the embassy is on fire. They must have had two or three hundred pounds of white phosphorus, and at least as much high explosive backing it up. They didn't gut us like they intended, but this place is going to burn and nothing is going to stop it."

"We need to evacuate now. I'll get the top floor. You take everyone out the rear. Watch out for opposition. Tell Grimaldi to get to a radio and get us some backup."

"Affirmative."

Bolan put his hand against the hallway door. It wasn't hot, at least not yet. The soldier crouched as he opened the door. Smoke filled the air overhead. Orange light lit the hallway as the outer walls of the embassy began burning in earnest. Bolan moved to the doors along the hallway to evacuate the staff.

The enemy had hit back, and they had hit back hard. Almost as fast as Bolan and his team had hit. Bolan grimaced as he kicked in a locked door. The enemy was serious, and they had just announced themselves as real players.

5

Berlin, Germany

Andy Reed looked better. He had an IV unit in his arm, and an oxygen tube rested beneath his nose. The left side of his chest was heavily bandaged and his left arm immobilized. He looked pale and his face was drawn. However, for an asthmatic who had been shot in one lung and had the other filled with tear gas, he was in remarkably good spirits. As soon as he had been stabilized in Macedonia, he had been flown to the military hospital in Berlin. The AK-47 rifle bullet had entered and exited cleanly and not disrupted to much soft tissue or shattered any bones.

The automatic bed was adjusted into a shallow sitting position. Reed looked up from a copy of the *New York Times* and smiled as Bolan walked into the room. "And there's the man I want to thank." He grinned at Hedner. "Hey, pretty lady."

Hedner blushed. "How are you, Andy?"

The journalist's face grew serious. "Better. A lot better. For a little while there I didn't think I was going to make it." He suddenly grinned again. "With one lung down and the other full of Tabasco sauce, I wasn't really sure I wanted to. Our friend here convinced me otherwise."

"Part of my job. Do you feel up to answering some questions?" Bolan asked.

"Sure." He waved the paper in his hand. "I've been reading about what happened to our embassy in Macedonia. It looks like they burned it up."

Bolan nodded. "It could have been worse. They could have

burned up the entire staff. As it is, they took a real good stab it.''

"You want to know about what I saw in that Serbian bunker."

"We've thwarted these people, but we still don't know who they are or what they represent. Anything at all you can remember might be helpful. Our leads are growing cold," Bolan stated.

"Well, I can tell you what happened, but I don't know how useful it would be to you. It was a short interrogation, and then I was back in the room with Sarah."

"What did you see in the bunker outside the room?" Bolan queried.

"They had some very sophisticated communications gear—I could recognize that much—and they had some computers. They had a whole lot of guns and some very unpleasant-looking dogs, let me tell you. They told me they were going to feed me to them unless I cooperated."

"What kind of cooperation were they demanding?"

"That was kind of funny. First of all, they told me that their intelligence sources knew that I was really a CIA agent masquerading as a journalist."

Both Bolan and Hedner kept straight faces. Bolan nodded. "What did you tell them?"

"I told them that was the most damn fool thing I've ever heard. What kind of a secret agent has his face on the cable news networks every day? Most of the CIA spooks pretending to be journalists I've found about are usually masquerading as behind-the-scenes people. Reuters or independents, and usually print media rather than television. People with Sarah's kind of job," Reed said, winking. "But I didn't tell them that part. I just told them that they were nuts."

Andy Reed had been a journalist for over forty years. Behind his twinkling eyes and folksy drawl, Bolan wondered how much he knew or suspected. "What else can you tell me? Was there anything in the bunker that was noticeable or different?"

"Well, like I said, lots of guns and guys with hard faces. There were some tech geeks there, as well."

Bolan raised an eyebrow. "Tech geeks?"

Reed shrugged his good shoulder. "You know, computer geeks. They're the same the world over. The gunmen were hard-cases. You could tell by the way they walked and held themselves. I've covered a number of wars. These guys had the look. The other guys, there were at least three, hovered over the equipment."

"What happened?"

"They slapped me around a bit, but after that I figured I was going to be all right. You're not really serious if you slap people and threaten to sic the dogs on them. I think if they had really suspected I was a spy, they would have started in with real torture or just killed me. As to what I noticed..." Reed took a moment to breathe and collect his thoughts. "They had area maps on the walls, and charts. There were banners on the walls with slogans, but I don't read or speak the language. They had some Serbian flags on the walls. They had a black-and-gray flag with a two-headed bird on it, but I've heard that's the ancient symbol of Serbia. They—"

"What kind of charts?" Bolan interrupted.

"Well, not exactly charts, but more like math equations or something."

"Could you tell what they were?"

"No. I got one look, and then they slapped me to attention and began asking questions. I can show you, though."

"Really?" Bolan asked.

"Really."

"Andy has a photographic memory," Hedner stated.

Bolan took a pad of paper from a desk and handed Reed his pen. "Show me."

"Now, I'm not much of an artist, so this is just the best that I can approximate of what I saw, and I couldn't see close enough to read any of the numbers."

"Take your best shot," Bolan directed.

Reed began drawing on the paper. He quickly finished one and tore off the page and handed it to Bolan. He did two more just as fast. Bolan looked at them. They were very simple. Each showed a half circle at the bottom of the page. There was a point at the top of the half circle. Two lines projected up and out from that point to form an angle as wide as the half circle. It looked for all the world like a pie wedge balancing point first on a bowling ball. The top of the pie wedge had a series of dots along its arc.

Bolan stared at the pictures in turn. For thumbnail sketches, they were excellent. Each was nearly identical. The only difference was that each picture had a straight line drawn through the point of the pie-wedge that intersected one of the dots in the arc, and each line intersected a different dot.

It was very clear.

The half circle was the earth.

The pie wedge balancing on top of it was an arc of fire.

The point where the two intersected was the location of an earth-based weapon.

The series of points on the arc of the pie wedge were satellites.

The line intersecting the point on the earth and the points of the satellites was the trajectory of a weapon.

The United States had lost three satellites. Andy Reed had drawn three sketches.

Bolan stared at them long and hard. "You couldn't see any writing on the charts?"

"Not really, not enough to read, and they sure weren't in English," Reed said, shaking his head. "I'm sorry, but a photographic memory doesn't quite work like people think. The words or numbers you see have to be something your mind can recognize or reference. For example I can read a page out of the New York City phone book and then close it and read it back to you. It's all names, addresses, and numbers written in a language I understand. But give me that same page of the phone book written in Chinese pictograms, and there just isn't anything there my mind can wrap itself around. I don't know Chinese. A page of Chinese writing is just a page of very complicated abstract symbols. Without knowing any Chinese, I would have to study the pictograms for days and weeks to memorize them, just like you. I might be a little faster at it, but it would still take a long time. Numbers I can do, but the numbers on the chart were mixed in with the writing, which messes up the process. I'm sorry, I wish I could give you more.''

Bolan shook his head. "No, you've given me more than you know." A thought occurred to him. "You saw the writing on the charts, though, right?"

"I saw it, but it meant nothing to me. Sarah could have gotten more out of it than me. She knows some Slavic."

"You said there were banners on the wall with slogans on them," Bolan probed.

"Yes, definitely. They were regular letters, but like I said, it was still a foreign language, and I only saw them for less than a second or two. I looked harder at the charts because I figured they meant something."

Bolan locked his gaze with Andy Reed's and held it. "Okay, but think. Think hard. Was the writing on the charts and the writing on the banners the same?"

Reed tried to sit up and winced at his wound. "Well, damn it! No, they weren't. I can remember that much. I swear they were different."

"You said there were tech geeks among the soldiers."

"I think so. They just had that look about them. They weren't armed, and they flinched when I was being slapped around."

Bolan nodded to himself and took the pad of paper and pen. He wrote several short sentences. "Did the writing on the charts look like this, as opposed to Arabic numerals?"

Reed stared at the pad. "It did."

"Do you mind if I hold on to these sketches?"

"I can draw you a hundred copies if you want."

"These three will be enough."

Reed looked at the writing on the paper Bolan had given him. "What kind of writing is this?"

"Cyrillic."

Reed sat up straighter in the bed. "Russian?"

Bolan nodded grimly. "That's right."

STASNY WAS NERVOUS, while Commander Nemanja was calm. He was entirely too calm. It would have been better if the commander were screaming or having a fit and demanding people's heads. It would have been better if he had said he was getting on a plane and coming to kill every incompetent bastard involved in the debacle. Stasny knew Nemanja from past experience. He knew the worst was yet to come.

Instead there was nothing on the other end of the phone line but icy silence.

"We burned down their embassy," Stasny offered hopefully.

"Yes. The American Embassy in Macedonia has been burned. By 'Serbian terrorists.' I have read about it in the newspapers, and saw it burning on the news. I have also heard that four heroic Marine guards are the only casualties among those who were in the embassy at the time."

"The operation was undertaken at your order, Commander," Stasny said, almost immediately regretting the remark.

Nemanja was silent for more long moments. "That's correct. I called for the tactics used. I can't blame the men involved. They died heroes. The fault is mine."

"What do you believe is the next correct course of action? Informants tell us that the news correspondent, Andy Reed, is recovering from a chest wound in Berlin. We have contacts in Germany. We could put together a strike team and kill him."

"No. That would be a foolish course. Kidnapping the journalists as bait to kill a special-operations force was an interesting strategy. I admit it would have been a tremendous coup had it been successful. American prestige would have been severely affected internationally. In their own country the effect would have been worse. Since the Vietnam war, American politicians have had a terrible fear of seeing their own men come home in body bags. If we had wiped out or captured the rescue team, the American willingness to deploy special-operations forces would have been curtailed for years, if not a decade.

"However, that opportunity has been lost. Killing Andy Reed now, after he has been heroically wounded and rescued, would be perceived by the world over as a vindictive act. The work of animals rather than freedom fighters. It wouldn't serve our cause."

The commander's voice became steel again. "Forget the journalists. It's time to go on to a higher-stakes game."

"But wouldn't such an act rally the American people, rather than intimidate them?" Stasny questioned.

There was derision in Nemanja's voice. "Your suspicions are only partially correct. I have had some ideas. I have been speaking with the technicians. I believe that we possess something with capabilities far beyond what we have envisioned."

Stasny was both frightened and confused. "What are you thinking?"

"My original plan was rejected by the leaders. I see that it was rash. I now have another plan. One that will serve us much better."

"Oh?"

"Yes, it is a question of character," Nemanja stated.

"Character?"

"Yes. I'm reminded of the words of Admiral Yamamoto before the Japanese fleet attacked Pearl Harbor during World War II."

"What did he say?"

"He said, 'I fear we may wake a sleeping giant, and fill it with terrible resolve.' He was correct in this assumption. The American people were outraged at the bombing. The American war machine went into full gear. For both Germany and Japan, declaring war against the United States was the beginning of the end," Nemanja said.

"I don't understand."

"As a nation, Americans are the fattest, dumbest, happiest, wealthiest, laziest and most ignorant people in the world. Even today most of them couldn't find Serbia on a map. It's best to keep them that way. Their politicians are aware of this. It's something they play upon. Their people and their news media have very short attention spans."

"These things are true, but I—" Stasny said, confused.

"Listen. The leaders wish to humiliate the United States, to force them to change their policies. The strategy of kidnapping journalists and using them to publicly humiliate their Special

Forces was simple. We put the giant into a situation where he reaches his hand into our affairs and burns it. He pulls back his hand back, and doesn't stick it back into the fire again for fear of being burned.''

"I'm still not sure what you are suggesting."

"What I am suggesting, my friend, is to strike fear into their politicians, but not arouse the American people."

"What do you—?"

The commander's voice filled with cold amusement. "I'm suggesting we let the giant sleep, but his fill his slumber with terrible dreams."

6

Budapest, Hungary

Mack Bolan sat in the secure communications room of the American Embassy in Hungary. It had been decided that Macedonia was too unstable to act as a reliable base. The charred ruins of the embassy there were testament to how hot the situation was becoming. Hungary was a prosperous and stable nation, it was a member of NATO and had very friendly relations with the United States.

Geographically, Hungary perched directly over the former Yugoslavia, and Serbia in particular.

Bolan checked his watch and pushed the button on the satellite link intercom. "Bear, did you get what I sent you from Berlin?"

Aaron Kurtzman came back across the line from Stony Man Farm. "I did. We've been going over it all night. I also forwarded it to Pentagon."

"Those look like firing coordinates to you?"

"I think you hit the nail on the head, Striker. We superimposed those three sketches of Andy Reed's you sent us onto the orbiting patterns of the three satellites we lost. The sketches were crude, but they were good enough for me. I'd call them a match. I would say someone had very accurate information about the orbits of our satellites and then took them out with some kind of weapon."

"How did they track them? From what I know about it, it would take a very powerful earth-based radar to track the orbits accurately, and some very sophisticated equipment to aim the weapon."

"Oh, indeed it would. Not many nations have that kind of sophisticated technology. The process of elimination as to what kind of system it was, who built it and who got their hands on it would be difficult, but not impossible to run down."

Bolan knew Kurtzman's tone all too well, and it didn't fill him with hope. "You don't sound happy."

"I'm not. I've told the Pentagon my suspicions, and they aren't very happy, either."

"Why?"

"I don't think our satellites were tracked by radar or any other kind of sophisticated imaging system."

"Then how did they do it?"

Kurtzman sighed. "I think the opposition took a high-tech weapon and used a low-tech targeting technique."

"What kind of targeting technique?"

"Well, I suspect they used math," Kurtzman replied.

"Mathematics?"

"Geometry, to be precise."

"What are you saying, Bear?"

"Let me tell you a little secret in the world of satellite surveillance."

"What's that?"

"Our satellites aren't very secret. Neither are anybody else's."

"What do you mean?"

"I mean there are three branches of amateur astronomy. There is deep-sky, where you observe nebulae, star clusters and galaxies. Then there is solar-system astronomy, where you observe the sun, the planets, the moon and the objects in our solar system. The other one, and much less talked about, is satellite observation, and anyone with a good telescope and access to the Internet can do it."

"You're kidding."

"No, I'm not. I remember when I was a kid and I first saw the Russian *Sputnik* satellite cross the sky. Today there are approximately eight thousand satellites up in orbit that are being tracked by United States Space Command. About two hundred of those belong to the United States military and cost over several hundred million each. How many of those two hundred are actual spy satellites that are transmitting visual images in real time is highly classified. What a satellite is doing is, indeed, top secret. But its position in orbit at any given time is not."

"So you are saying they got all the targeting information they needed right off the Internet?"

"They just have to search the right places. It's all there," Kurtzman said.

Bolan rolled his eyes skyward. He believed in freedom of information, but it didn't make his job any easier.

"Like I said, Striker, sky-watchers love to watch satellites. In 1983 the United States government stopped publishing orbital data of our military satellites. However, the orbits of most satellites were already known. Today the launching of anything into space is a worldwide event. Ever since 1983, whenever any nation launches something into space, dozens of amateur satellite watchers armed with nothing more than celestial charts, stopwatches and backyard telescopes began their own tracking operations. There are dozens of Web sites on the subject. Right now I have a downloaded chart of the orbits of over six thousand satellites, owned by the United States, China, Russia, France, Israel and Japan. It's like a computer hacker who hacks into government files. Tracking secret satellites is the same kind of rebellion and sleuthing, except it's done by astronomers.

"The thing is, until now, this kind of information was only useful to governments and terrorists who wanted to do something out of sight. They could determine whose satellites would overfly them and calculate how long the satellite could observe them before it went over the earth's horizon. That gave them their window of opportunity while they weren't being watched. The satellite observation itself was passive."

"And now someone has gone active with that same information and reached out and touched our most sensitive satellites," Bolan stated. "They can do that? Just by doing the math?"

"Striker, give me an earth-based weapon that can reach up and touch a satellite, then all I need is its orbit and its speed. After that, all I need is a calculator. The reason why no one has given the problem much thought is that no one has had a decent land-based weapon. The United States found the best way to take out a Russian satellite was to fly an F-15 as high as possible to intercept the satellite and fire a missile at it."

"Nevertheless, someone has gone ahead and done it."

"So it seems," Kurtzman acknowledged.

"How did they reach our satellites?"

"Well, there are three possibilities that I can see. One is a hypervelocity rail gun. We were developing these during the Star Wars program under President Reagan. What you basically have in a rail gun is between three and five conductive rails that make up your barrel. You send a huge electromagnetic pulse down the rails, and this yanks your cannon shell out of the barrel at tremendous velocity."

"You don't sound convinced."

"I'm not. Theoretically it's possible, but to do it you have to get your cannon shell going at least seven miles per second to escape earth's velocity. You would need a gun at least the size of the sixteen-inch guns on one of our battleships. It would need a mount the size of a train car, and probably a whole train, as well, to hold your electromagnetic generators. Then there is the problem of accuracy. Launching a cannon shell into space, you have to deal with the atmosphere, and unless you time it exactly so that you shoot when the satellite is directly above you, you have to worry about the arc of your fire. With present technology, there is just no real guarantee of a hit, and our friends hit us, one, two three."

"What's the second option?" Bolan asked.

"A particle-beam weapon. Once again it is theoretically possible. But a particle beam is literally just that, a beam of particles. You charge them and accelerate them at a target. They are literally smaller than an atom, but you are accelerating billions of them at a significant portion of the speed of light. They tear anything they hit to shreds."

"So what's the problem?"

"Your particle beam literally has to blow a hole in the atmosphere to reach its target in space. That would take tremendous amounts of energy, and just like a rail gun, atmospheric conditions affect accuracy. Once again it's technology of the kind of mass and expense no Serbian terrorist group could get ahold of, much less use or maintain.''

''And the third option?''

''Can't you guess?'' Kurtzman challenged.

''A laser?''

''That's right. A laser is just a beam of almost perfectly focused light. It can pass through our atmosphere without having to smash through it like a particle beam or a ballistic projectile. There is no arc in a laser's trajectory, and its velocity is the speed of light itself. Lasers are proved technology—they've been around since the fifties. People wave them at each other at sporting events. I've seen them mounted on a number of weapons you take into the field.''

''We're talking about a laser capable of burning a satellite into slag,'' Bolan said.

''Well, that does narrow things significantly. If I had to bet, I'd say the only nations with that kind of technology currently are the United States, Russia, Japan and possibly France.''

''That leaves it getting into the hands of a Serbian terrorist group.''

''You said in your report that Andy Reed saw Cyrillic writing on the targeting readouts.''

''That's what he said.''

''What are you going to do?''

''I'm going to Russia. We need to track down what kind of weapon it is and how it got in Serbian hands. We can't afford to wait for them to hit us again. We foiled them in Serbia and Macedonia. I don't think our friends are too happy with us. They're going to hit us again, and hit us soon. They have an agenda, and I think the stakes are going up,'' Bolan warned.

''HAVE THE AMERICANS changed their timetable?''

Viktor Stasny was almost giddy with excitement. ''No, Commander. They're conducting business as usual. They don't seem to even suspect what you have envisioned.''

Branko Nemanja allowed himself a thin smile. "They don't suspect it. Even if they had thought of it, they don't think we would dare."

Stasny's voice dropped conspiratorially. "I believe you would dare to do it."

"I would. If I believed the situation warranted it. However, in this the leaders are correct. The consequences would be astronomical. My revised plan is much more sensible, and it leaves the final option open if we should deem it necessary. Even then, I believe our plan is enough. It's a price the Americans won't be able to pay."

"You believe they will capitulate."

The commander leaned back in his chair. Monkeys shrieked outside of the command shack. "They'll have no choice. Remember, it's not the American people we must strike, but the hearts of their leaders. This is what we will do. Politicians are politicians the world over. All of them think the same way in a crisis. They will take the path of least resistance. Threaten them, but leave them with a way out, and they will find their level, like water. It is simple. We give them two choices. One is a threat, a national disaster too horrible for their hearts to bear. The second choice is to accept being crippled for years by the fear of the threat. Given two unacceptable options, we'll allow them a third option."

"Capitulation," Stasny stated.

"Yes. Quiet, face-saving capitulation. The American politicians will do what we tell them to do. We won't rub their faces in it. We'll tell them what to do quietly, through the highest channels. We'll allow them to clothe their changes in policy it in any politically face-saving garb they want. We will offer them no acceptable alternative." Nemanja took a deep breath. "Time is fleeting. We only have a few hours before the opportunity will be lost, and it could be a year before it presents itself again."

"I have spoken with the leaders. They like your revised plan. They commend your cleverness. They say you are going to rise high."

The commander steeled himself. "And?"

"And they say the mission is a go."

A slow smile spread across Nemanja's face. The smile reached his eyes. He had no doubt he would rise high. It wouldn't surprise him if rose to be president. All of the leaders would have to be killed first, but that wouldn't present a problem. The commander focused himself on the task at hand. He was about to decide the fate of nations.

"Very well. Tell the leaders I will fire as soon as the target comes into range."

Space shuttle *Atlantis* was swiftly approaching its launch area. It was orbiting the Earth over two hundred miles above the planet's surface. The shuttle had turned belly-up to space. The cargo doors surrounding the shuttle's midsection had been thrown open, and its cargo was locked onto the robot arm and ready to be deployed. The payload was a highly classified Pentagon satellite rumored to be worth more than the shuttle's original launch price.

Captain Steven Henderson watched the blue planet beneath him. The miles upon miles of deep water passed over Asia. The flight and final countdown items would soon be in sight. Within minutes he felt would move without the return crews of...

But before Virginia, something about it.

The satellite was highly advanced. Once it was launched in orbit it would sit in orbit over time and some of Pegasus and the surrounding territory under sunlight. The satellite had its own orbital thrusters that would allow it to move about once it was deployed.

What it meant to Steve, all that Clinton relied on him was the civilian payload coordinator. Henderson was the captain of the mission, but his job was little more than being a tech drive. Clinton was the brain of the operation and would decide the actual deployment.

"Two minutes. Prepare for final systems check."

The other two men came within the through a check of the deployment arm and the satellite's systems. Clinton ran his fingers on the satellite itself. He looked up from the console with a satisfied smile. There were still a million things that could go...

Space shuttle *Atlantis* was swiftly approaching its launch area. It was orbiting the Earth over two hundred miles above the planet's surface. The shuttle had turned belly-up to space. The cargo doors on top of the shuttle's fuselage had butterflied open, and its cargo was locked into the robot arm and ready to be deployed. The payload was a highly classified Pentagon satellite rumored to be worth about as much as the shuttle's original asking price.

Captain Steven Henderson watched the blue planet beneath him. The skies were clear as they swiftly passed over Asia. The Tigris and Euphrates Rivers would soon be in sight. Within minutes nothing in Iraq would move without the technicians in Fort Belvoir, Virginia, knowing about it.

The satellite was highly advanced. Once it was stationed in orbit, it would sit in orbit over Iraq and stare at Baghdad and the surrounding territory unblinkingly. The satellite had its own orbital thrusters that would allow it to move about once it was deployed.

"What's our ETA, Steve?" Jeff Clarkson asked. Clarkson was the civilian-payload coordinator. Henderson was the captain of the mission, but his job was little more than acting as a truck driver. Clarkson was the brain of the operation and would do the actual deployment.

"Two minutes. Prepare for final systems check."

The other two astronauts swiftly ran through a check of the deployment arm and the shuttle's systems. Clarkson ran his checks on the satellite itself. He looked up from his console with a satisfied smile. There were still a million things that could go wrong, but he had a green light. "All systems operational. We're a go from my end."

"Roger that," Astronaut Marcus Caron said as he looked up from his computer. "Deployment system is fully operational. All systems are go."

Henderson nodded to himself and watched the Earth spin under him. He spoke into his mike. "Houston, our ETA is one minute. All systems go."

"Roger, *Atlantis*. We read go from down here. You are cleared to deploy."

"Roger, Houston. Preparing to deploy."

The shuttle vibrated slightly as the deployment arm began to unfold with its payload clasped in its padded claws. Henderson watched his cargo-bay TV monitor. The satellite sat cradled in the claw and looked like a great beer keg wrapped in gold foil. "All systems are functioning within parameters, Houston. Smooth as silk."

"Roger, *Atlantis*, we're reading a perfect deployment."

The claw opened and the satellite was suddenly floating freely in space. It seemed to just hover next to the shuttle. There was no air or drag in space so the satellite continued in orbit at the same speed as the space, shuttle.

"That's my baby," Clarkson said, grinning. "Preparing to erect solar arrays."

"Roger, *Atlantis*."

Clarkson typed in a command, and the solar-power arrays began to extend themselves from the satellite like the vanes of a windmill. "Solar arrays deploying." Clarkson looked back at Caron. "Sorry, Marcus."

The big redheaded astronaut had a wistful look on his face. He had been hoping the solar array would have problems. If it did, it would have been his job to go outside and erect the solar power arrays manually. Caron wanted a space walk, and he wanted it bad.

Clarkson ran a systems check on the satellite. The arrays were taking in the sun's rays and converting them to electricity to power the satellite. "Solar array erected. All systems are on-line.

She is under her own power. Preparing for boost to final orbit burn."

"Roger, *Atlantis.*"

Clarkson began the burn sequence. The maximum altitude the space shuttle could reach was only a few hundred miles. The satellite would boost itself up with its own rocket motors to its final destination 22,300 miles up from the Earth's surface. The timing of the burn going up and the burn of the retro-rockets to slow it back down and deposit the satellite into final orbit had to be exact. "Booster reads green, ready for burn."

"Roger, *Atlantis,* you are a go."

"Initiating burn sequence. Five...four...three...t—" Clarkson stared at his screen in alarm. "Houston! The attack-warning system has activated! Satellite has been illuminated!"

The man in Houston sounded close to panic. "Roger, *Atlantis.* Run systems check, could it—?"

"Houston! Attack-warning system reads continuous illumination by low-intensity laser! Ground based. Laser is locked on to the satellite and tracking."

"Jesus!" Captain Henderson shouted as he stared out of the window of shuttle's cockpit. The satellite sat in space alongside them. A pale blue beam of light seemed to have magically grown out of the bottom of the satellite and extend down to Earth and disappear into the atmosphere like a perfectly straight umbilical cord of light. "Houston. This is no malfunction. The satellite is being tracked. I have visual confirmation."

"*Atlantis,* what do you see?"

Henderson squeezed his eyes shut as the blue beam pulsed into a white light that blocked out the stars. He shook his head and blinked at the pulsing images that continued to wink across his vision. He craned his neck and looked out the cabin window. His jaw dropped in shock.

Clarkson was furiously punching keys on his console. "Something's wrong. Nearly all systems are off-line."

Henderson blinked again and shook his head.

The satellite was burning. Smoke and orange fire were geysering out of fissures in the superstructure. The booster rockets were burning. The satellite suddenly came apart silently as the booster rockets detonated. The solar arrays tore, and bits of satellite flew away in all directions streaming fire and smoke. The fuselage of the shuttle vibrated as pieces of satellite struck it like hail.

"Close the damn doors!" Henderson roared.

"Captain!" Caron's voice broke in panic. His eyes were glued to the screen that monitored the cargo bay. Henderson looked at his own monitor. A thin blue beam was shining up from the Earth's surface and locked on the floor of the cargo bay.

"Jesus H. Christ." The shuttle shuddered as Henderson fired his control thrusters. "Houston, we are being illuminated. Initiating rollover sequence."

Henderson prayed as his rockets fired. The satellite they had deployed was extremely advanced. One drawback of its incredible viewing ability was the need to launch the satellite with the shuttle belly up so that the surveillance sensors could be tested looking at the Earth. This had left the shuttle terribly vulnerable to their attackers. The only hope they had was to bring the shuttle's belly toward Earth to bring its heat resistant reentry tiles to bear. The ceramic tiles lining the shuttle's belly were made to withstand thousands of degrees.

Something had cut through the satellite like a knife. The reentry tiles were their only defense.

The shuttle turned with agonizing slowness. Henderson's hand clutched the Saint Christopher's medal he wore against his chest. He waited for the hull to suddenly rupture and explosive decompression to turn himself and his crew into jelly. The shuttle completed its rollover and the opposing attitude thrusters fired to keep them in their new alignment.

Henderson let out a breath. Houston was screaming in his ear. He released his Saint Christopher's medal. His hands were shaking. "Houston, rollover complete. Satellite has been destroyed by hostile ground-based action. Request instructions."

There were long seconds of silence from Houston.

"Repeat, Houston, this is *Atlantis*. Satellite lost to hostile action. Request instructions."

"Roger, *Atlantis.* We're bringing you in. Prepare for ignition of main rocket motors and reentry."

"Roger, Houston. Preparing for reentry."

The rest of the crew silently looked at one another in shock.

Clarkson stared at his screen in utter disbelief. "They shot us. Someone shot us."

"No." Henderson kept his eyes on his controls. "They shot the satellite. We got illuminated."

"What does that mean?"

"It means for the next two hours we are sitting ducks."

Washington, D.C.

THE PRESIDENT of the United States was furious. "You're telling me they shot at the shuttle with a laser?"

The director of NASA, the director of the CIA, the secretary of defense, and an Air Force and Army general all sat in their chairs with exceedingly grim looks on their faces.

The director of the National Reconnaissance Office cleared his throat. "Technically that's correct, Mr. President. However, it's more realistic to say they shot the satellite being deployed with the intent to destroy it, which was successful. *Atlantis* herself was illuminated with a target-acquisition laser, but wasn't fired upon by the main weapon."

The President controlled his temper. "Just what are you saying?"

The SRO director consulted an extensive file folder before him. "Well, sir, according to the records of both Houston command and the shuttle itself, the satellite was illuminated by a LADAR. A LADAR is simply radar that uses light rather than radiowaves. The light hits the object and bounces back, giving you range, speed and, once it locks on, tracking. This was also confirmed by the satellite's own attack-warning system and with visual confirmation by the *Atlantis* pilot, Captain Steven Henderson. He reported a clearly visible pale blue beam striking the satellite just after it had been deployed."

"So, they sighted in with this LADAR?"

"Exactly, Mr. President. Then Henderson reported a blinding flash, which is confirmed by shuttle camera monitors and other astronauts who said the shuttle's cabin filled with light like a bright strobe. At this point we lost contact with the satellite. Henderson gave us visual confirmation that the satellite had been severely damaged and was on fire. He reports seeing the rocket booster and maneuvering rockets detonating and the destruction of the satellite as it exploded. Camera monitors didn't see this directly—however, the monitors do show fire and smoke on the edge of their visuals. The astronauts reported pieces of the destroyed satellite striking *Atlantis*. This is confirmed. They have actually found burned pieces of the satellite that flew back into the cargo bay."

The President wasn't pleased at all. "Is everyone on the shuttle all right?"

The director of NASA spoke. "Yes, sir. As you have probably have already been informed. The shuttle made an emergency re-entry and landed in the Mojave two hours ago. The shuttle itself is undamaged save for some scratches on the fuselage and inside the cargo bay from flying satellite debris. None of the crew were injured during the attack."

"So, why did they illuminate *Atlantis?*"

The SRO director scanned his notes again. "Well, their targeting procedure was very unorthodox. According to our records and the satellite's warning system, they illuminated the satellite for exactly ten seconds with their LADAR. That is very anomalous behavior."

"Anomalous?" The President looked hard at the director. "How so?"

"Well, they didn't need to. A LADAR is not a radar in the strictest sense. Instead of a wide-band pulse of radio-frequency energy, you are literally firing a low-power laser. Its beam hits the target and bounces back. This happens at the speed of light, it's nearly instantaneous. They would only need fractions of a second for a human operator to confirm LADAR lock and then fire their main weapon. Even less if it was all being done by computer. Indeed, they could have done it so fast the satellite's attack-warning system might not have picked it up at all. But they kept LADAR lock for a full ten seconds. It is also strange to note that they seem to have illuminated the shuttle in a similar fashion. The shuttle has no attack-warning system, so the exact time of LADAR illumination can't be verified, but Captain Henderson reports seeing the LADAR beam in his cargo-bay monitor for several seconds as he began his defensive rollover maneuver.''

The President leaned his hands against the desk top. ''We're sure they didn't fire their main weapon at the shuttle?''

The NRO director frowned. ''No, we can't be absolutely sure. However, none of the astronauts reported seeing a second flash, nor did any camera monitor record one. The shuttle's hull has been thoroughly examined, and there is no discernible burn damage or evidence that it was fired upon.''

''So, what the hell was that all about, then?''

''Psychological warfare.'' All the men in the room turned to look at the general who had spoken. He was a small man, and his highly decorated dress uniform identified him as a three-star general in the United States Marines. ''And a damn fine example, I might add.''

The NRO director cocked his head. ''What are you saying?''

The Marine shifted in his seat. ''I flew Phantoms. On numerous occasions I flew patrols near borders of Communist countries. We would shadow their fighter patrols. They would shadow ours. We were always jockeying at one another. If you wanted to bring the situation as close to an international incident as you could, and scare your opposing number, you lit him up with your radar, you illuminated him. It meant, 'I've got you locked and I can kill you whenever I want.' I did it a number of times. That's what they wanted. That's what they got. The satellite wasn't their target at all. Neither was the shuttle.''

The director of NASA blinked. ''You're saying the satellite or the shuttle wasn't their target? What the hell are you saying?''

The Marine general visibly remained patient. ''Their target

was every man in this room.'' He turned his gaze on his commander-in-chief. ''You in particular, Mr. President.''

The President nodded. ''So the destruction of the satellite was just a means to an end.''

''Exactly. They held LADAR lock on it for ten full seconds. They wanted the satellite's attack-warning system to light up like a Christmas tree. They wanted the shuttle crew to see the LADAR beam. They wanted Houston to freak out, which they did. Then they slagged the satellite. While that was blurring our minds, they illuminated the shuttle, to send us into a complete panic. A panic that lasted during the entire reentry of the shuttle. They made us sweat bullets until the shuttle actually touched down on the runway.''

The general consulted the file before him. ''According to this file, we lost three satellites last week. Now we've lost a fourth, in middeployment, and they lit the shuttle and let us know about it. I believe the situation is very clear. We are being told that they can shut down our entire space program anytime they want. They can slag any U.S. satellite in orbit and there is nothing we can do about it. They are letting us know that any future space launch of any kind will only be done on their sufferance.''

There was total silence around the conference table.

The Marine general met the President's gaze and held it. ''I believe they'll start making their demands very soon.''

8

Moscow

"They've actually threatened the space shuttle?" Bolan sat back in his chair in the American Embassy's secure communications room.

Aaron Kurtzman sounded distinctly unhappy over the satellite link. "They're threatening the entire United States space program. This also includes our satellite web, which services our television transmissions, our cellular phone networks—hell, they can punch gaping holes in every form of communication the U.S. uses both militarily and economically. If they starting popping our satellites one by one, they can start shutting down the whole country, and they can threaten anything we put back up to replace it. Illuminating the shuttle was the real bomb they dropped."

Bolan nodded. "They won't do that. We all remember how the whole nation came together when *Challenger* blew up. If Americans thought that someone had blown up one of our shuttles and killed the crew, the President could probably get away with calling for nuclear strikes as long as someone was made to pay."

"You're right, Striker. But they didn't. They just gave us the nightmare of the threat. Their real action of destroying four of our best spy satellites is more than threat enough. The President will never come out and admit publicly that a foreign terrorist organization is holding the entire American space program hostage. They have us dead to rights."

Bolan stared at the wall coldly. "What kind of demands are they making?"

"They're being very subtle about it. They want us to start removing American forces from the Balkans. They're not demanding that we do it all at once. They aren't trying to humiliate us by revealing to the world what they have done. They will allow us to say we lost some satellites due to systems malfunctions. They are going to let us 'make policy decisions' that will permit us to start retreating out of the Balkans slowly without raising any eyebrows. They want us to start using diplomatic pressure to get NATO to go along with removing their own forces out of the area. All of this is very hush-hush. They don't want to raise a stink. They want us—"

"They want us to capitulate." The words tasted like bile in Bolan's mouth. "And they're going to let us publicly save face while we do it."

There was a long pause on the link. "You're right."

"What is the President going to do?"

"Initially he's going to start acceding to their demands. He will make noises about changing our policy toward Serbia and the Balkans, and he's going to shuffle some troops."

"What are my orders?"

"Your orders are unchanged."

Bolan let out sigh of relief. If he had been ordered home, the new millennium would start with the United States letting terrorists decide her foreign policy. It was an age Mack Bolan had no desire to live in.

Kurtzman continued. "Find out what this weapon is, where the enemy got it and where it is being deployed from. From there we are likely to destroy it with surgical air strikes."

Bolan looked at the map of the world that dominated the communication room's wall. "What else have we been able to figure out?"

"Well, the weapon has to be pretty advanced technology. They destroyed our satellites one at a time, and they destroyed the satellite *Atlantis* was deploying and then illuminated the shuttle. We are suspecting it must be some kind of prototype, and we suspect the bad guys only have one weapon. We are betting it is some kind of high-frequency laser, and it has a low-frequency LADAR laser attached to it as an aiming unit.''

Kurtzman's voice betrayed grudging admiration of their opponents as he explained the LADAR. ''It's the low-tech simplicity of their aiming that makes the system so dangerous. If it was using radar to track its targets, it would have to send out radar pulses, and that would alert everyone and their brother as to where the weapon was. Once we knew about it, every time they fired the weapon it would attract antiradar missiles fired in retaliation like flies. But, like I said before, our friends are using ordinary math to plot the courses of their targets. When they figure their target is aligned, they fire the LADAR. The LADAR doesn't fill the sky with telltale electromagnetic static like radar. It's literally a beam of light, barely wider than a flashlight beam. There is nothing to detect. No countermeasures to take. If their math is good, the LADAR hits the target and bounces back, confirming their target, and tracks it. Then they fire their main laser weapon to destroy the target. The system is just about foolproof, and just about undetectable. There is no warning, and it happens so fast there is no way to track the weapon's firing angle back to its source.''

''What about those sketches we got from Andy Reed? Have you been able to do anything with those?''

''Well, they mostly served to confirm our worst suspicions, but we were able to do a little math of our own. When we compare them with the attacks on the satellites during your mission in Serbia, and against the attack on the shuttle's satellite deployment, we have figured pretty conclusively that they must be firing from a point very near or on the equator.''

Bolan looked upon the wall map before him. He ran his eye along the line that formed the Earth's equator. ''Can you narrow that down a little?''

''We have. Assuming one weapon, firing from one location, attacking the five known targets, we are assuming equatorial Africa.''

Bolan gazed at the African continent and the band of territory that ran beneath the Sahara Desert. The land was nearly three thousand miles across, and some of the most hostile terrain on the planet. "Well, Bear, that narrows it down a little."

"That's also assuming the bad guys aren't firing their weapon from a ship slightly off either African equatorial coast."

"That's comforting." Bolan's eyes bored into the map. "How big is this weapon system?"

"My bet is that it's fairly portable. Design wise, if the weapon was fixed to a permanent site like a telescope in an observatory, there is too much chance of it being found and bombed into oblivion during a conflict. If I had to bet, I would say it is at least truck towable, or perhaps has its own special armored vehicle built around it."

A deep line drew down between Bolan's brows. A mobile weapon system, undetectable during acquisition or firing mode, most likely situated in an unknown and impenetrable part of the African bush where the United States had few friends and little clout. That, of course, assumed the weapon system wasn't on a boat and changing locations already.

Bolan shook his head. "We're never going to detect this thing, Bear. No spy plane or satellite is going to find it unless we catch some freak luck. We're going to have to get down in the mud and sleuth this thing to its lair one clue at a time."

"That's what I told Hal," Kurtzman said, referring to Hal Brognola, the director of the Sensitive Operations Group. "That's what he told the President. Neither the NRO director or the Pentagon are very happy about the news. What are you going to do?"

"We're assuming this may be some kind of Russian prototype. The first thing is to find out exactly what this weapon is and how it could have gotten into Serbian hands."

"You have an idea where to start looking?"

"No. But I have a contact in mind who might be able to help."

BOLAN WALKED DOWN the hallway that split rows of tiny gray offices. Two armed guards marched stiffly behind him. The building had changed little since Bolan had last seen it. The attitudes of the employees he saw were unrelievedly grim. They marched on down the hall to a corner office, and one of the guards rapped on the opaque window pane in the door.

A woman's voice spoke in Russian. "Enter."

The guard opened the door, saluted and closed the door as Bolan entered. A woman looked up from the desk. Blond hair that was usually bound in a severe bun hung down about her shoulders. She wore well-tailored but clearly well-worn suit jacket and skirt rather than her green service uniform. Cobalt-blue eyes met Bolan's.

The Executioner stood tall and saluted. "Captain."

GRU Captain Valentina Svarzkova raised an eyebrow but returned the salute. She spoke in heavily accented English. "You."

Bolan smiled. "Me."

The military intelligence officer smiled in weary amusement. "I must admit I had some misgivings when I was informed that a man named Mike Belasko wished an appointment. So did my superiors."

Bolan shrugged. "I appreciate your seeing me despite your reluctance."

"You make my superiors nervous. The first time we worked together was to clean up a very embarrassing matter to my country. The second time you nearly sparked a war between the GRU and the former KGB." The woman returned his shrug. "My own misgivings are personal in nature."

"Oh?"

"They are more related to my health. The first time we worked together my nose was broken and my left femoral artery was severed. The last time I saw you I took two .22-caliber bullets through my left lung."

Bolan looked about the office. A woman's GRU dress uniform hung on a coat rack, and the four stars on the shoulder boards revealed the rank of captain. Hanging from another peg was a shoulder rig with a cocked and locked CZ-75 9 mm pistol hanging in the holster. Various citations and commendations hung on the wall, including one for the Russian Medal of Valor. There was a framed and autographed photograph of Chuck Norris on the wall, and beneath it a small wooden frame held six tightly coiled and tied cotton belts tiered downward from white to black. All of the belts were faded and worn from many washings except for the black, which was so new it almost gleamed. Beneath the rack of belts was a certificate from the All Russia Karate Federation, signed by the head of the Tang Soo Do affiliate.

"I see you made black belt."

Svarzkova nodded.

"How have you been?"

Her smile died on her lips. She looked at Bolan matter-of-factly. "Since London? I have been married and divorced. I was recommended for rank of major and rejected. The Russian ruble is worth nothing, yet pay has been reduced." Svarzkova stared bleakly at the wall of her office. "Yet, I am lucky. GRU is elite service. Many soldiers in the field haven't received pay for months. Corruption has penetrated the highest levels of our government."

Bolan had seen that corruption firsthand, and fought it when it had threatened the United States. The Union of Soviet Socialist Republics had fallen, and the new Russia that had replaced it was a superpower with feet of clay. Russia was tottering under hyperinflation, massive governmental corruption and brazen organized crime. The black market accounted for more of the Russian gross national product than her legitimate business. Valentina Svarzkova was a trained GRU field agent, sworn to seek out and destroy the enemies of the Russian people. Now the enemies she fought were more often than not her own countrymen.

"Buy me dinner and we'll catch up," Svarzkova suggested. "Besides, you wish to pump me for information."

"WHAT IS IT you wish to discuss?"

Bolan refilled Svarzkova's glass from the bottle of Hungarian red wine. "Serbia."

Svarzkova ceased chewing for a moment. She swallowed and then finished most of her wine before she spoke. "This is perhaps not a good topic for conversation. My government isn't pleased with the way yours has conducted itself in the Balkans. Serbia is a Russian ally. The United States didn't endear itself to us with her actions there.''

''I'm aware of that. But you and I have had mutual problems there before.''

''This is true.''

They both remembered a certain renegade Russian special-forces soldier who had sold his services to a Serbian terrorist group. Bolan and Svarzkova had tracked him halfway across the globe to bring him down. Both of them had nearly paid for it with their lives.

''What is the mutual problem you and I have in Serbia?''

Bolan chose his words carefully. ''I have been authorized to tell you that some of our intelligence operations have been compromised. We believe a faction of Serbian terrorists are responsible, with or without the sanction of members of the government, we can't be sure.''

Svarzkova frowned as she poured herself more wine. ''Well, I offer my personal regrets. Of course, this is a matter of interest to GRU, but I do not see how this is a GRU concern.''

''We believe they are using Russian weapons.''

The agent shrugged. ''Serbians are allies of Russia. I would guess ninety percent of the Serbian military is equipped with weapons of Russian manufacture. If Serbian terrorists are acting against the United States, it is natural they would be equipped with Russian weapons. It's what they would have access to.''

''I understand that.''

''Good.''

''But those weapons included high-frequency ground-based antisatellite lasers.''

Svarzkova snorted. ''Impossible.''

Bolan took her gaze and held it. ''Are you absolutely sure?''

The Russian agent scowled. The ruble was nearly worthless and her economy was in shambles. Most of her industry was ten years behind the times and couldn't compete. She was starved for hard currency. One of the few industries Russia still excelled at was the arms industry. The Russians would sell just about anything to anybody. What's more, vast numbers of her weapons were available illegally on the black market. Valentina Svarzkova was a military intelligence officer. The fact that everything from small arms to battlefield missile components were leaking out of her borders like water through a sieve wasn't something she enjoyed being reminded of.

"What you speak of is a matter of the highest level of military security. Do you have proof?"

"No. The evidence is spectacular, but it's mostly circumstantial. We have lost some satellites. Your own space command monitors American satellites in orbit. You can easily confirm this. I have some diagrams, some calculations and a rather amazing piece of videotape footage along with radio transcripts from our space shuttle during a satellite deployment. I'm authorized to release these to you and your government."

"Very well. I'll show it to my superiors. It will be considered. I can't guarantee cooperation from me or my government." The woman stared down at her plate for long moments. "I'm no longer hungry. Let's go to your embassy at once."

9

Mack Bolan strode down another hallway. It was the same building that Valentina Svarzkova's office had been in, but the corridor down which he walked was many levels underground. The walls were unrelieved gray concrete and ribbed with exposed steel reinforcement girders. This area of the facility had been designed to withstand direct strikes from nuclear weapons. The men who escorted him weren't men in suits as had been the case above ground, but were grim-faced soldiers in uniform armed with AK-74 automatic rifles.

Bolan wasn't entirely comfortable. There were many people in the former Soviet Union who would be delighted to see him dead. The fact that he had successfully worked with this branch of the GRU and had been a valuable ally to them in the past wasn't enough to guarantee his safety in Moscow. Perhaps not even enough to guarantee his safety in this very facility.

Nevertheless, no one was going to allow him into the very bowels of Russian military intelligence armed with a .44 Magnum Desert Eagle semiautomatic and a 9 mm Beretta 93-R machine pistol.

They came to a windowless steel door with a camera unit mounted over it. The guards saluted the camera lens. A moment later the door seals hissed open.

Three people sat around a large wooden table that had been designed to hold well over a dozen people in a meeting. Bolan recognized two of them. Valentina Svarzkova sat in her dress green uniform and at the head of the table sat Uri Ozhimkov. Bolan had met the man once before when he had worked with

Svarzkova. He was her superior officer and in certain situations the only man she reported to. When Bolan had last seen the man he had worn the stars of a colonel. He now wore the shoulder boards of a major general.

Another man sat at his left in civilian clothes. He looked to be in his late thirties. He stared at Bolan with such frank curiosity the Executioner didn't take him to be an intelligence officer.

Ozhimkov rose and offered Bolan his hand. The general was nearly bald, and his eyes and mouth threatened to sink down and disappear into the frown lines in his face. He was a large man, and the straight line of his massive shoulders belied the more than sixty years he carried across them. His English was heavily accented but his grammar was nearly perfect. His grip was like a steel vise that was straining to behave itself. "Greetings. Welcome to Moscow. I hope that you are well."

"Thank you, sir. Congratulations on your promotion."

The deep lines of the Russian's face shifted for a moment into the briefest of smiles. "Thank you. Please be seated." The general settled his massive bulk into his chair with a grunt. "It pleases me to see that you are well, but I can't say that I am pleased to see you. You have never been a bringer of good tidings, Mr. Belasko."

"I appreciate that, sir, but it is my hope our business here can once again prove successful." Bolan took the seat next to Svarzkova. "You have reviewed the materials I gave to Captain Svarzkova?"

Ozhimkov grunted. "Indeed, I have. I found them extremely interesting."

"What is the opinion of your superiors?"

"I haven't shown them to my superiors."

There was silence around the table. Russian intelligence officers almost never gave anything away. Discussions with them often led to jockeying back and forth to see who could get more information out of whom. Ozhimkov had just dropped a bomb in the opening round. It was a testament to the gravity of the situation.

Bolan nodded slowly. "I believe I understand."

"I'm sure you do. If such an antisatellite weapon exists, much of its development and control would fall under the auspices of the Directorate of Cosmic Intelligence, which is attached to the GRU. The escape or loss of such technology could only occur with cooperation from officers of the GRU."

Bolan sighed. He had already suspected as much. It was one reason he'd felt there was some likelihood of never seeing the Earth's surface again once the elevator had started downward. "It is possible that someone above your pay scale is involved."

"It is more than possible. If the circumstances toward which your evidence points prove true, there can be no other alternative." The general gestured toward the man in civilian clothes at his left hand. "This is Dr. Sergei Gareyev, a scientist from the Institute of Advanced Physics."

Bolan rose and extended his hand. "I'm pleased to meet you."

The man spoke excellent English. "I'm pleased to meet you, as well. It is fascinating what you have presented to the general."

Ozhimkov rested a hand on the diplomatic satchel that sat before him. "I will tell you now. The four of us in this room are the only people in Moscow who have reviewed these materials. I have absolute faith in Captain Svarzkova's loyalty to the motherland. Sergei is my grandson-in-law, and it was I who oversaw his enrollment in at the institute. I trusted both his loyalty and his scientific knowledge to show him these materials before showing them to anyone else. You will have to take my word for this. As for myself, if I were involved in a conspiracy such as this, Mr. Belasko, you would never have stepped out of the elevator onto this level alive."

"I have absolute faith in your loyalty to Russia, General. That is why I came to Captain Svarzkova first, and why I stepped into the elevator when I received your invitation."

"Hmm." Ozhimkov grunted again and shifted his bulk in his chair. "Thank you. I appreciate your candor." He gestured again to Gareyev.

The doctor flipped open the file before him. It was full of transcripts of the information Bolan had given Svarzkova and many stills taken from the shuttle *Atlantis*'s camera monitors.

"The weapon you are postulating would require at the very least ten thousand megawatts of power. Both the United States and Russia have developed lasers of such power in the laboratory. This is documented. The question is using the technology to develop a deployable weapon. As I have said, it would require vast amounts of power. Such sources often involve highly volatile materials. There is the question of making both the weapon and the power source portable. In such a case the weapon would have to be relatively small. When the weapon becomes small, cooling it becomes a serious problem."

Gareyev held up a color photograph. On it was an American C-135 transport jet. It had a large hump on its back that ran a third of the length of the aircraft. "Your own government fielded the NKC-135 Airborne Laser Laboratory aircraft. According to our intelligence, it was designed to test the feasibility of using a laser from an airborne platform against an airborne target. We also have intelligence of an American tracked vehicle that mounted a high-frequency laser, but it was intended to be used against aircraft operating in the atmosphere. According to our intelligence both projects were prohibitively expensive, and extremely delicate. Russia herself worked on similar projects, whose nature is highly classified. However, we came to many of the same conclusions. Like your nation, we found that high-frequency lasers, if ever deployed in the field, would best be deployed in space, to be used against targets also in space."

Bolan nodded. Aaron Kurtzman had told him the same things. "I understand your position, Doctor. Nonetheless, something has sliced four of our satellites out of the sky and forced the shuttle *Atlantis* to make an emergency reentry when it was illuminated by LADAR."

Dr. Gareyev nodded. "Yes, I reviewed the videotape. Quite remarkable. I have also reviewed your theory that no radars or tracking satellites were used to aim or coordinate the weapon. Your mathematical aiming theory, as it were, using downloaded information from the Internet to predict the locations of targets is quite ingenious. A low-tech approach to a high-tech problem."

"There are a number of questions my government needs answered. For one, how did the Serbians get ahold of such a weapon?''

Ozhimkov's frown lines deepened even further. ''I have given this much thought. I don't believe the Serbians bought this weapon. They would never have heard of it. If I myself were to sell such a weapon for profit, Serbia wouldn't be my first choice. China could afford to pay much more, as could India. For that matter, I believe France or the United States would be willing to pay great amounts of money to acquire such a weapon system. I believe the weapon was given to these Serbians, and given to them for political purposes.''

''I'm afraid I agree with you, General. I'm not at liberty to discuss any communications between my government and that of the terrorists, but I can tell you their goals seem to be political rather than monetary.''

Ozhimkov nodded. ''I can guess at what some of their demands may be, but that doesn't matter at the moment. What matters is there has been a gross breach of Russian national security. It seems likely that some of our very most advanced technology has been given into the hands of terrorists. Once in those hands, the technology is no longer ours to control. It is quite conceivable that it could fall into the hands of others, or be deliberately sold into other hands by defectors. Terrorists have always had the power to convince themselves that anything they do is justified. It's possible that in the future this technology could be used against my country, and we, like you, Mr. Belasko, have no current defensive measures against it. We would be subject to the same blackmail of our space program that I assume your nation is.

''This situation is intolerable. The weapon must be found and returned to GRU where it belongs. Barring that, it must be utterly destroyed. Those responsible must be ruthlessly eliminated. In this, I'm willing to offer my direct assistance.''

''Thank you, General. I appreciate your candor, as well.''

The general let out a heavy sigh. ''I believe this act of treason was committed for political purposes. There is only one group in

Russia who would engage in such an act of rash stupidity and treason and then justify it to themselves for political reasons.''

"The KGB," Bolan guessed.

Ozhimkov nodded slowly. "Yes, the former KGB." The old man glared darkly at the wall. "I will make no protestations of how much better we are. The GRU has committed many crimes over the years. Our hands are as red with blood as any intelligence service in the world. However, we have one salvation. We are soldiers. We are patriots. Always, in our hearts, our loyalty is to Russia. Our whole might, until very recently, has always been directed against foreign powers. The KGB—they were, and still are, despite their new names and departments, a political entity. Their loyalty has always been to communism, and to themselves.''

Bolan nodded. The atrocities the KGB committed against its own people were far worse than anything they had ever managed to accomplish internationally. "You believe a faction of the former KGB has corrupted someone high enough in the Directorate of Cosmic Intelligence to accomplish the transfer of the weapon system to the Serbians."

Svarzkova looked angry enough to spit. "It is typical Byzantine logic of KGB scum. They should all be shot."

"I'm currently sending out feelers. I am contacting those I think I can trust, looking for leads. It had been my experience that most scientists are unable too keep their mouths shut. The exchange of ideas is to strong a lure for them. My grandson-in-law is making discreet inquiries among his colleagues. I'll inform you as soon as I have developed a lead, or suspect that we ourselves are discovered. Were I you, I would go back to the American Embassy—it is the only place in Moscow where you may enjoy some immunity from reprisal.''

"Thank you, General.''

"Captain Svarzkova, you will take a detachment of guards and escort our guest. His safety on the streets of Moscow is your responsibility.''

Svarzkova sat up straight in her chair. "Yes, General.''

"Good. Mr. Belasko, your weapons will be returned to you once you are above Level Four."

Svarzkova rose and saluted. Bolan followed her outside of the steel door. The uniformed guards stood waiting for them with their rifles at port arms. They fell into rank behind Bolan and Svarzkova as they walked down the hall.

Bolan spoke mildly. "So, how is your French these days?"

The captain's accent would have sent a Parisian into fits, but her French was understandable. "It's my third language. English was my priority. Why do you ask?"

"These are not the same guards who escorted us before. Do you understand?" Bolan asked in French.

Svarzkova leaped and spun. A sound tore out of her throat like the scream of a wounded leopard. The heel of her right dress boot scythed through the air at head level and crashed into the ear of the guard behind her.

Bolan whirled.

The unmistakable sound of an AK's selector lever being flicked from safe to full auto greeted him. His left hand chopped down and struck the rifle's barrel out of line with his body. The concrete hall thundered with the sound of automatic rifle fire. Full-metal-jacketed bullets sparked and shrieked off of the hardened concrete walls.

Bolan's right fist drove into the man's solar plexus. Pain jagged up his wrist as the bones and ligaments compressed. His fist smashed into the unyielding wall of titanium and spun fiberglass that was Russian body armor.

The blow shoved the man backward. Bolan ignored the pain in his wrist and seized the AK-74's barrel in his left hand. He held the barrel away from himself as the guard twisted the rifle and fired off another burst. Heat seared the Executioner's hand and he ignored it. The man suddenly stepped forward and rammed his knee upward. Bolan raised his own leg to defend his groin. The man lunged forward to bowl Bolan over.

Bolan let him.

The Executioner seized the man's rifle in both hands as he fell backward. The sentry instinctively held on to his rifle, and Bolan pulled him down as he fell. He rammed his foot into the man's groin and kicked up with all his might as he rolled.

The Russian flew over the soldier and landed heavily on the concrete.

Bolan twisted as the other guard lunged at him with his bayonet. Both the Russian's rifle and Svarzkova lay on the floor. He hadn't stopped to retrieve the weapon. Bolan's back presented too great a target. Bolan whipped up the rifle he had wrested away as the knife plunged home.

The knife sank through his leather jacket and punched into his armor. Bolan wasn't wearing the full Threat Level III armor he would on a raid. The armor he wore was designed to remain concealed under clothes and had no hardened ceramic trauma plate, but the clipped point of the bayonet slowed and snagged in the tightly woven Kevlar fibers of Bolan's vest.

The Executioner whipped the rifle butt around to crash into the guard's teeth. The Russian staggered back spitting blood. Bolan leveled his rifle.

The first Russian seized him from behind.

The second came forward again with his bayonet held low.

Valentina Svarzkova's forearm whipped around his windpipe. The Russian gagged and his eyes flew wide. A bloodied knife glittered in Svarzkova's hand as she yanked back the man's head and drew the blade across his throat.

Bolan raised his feet in the air and kicked against the wall of the narrow corridor with both feet. He drove the Russian holding him back against the opposite wall. The grip on the rifle loosened, and Bolan ripped it free and whirled. The Russian's hand went to his knife.

The AK-74 in Bolan's hand erupted into full auto. The bullets hammered the armored man backward. The burst climbed up his chest and then tore into his throat. Bolan's finger flicked off the trigger.

Alarms howled loud enough to shake the walls, and red lights up and down the corridor began pulsing in alert. Steel doors along the hall hissed open. Bolan threw down his rifle and Svarzkova dropped her knife. Armed guards filled the corridor with

the sound of pounding feet. Bolan didn't relish the idea of the
killer's backup shooting them down in the corridor, but he was
an American, and two Russian soldiers lay dead. Both he and
Svarzkova would be shot to pieces if he didn't surrender.

Guards seized him and rammed him face first against the wall.
Svarzkova was held at gunpoint but not physically accosted.

General Ozhimkov lumbered down the hall with Dr. Gareyev.
Both men held pistols in their hands. The general stared down
at the dead men. "What is the meaning of this? Are you insane?"

"Those men aren't the guards who escorted us down the hall
or took position on the door once we entered the meeting room."

Ozhimkov scowled.

Bolan jerked his head at the bodies. "They are wearing concealed body armor."

Ozhimkov barked at one of his soldiers. The man knelt. He
ripped open the man's uniform blouse. The tears of Bolan's bullet
strikes in the titanium armor formed a trail up his chest. He
snarled in rapid Russian but Bolan understood enough. The general wanted to know who the hell these men were.

The soldiers released Bolan. They nodded apologetically and
Bolan shook his head for them to forget it. He and Ozhimkov
looked at one another long and hard.

"They're on to us."

10

"The Americans have sent someone."

Commander Branko Nemanja pondered the statement before asking, "Sent someone where?"

"To Moscow. He went to GRU headquarters."

"One man?"

"Only one that we know of."

"Who is he?"

"We don't know."

"With all the assets at our disposal in Russia, you don't know?"

"No." Stasny was getting nervous again. "He doesn't seem to exist in any files we have access to."

The commander considered that. In the end the Americans had few options. Russia was one of the few places they could go to try to track down their problem. With the fall of the Communist government and the new openness, there was even some chance that someone might actually try to help them. It was something Nemanja had expected, though it seemed the Americans were working remarkably fast. "Very well. The only place where this man might find anyone or anything useful would be at the GRU. We have people in place for just such a contingency. Contact our friends, have our assets activated. Push our contacts, they have access to more information. They are just afraid to risk their own necks. I want to know who this man is, and I want him terminated."

"The attempt has already been made. In GRU headquarters, at the Sixth Level."

"What do you mean, attempt?"

"It failed, Commander."

Nemanja thought upon this for long moments. "I have been to GRU headquarters. Sixth Level is a high-security area. Whoever this man is, he is a foreign national. He would have been disarmed, helpless. How could the attempt have failed?"

"I don't know, commander. Our contacts say they had two very competent and trusted men on the job. Both were wearing body armor and were armed with automatic rifles. It seems the American defeated them in hand-to-hand combat."

"This stinks of their special forces."

"It seems he had some assistance from a GRU agent who accompanied him. Our sources say she was the first person in the GRU he contacted upon arriving in Moscow."

"She?"

"Captain Valentina Constantina Svarzkova."

"Find out everything you can about her."

"It's already being done."

"How long ago did this happen?"

"Twenty minutes ago."

"Good. For once we are acting swiftly. We must be even quicker. The American is probably being debriefed in GRU headquarters. From there he will go to the U.S. Embassy. Have our contacts get men into the street near the embassy. Make sure they have heavy weapons. Kill the American and whoever is in his convoy before they can reach the embassy."

"I will arrange it."

"Good. Contact me when the American is dead." The commander hung up the phone. It was only to be expected that the Americans would try something. Sending someone to investigate was about their only option other than complete surrender. He couldn't really blame them. The commander smiled.

But he'd punish them for it.

BOLAN STOOD AND WATCHED while a GRU team swept Valentina Svarzkova's apartment for bombs and electronic bugs. Svarzkova watched them as they pushed her meager furnishing about. She had a wooden table and three chairs that crowded half of her apartment. There was an ancient refrigerator and a stove crammed into the kitchen nook. A magnificent brass-and-copper samovar and tea service sat in a place of prominence and must have been a treasured family heirloom. A tiny counter folded out of the wall and formed a kitchen table and ironing board. Her bed folded down out of the wall, as well. She had a tiny closet and a bathroom and little else. Her prize possession was a twelve-inch color television and a decade-old VCR.

Svarzkova returned the salute of the GRU corporal as he pronounced her apartment devoid of bugs and explosives. The team filed out the door. Two of soldiers stationed themselves outside, while the others went downstairs. All of them carried sound-suppressed 9 mm Stechkin pistols concealed under their jackets.

The door closed and Svarzkova turned on Bolan. "General Ozhimkov ordered me to take you back to American Embassy."

"No, he suggested that it was one of the few places I might be safe," Bolan stated. "Your exact orders were to ensure my safety on the streets of Moscow."

The woman's eyes narrowed slightly. "I had heard United States was a nation of lawyers."

"Listen. We were attacked, on the sixth underground level of GRU headquarters. That tells us something about how deeply embedded they are in your organization. It also means our enemies will have fallback plans. Their initial assault on the two of us has failed. That probably shocked them. Right now they are trying to figure out who I am and yanking your service records. Tactically they will be expecting me to be burning rubber for the embassy in a small convoy of unmarked GRU cars. They will have men waiting, probably with RPG-7 antitank rockets. I'm not ready for that to happen quite yet. Your apartment is the last place they'll expect us to go. Though since you're the first person I contacted, I bet they're having it watched already. I'd give it fifty-fifty that right now they are more than likely trying to scramble something together to hit us here."

"Ah. So, what shall we do now?"

"Wait."

She glanced at her watch. "How soon do you think until we are attacked?"

"Oh, I'd say within the half hour."

"Ah."

"Do you have any more guns?" Bolan asked.

"Yes."

"Go get them."

"Okay." Svarzkova went to her closet. She pulled out an AK-74 rifle with a 30 mm grenade launcher attached to the barrel and a Dragunov semiautomatic sniper rifle. "Which would you prefer?"

"I've got my own coming."

Svarzkova perked an eyebrow as she pulled out ammo bandoliers and began loading her rifles. "We're expecting company?"

"Yeah, we are."

The Dragunov clacked as the captain racked the bolt on a loaded magazine. Svarzkova looked down as her cellular phone rang. She answered it in Russian. She listened for several moments and then held out the phone and spoke in English. "Someone wishes to speak with you."

Bolan took the phone. "Yes."

Carl Lyons spoke. "Tell the captain to let us up. We've got some serious GRU muscle down here and they want verification that we're friendly."

"One second." He nodded at Svarzkova. "They're on our side."

The Russian took the phone and ordered her men to let the visitors in the building. "They are on their way up."

"Call General Ozhimkov. Tell him we're about to be attacked."

"Okay." Svarzkova pushed buttons and began speaking rapid Russian into the phone.

There was a knock on the door.

"Who is it?" Bolan challenged from beside the doorjamb.

"Me."

Jack Grimaldi's voice chimed in behind Lyons's. "Us."

Bolan unbarred the door. The two men from Stony Man Farm were wearing long coats and carrying canvas rifle bags. Lyons also had a something rolled over his shoulder in a tarp.

Svarzkova looked at Grimaldi. "Him I remember. The pilot."

Grimaldi grinned. "Give the lady a cigar."

Lyons had two square sections of rolled chain-link fence. Svarzkova had already drawn the drapes on the two windows on her apartment that faced the street. Lyons produced a bolt gun and began nailing the sections of fence in place.

Bolan began donning the Threat Level III armor they had brought him and he quickly checked his weapons. Grimaldi took four coils of rappelling rope from a bag and Lyons punched three eyebolts into the floor. Grimaldi tied the ropes fast and tested them with a yank.

Valentina Svarzkova looked at Bolan accusingly. "General Ozhimkov wishes to know why you're in my apartment and not at the American Embassy."

"Tell the general it is what the enemy would have expected me to do."

The Russian agent spoke into phone. "The general agrees." Her eyebrow rose as she listened. "However, General Ozhimkov says he can think of better strongholds than my apartment."

"Tell him the enemy will come to the same conclusion."

"Ah." She spoke briefly to the general and nodded. "General Ozhimkov says you're very clever. He says he's scrambling men to our position."

"Unless they're wearing GRU uniforms, how will we be able to tell them from the bad guys?"

Svarzkova relayed the question and then smiled. "General Ozhimkov says you will know." She clicked the phone shut. "So, now we wait."

Bolan jacked a 40 mm grenade into the breech of his M-203. "Yes. Why don't you load a frag."

Svarzkova broke the breech of her grenade launcher and loaded a 30 mm round. "What if the enemy doesn't come?"

"Then we order pizza."

"Ah." She looked at the additions Lyons and Grimaldi had

made to her apartment. "What is the purpose of fencing the windows?"

"It's an old American trick from Vietnam. The VC used to pass out RPG-7 antiarmor rockets like candy to their troops. At the time, RPGs were capable of taking out our armored personnel carriers. But metal fencing around the carriers would detonate the RPG's fuse before it struck the carrier's armor, and thus disperse the explosion. We ended up putting fencing around just about everything we could. The outer walls of your apartment are brick. They'll stop small arms and rockets, but we want any RPG rocket hitting the windows detonating outside your apartment rather than in."

"I agree. Very clever."

Grimaldi and Lyons were busy taking pans of water and soaking the curtains.

"And ropes in my floor?"

"We're on the eighth floor. Rappelling will be a lot faster than the elevator if we want to make a quick exit. Here." Bolan reached into her bag and handed her a rappelling harness and gloves. "Put on some pants."

Svarkova shucked her dress and pulled pants and a University of Moscow sweatshirt from her dresser. A tiny PSM .22-caliber assassination pistol was strapped to her right thigh. An AK-47 bayonet blade with the handles and guard removed was strapped to the other.

Lyons overturned the table and then pulled the mattress off of her bed and laid it behind the table.

Svarzkova pulled on sneakers and then began rapidly donning her weapons and armor. She stepped into the rappelling rig and hiked it up around her hips. "I'm ready."

The phone on the kitchen counter rang. "Captain Svarzkova." Her head cocked to one side. "Hello? Hello?" She slammed the phone down and moved to the makeshift bunker.

"Who was it?"

"The enemy, establishing we are still in apartment. They will hit us now."

Gunfire erupted down in the street. The two men outside the

door shouted. Svarzkova shouted back at them to maintain position. Her cellular phone rang. She listened for a few seconds before announcing, "Our men in front of building are being engaged."

Bullets shattered the glass windows in the apartment. Outside a shrieking hiss sizzled over the sound of gunfire.

Bolan gritted his teeth. "Here it comes!"

High-explosive warheads hit the fencing. Orange light lit up the apartment. Fragmentation tore through the room at neck level, and a jet of molten fire six feet long sent waves of heat rolling over the barricade before it burned out. A second explosion roared outside the window, and another lance of fire shot into the room. Thunder rolled through the tiny apartment, and the room plunged into darkness as the lamps shattered. A third weapon hit the kitchen window, and the armor-piercing fire jet lit the room with lurid flame and blackened the front of the refrigerator. The air in the room was almost too hot to breathe and reeked with the smells of burned high explosive and rocket propellant.

Bolan leaped to his feet. "Now! Hit them! Two on each window."

All three Americans held M-16 rifles mounted with M-203 grenade launchers. Svarzkova was armed with the exact Russian equivalent. Bolan and Svarzkova went to the bedroom window while Grimaldi and Lyons took the kitchen. The RPG-7 was a rocket-propelled grenade launcher. In the Moscow night the trails of white rocket smoke led straight back like accusing fingers to two windows in the opposite apartment complex, and the third led to the roof.

Bolan aimed his M-203 at the roof and fired. Svarzkova's weapon fired beside him while Grimaldi and Lyons looped their own grenades into the offending windows across the street.

Bolan racked open his M-203's smoking breech. "Hit them again. Gas."

The grenade launchers thumped in unison, and CS grenades arced through the air.

"Gas again. Hit the men in the street."

Rifle fire had begun to climb up from the street and impact around the windows of Svarzkova's apartment. Bolan and his men fired gas grenades in flat trajectories down at the riflemen below on the street. They were using cars for cover but they had no cover against clouds of tear gas.

"Captain. Get your men in here to cover us. We're going down." Bolan directed.

Svarzkova barked out orders, and the two GRU men stormed into the room. Bolan and Lyons hooked their ropes through the D-rings on their harnesses.

"All right, by twos. Let's do it."

Bolan kicked out the burned and twisted fencing in the window and stepped out into space. He went face forward and ran down the side of the building in the Australian assault technique. Grimaldi ran right behind him. Rifles cracked from above, and tracers streamed down into the men in tear-gas clouds. On the street people screamed.

Bolan kicked out as he neared the sidewalk and squeezed down on his handbrake. He hit the quick-release buckle and took cover behind a car next to a GRU man. Grimaldi followed.

Lyons and Svarzkova were flying down the side of the building like heavily armed spiders. They braked at the last second and stalled into gentle landings.

"Captain. We need that building sealed off. Get two men on each side. The men in your apartment can cover the front. Deploy on go," Bolan ordered.

Svarzkova shouted at the GRU men. Bullets whined through the air as the men in the tear-gas cloud tried to engage them. Bolan brought the muzzle of his M-16 over the hood of the besieged Zil sedan he was using for cover and flicked his selector lever to semiauto. He put his front sight on a man with a submachine gun and squeezed the trigger. The man jerked back and toppled behind a car.

The Executioner scanned the street. People had fled in all directions, and the street looked empty. Bolan pulled a grenade from his bandolier. "Frag them."

Bolan and Lyons hurled fragmentation grenades over the cars

across the street. Grimaldi tossed a third and orange light flashed. The windows of the cars shattered and spiderwebbed as metal fragments hissed through the air. Men screamed.

Bolan rose. "Go! Go! Go!"

He vaulted over the hood of the Zil and charged across the street. He and Grimaldi broke right, and Lyons and Svarzkova broke left to skirt the gas cloud. Svarzkova's six GRU men ran wide to cover the back and sides of the building.

Nothing moved in the gas cloud. The assassins had been using two parked cars for cover, and the three fragmentation grenades had achieved lethal interlocking circles.

Bolan and his team ran up the steps of the building. Bolan didn't wait to be buzzed in. He and Lyons put their boots into the center of the double door, and it shattered inward on its hinges.

An old man in a red doorman's uniform stood behind his counter and started at the four of them in terror.

"I am Captain Svarzkova of military intelligence! You will obey my orders without question," Svarzkova roared in Russian.

The old man nodded. He answered the Russian agent's questions breathlessly.

Svarzkova jerked her head up at the ceiling. "His name is Pietor. He says eight men he didn't recognize came in carrying large bundles. Two men who rented a room earlier today buzzed them up. They went to the eighth floor. None of them have come down."

Bolan grimaced. That meant more than two to one. With luck they had gotten some of their adversaries their opening grenade salvo from the apartment.

Svarzkova cocked her head. "Gunfire has stopped."

It had, and none of Svarzkova's men had called in. The woman clicked her phone open and spoke. She clicked the phone shut. "My men report no movement. No breakout has been attempted."

Grimaldi looked leerily at the roof above him. "I don't much like the idea of going room to room with them having two-to-one odds on us."

Bolan flicked his M-16's selector to full auto. "They should have tried to get away once the ambush was broken. If they try and hide or set an ambush in the building, it'll waste too much time. The Moscow police will be here in minutes. GRU fast-reaction teams will be right behind them."

"Maybe they don't care if they're captured," Lyons suggested. "Maybe they're betting on their KGB buddies bailing them out and then disappearing."

Svarzkova shook her head. "No, Ozhimkov is the GRU general. He has friends in high places. Even if the directing council of former KGB orders release, he could still delay it for at least twenty-four hours. During that time, General Ozhimkov would personally direct the interrogation. I believe the men upstairs will take extreme measures to avoid capture."

Grimaldi glanced around. "Then why haven't they busted out?"

"They're expecting backup?" Lyons said as he shrugged.

Bolan's face split into a sudden grimace. "They're expecting extraction. Valentina, get on the horn to the general. Tell him our friends are going to try and extract by air." He turned to his men. "We're heading for the roof."

Svarzkova put her phone away. "I have spoken with General Ozhimkov. He says he's on his way. He says he has considered this contingency."

Bolan jerked his thumb upward. "Let's do it. Watch for anyone in the building displaying signs of tear-gas exposure."

Lyons punched the buttons on both elevators and frowned. "They've knocked them out."

"Stairs." Bolan kicked open the stairwell door and lunged aside. No bullets came streaming out of the doorway. "All right, by twos. Captain, you with me."

Bolan and Svarzkova took the stairs, craning their necks and aiming their weapons at each landing above. Grimaldi and Lyons hung back by one landing. They reached the eighth floor, and Bolan motioned them to go on without stopping. They swiftly reached the door that led to the roof. Bolan stepped back down the risers and loaded an antiarmor round into his M-203. He motioned Grimaldi and Lyons forward.

Bolan fired.

The munition struck the steel door at the knob and flung it open.

The concrete interior of the stairwell sparked and shrieked as full-metal-jacketed bullets whined and ricocheted. Bolan reloaded and then pulled a frag grenade from his bandolier. He pulled the pin and the cotter lever pinged off as he hurled it up the steps and out the door. The grenade detonated with a crack. Bolan followed it with a flash-bang and moved up the steps. White light pulsed and thunder rolled.

The Executioner came out of the stairwell with his M-16 snarling on full auto. A bullet struck his chest, but the ceramic trauma plate of his armor held. Bolan aimed at the muzzle-flash and fired his launcher. The gunman was partially covered by a large and obsolete satellite dish. The dish crumpled, and the man was flung from his feet as the high-explosive grenade detonated.

Bolan whipped around the concrete housing of the stairwell and shouted back. "Frag them!"

Grenades began lobbing out of the stairwell and detonating. Bolan reloaded his M-203. After the third detonation he took a quick look. There were at least four gunmen on the roof. They took cover behind air-conditioning housings and chimneys. Two more men were down from the grenades. Rifle fire sparked off the concrete as Bolan ducked back.

"Four hostiles. Fifteen yards from the door. They have cover."

An angry torrent of gunfire hit the stair housing at Bolan's words. The Executioner took two more grenades from his bandolier. "Hit them again. Two grenades."

Hand grenades lobbed up out of the stairwell. They couldn't get an angle to hit the men and instead detonated in front of their cover. But it made them duck, and the Executioner had no such limitations on his trajectory. The instant the second grenade detonated, Bolan stepped from cover. He tossed one of his grenades high and then bowled the other in a low underhand to skip it across the roof between one of the chimneys and an air-conditioning unit. He leaped back as a man rose to fire at him.

The grenades detonated like whip cracks. Men screamed. Bolan moved out to finish the attack and then leaped back as tracers reached out for him. A windstorm whipped up by the thunder of rotor blades ripped across the rooftop. The helicopter had almost fallen out of the sky. The Russian Mi-2 had struts affixed to its fuselage, and the machine guns affixed to them blazed and chopped at Bolan's cover.

Their plan was obvious. The helicopter was going to move around to flush him out into the guns of the riflemen.

Bolan pulled his last frag and looped it up and over his cover. It detonated with a crack. The firestorm continued unabated. He was out of frags, and tear gas wasn't going to stop a helicopter. There was a chimney directly behind the concrete stairwell.

Bolan ran for it.

He dived over it and ducked as the helicopter rounded his cover and fired off a storm of tracers into his former position. Bolan rose from the chimney and fired his entire magazine into the cockpit of the helicopter. Sparks whined and the nose of the helicopter spun to track him. The light-caliber bullets of the M-16 wouldn't penetrate the Russian crash-proof aircraft glass. Bolan dropped and the chimney began to come apart under the onslaught. He pulled his Desert Eagle. Its heavy .44 Magnum rounds were likely to smash through the cockpit of the helicopter, but he would have to stand up into the machine guns to do it.

Bolan's eyes squeezed shut in a sudden, hellishly bright glare. The blinding light of a spotlight held him crouched against the chimney. He considered firing into the light but he noticed the machine guns had ceased firing. The light lifted off of him and Bolan looked up.

A Russian army Hind gunship hovered over the apartment building. It was over sixty feet long and twenty-one feet tall. Its tandem bubble canopies and stub wings gave it the visage of some horrible man-eating insect. Beneath its stub wings were 57 mm rocket pods and twin pairs of AT-6 Spiral laser-homing missiles. Bolan's most immediate concern was the four-barrel

Gatling gun mounted under its chin. All four barrels were pointed at him.

One barrel suddenly ripped into life and sent a stream of fire across the rooftop. The Mi-2 seemed to shiver in place. The message was unmistakably clear. The squat little helicopter was out-engined, out-armored, and outgunned by the army gunship. It resembled a pigeon that had suddenly received the undivided attention of some new and terrible breed of raptor.

Bolan rose from behind his cover. Svarzkova and his men had left the stairwell. The remaining assassins had thrown down their rifles.

Svarzkova walked forward and handed Bolan her phone. "For you."

"Thank you, General. That was timely."

Ozhimkov's voice came over the shuddering of rotors. "You must not be found here. I can't guarantee your safety if you are taken into interrogation. You must flee. Go with Captain Svarzkova."

Bolan looked over the roof edge. Police cars were filling the streets below, and men with rifles were deploying all around the building. "Any suggestions as to how?"

"The gunship is too big to land on the roof. I must stay here. Captain Svarzkova informs me one of your men is a helicopter pilot. Take the Mi-2 to the coordinates I have given Captain Svarzkova. Contact me when you have gotten there. Go quickly. Police helicopters are deploying. You don't wish to be followed. I have radio contact with the Mi-2. They will land now."

On cue the Mi-2 landed on the roof of the building. Bolan jerked his head at Grimaldi and Lyons. Grimaldi gleefully pulled open the cabin door and yanked out the pilot. Lyons did the same to the copilot.

Grimaldi climbed in and donned the headset, glancing at the controls for a moment. He flashed Bolan the thumbs-up. The rotors surged with new power.

Captain Svarzkova grinned at Bolan. "Let us go for little ride in the country."

11

Smolensk

The Mi-2 helicopter touched down in a clearing. They had flown west out of Moscow, and as the lights of the suburbs had faded away they had kept on flying. They flew over small cities and towns until they gave way to scattered villages in the thick pine forest.

Bolan looked out the window. Beyond the clearing was a small farmhouse with a barn. No lights were on and no smoke came from the chimney. Bolan did some mental calculation.

"We're in Smolensk."

Valentina Svarzkova nodded. "Yes. Very good."

They leaped from the helicopter and fanned out. They quickly swept the perimeter and then approached the house from the rear. Svarzkova went into the woods and came back with a key in a black box. She inserted the key into the door. "The house hasn't been opened. There has been no breach in security."

"This is a GRU safehouse?"

"In a sense. However, only General Ozhimkov knows of it. It is his personal dacha."

Bolan examined the little farmhouse. It was almost all of stone construction. The roof was made of clay tiles. It would be almost impossible to burn. The heavy oak door was thick enough to stop rifle bullets and was bound with iron. The windows were narrow slits. Despite the rural trappings, it was clearly a bunker.

Svarzkova opened the door and flicked on the light switch. Wood paneling covered the walls. The door opened into a wide central room. Antique furniture was tastefully arranged before a huge marble fireplace. Trophy heads of deer, bear and boar were mounted on the walls, and thick Persian carpets covered the floor.

"We should be safe here. General Ozhimkov will contact us. We will wait."

Bolan dropped his gear bag in a corner and unslung his rifle. "All right. We'll take watches in twos."

Grimaldi looked at Bolan. "Lyons and I will take the first one. You two go ahead and get some shut-eye."

"Yeah." Lyons was already taking his rifle apart to clean it. "You two probably need to go talk tactics or...something."

Svarzkova looked at the two of them and then at Bolan. "Your men are very uncultured individuals."

Bolan nodded. "I know."

"I like them."

She turned and went up the stairs. Bolan felt his fatigue and the jitters of spent adrenaline as he followed her. Each riser of the narrow stairs felt like a mountain, and his web gear felt as if he were festooned with lead. There were three doors on the second floor, and she led him to the farthest. She opened the door and flicked on the light.

Bolan glanced around the room.

It was dominated by a huge bed. A pair of bearskins was thrown over it, and a third with its head and paws attached lay on the floor beside a small fireplace. There was a sideboard with a number of exquisitely cut crystal decanters. Beneath them was a small refrigerator set into the stone wall. Candlesticks and sconces were placed strategically around the room. In one corner was a tiny table and two chairs where a couple could take an intimate breakfast.

Bolan had to wonder about a seventy-year old Russian military intelligence general who had mirrors on the ceiling of his bedroom.

Svarzkova seemed to read his thoughts. "General Ozhimkov is rumored to be a man of exceptional virility."

"I suppose he must be," Bolan said as he bent to the small

fireplace. Firewood and kindling were expertly stacked inside. He struck a match and set flame to the kindling.

Svarzkova had unstrapped her knife and pistols and tossed them on the bed. She flopped down on the bearskin rug by the fire and watched him.

"Are you sure this is a good idea?"

"This is an excellent idea," Svarzkova confirmed.

Bolan's fatigue fell away from him as he shrugged out of his raid suit.

"THIS IS RIDICULOUS! Must I come to Russia myself," Commander Nemanja asked furiously.

Stasny was at a loss for words. "I don't know what to tell you, I..."

"Of course you don't know what to tell me! It's not in your nature to speak plainly and admit that you're completely incompetent."

"I didn't plan the assassination, Commander. You did."

"I told you to ambush them on the way to the embassy."

"They didn't go to the embassy."

The commander's voice dropped dangerously low. "Then you should have contacted me, and I would have spoon-fed you some intelligent tactics. Instead the incident has turned into a front-page debacle, just as the attack in Macedonia was."

"The assassins were trained paramilitaries. They began the fight with a salvo of RPG-7 antitank rockets. The American and Svarzkova should have been killed in the initial seconds of the attack."

"Apparently they were not," observed Nemanja dryly.

"No."

The commander mollified his tone. "Tell me what happened. I must assess and come up with a new plan."

Stasny brightened as the exchange went from an upbraiding to a war council. "As I said, the attack began with RPG-7s. The American and his henchmen returned fire with grenade launchers firing fragmentation and gas munitions. They then engaged our men on the ground. Our surviving men in the building called for extraction.''

''And?''

''And the American and Svarzkova led a force into the building. They captured the men, took the helicopter and flew away. Their whereabouts aren't currently known.''

''They just took an armed helicopter and flew away?''

''Yes.''

''What of the surviving attack force?''

''They are in custody or in hospital under heavy guard.'' Stasny cleared his throat before continuing. ''I can't verify it, but according to witnesses, a Hind gunship came to their assistance during the fight on the roof.''

''Ah,'' Nemanja said, leaning back in his chair. The situation suddenly became very clear to him. ''That would have been the work of General Ozhimkov.''

The commander nodded to himself. He knew Ozhimkov by reputation, and such unorthodox tactics were exactly the kind of behavior to expect from the old wolf. It was just such methods that had prevented him from attaining the rank of general until well after the Communist regime had fallen. His tactics in Afghanistan had been brilliant, but his independence hadn't sat well with the political commissars in Moscow.

''Yes, our spies tell us that Ozhimkov has been making discreet inquiries, and there is evidence he is mobilizing men he believes are loyal to him.''

Nemanja looked up at his wall map and gazed at Moscow. ''Ozhimkov won't stop. He won't be bribed or intimidated. His loyalties have always been first to Russia and then to his men. In his mind a great crime has been committed against his country. He will do everything in his power to rectify the situation, and he will give invaluable aid to the American.''

''Our spies have told us as much. Ozhimkov is to be feared. Are you sure he can't be bribed or brought into the fold? Is there no family that can be threatened?''

The commander suspected his contact already well knew the

answer to the question, but he was unwilling to say it first. Nemanja decided to cater to his squeamishness.

"I will tell you what we must do." He lightened his tone to sound almost jovial. "We must put a bullet in Ozhimkov's brain."

BOLAN AWOKE and glanced at his watch.

Svarzkova grinned. "Your friends saw fit not to wake us for our watch."

"Well, they're uncultured individuals, but they have their redeeming qualities," he said, relaxing back into his pillow. "I gather there has been no word from Ozhimkov?"

"No. The general hasn't contacted us yet."

Bolan decided he wouldn't mind Ozhimkov holding off for another hour or so, either. He looked down at Svarzkova. He had never seen a woman look more fetching in a bearskin. "How have you been?"

"Well, I was married. I was divorced. I wasn't promoted. I haven't had a pay increase in two years."

"What happened with the marriage?"

Svarzkova shrugged. "He said he didn't like me being a soldier, going into danger. I think perhaps he was jealous."

"Jealous of what?"

"I outranked him."

Bolan smiled. "I can see some guys having a problem with that."

A line drew down between her eyebrows as she stared into the distance of memory. "Indeed. He had a problem with it." She shook her shoulders as if she were shaking off the thought and grinned up at Bolan. "I am glad you are here."

"I thought you said every time you see me you get wounded."

The Russian agent nodded. "Indeed. This is true."

Svarzkova snuggled her head against his chest. "Sometimes I think of leaving Russia."

Bolan glanced down. "Really?"

"Yes. I have fought very hard, but she is falling. I think things will become much worse before getting better. Times are dark. I'm not sure if I wish to see it get darker."

Knuckles rapped twice on the door. Lyons spoke softly but urgently. "You awake?"

"Yeah. What is it?"

"We have company. A chopper's coming in. A transport, no open armament."

"On my way."

Bolan began to hear the thump of rotors as he dressed. He took up his M-16/M-203 combo and checked the loads in the rifle and the grenade launcher. The thumping turned into a steady thunder as the chopper orbited the dacha and then began to descend into the clearing.

Bolan opened the door and followed Lyons down the stairs.

Grimaldi cradled his rifle in his arms and peered out of the narrow slit window. He looked up as his teammates approached.

"It's an Mi-8. We've got four men coming up the drive. Three in uniform. One in civvies."

Bolan took a look out the window. Three of the men wore GRU military uniforms. The man in civilian clothes was Dr. Gareyev. "They're friendlies. Let them in."

Gareyev and a large man wearing lieutenant's stars came to the door while the other two soldiers stood at station several yards back. The men held short-barreled carbines low and kept their eyes on the trees.

Bolan opened the door. "Dr. Gareyev. It's good to see you."

The doctor looked haggard and had dark circles under his eyes. "I'm glad to see you, too. Your men and Captain Svarzkova are well?"

"Everyone is fine here. We needed the sleep. Tell General Ozhimkov we appreciate him opening his private dacha to us. Please, come in."

The Russians entered the dacha. The big lieutenant looked Bolan up and down. He was over six and a half feet tall and his hair was so blond and his eyes so blue that he looked more Swedish than Russian.

Bolan turned his attention to Gareyev. "I'm surprised General Ozhimkov hasn't made any effort to contact us until now."

"General Ozhimkov has been assassinated."

Svarzkova gasped from the top of the stairs. She spoke in such a torrent of Russian Bolan couldn't make out what she was saying. Emotion burst out of Gareyev for the first time. Willpower alone seemed to keep tears from spilling down his cheeks. After long moments of dialogue in Russian, Svarzkova looked at Bolan. "General Ozhimkov was murdered approximately two hours ago in his Moscow apartment. He was shot twice in the chest, penetrating the soft body armor he was wearing. He was then shot in the face with a 12-gauge shotgun. Dental records were required to identify body. Two of his personal GRU guards are missing."

"I'm sorry. I know he was your mentor. He was a good man."

The big lieutenant spoke for the first time. "General Ozhimkov was a Hero of the Soviet Union."

The award of Hero of the Soviet Union was the highest honor a Russian could receive under the Communist regime, and was the equivalent of the United States Congressional Medal of Honor.

"What has become of the prisoners from the firefight in Moscow?" Bolan asked.

The lieutenant's voice was a grate of rage. "They have been transferred into custody of the Foreign Intelligence Service."

Bolan let out a slow breath. The Russian Foreign Intelligence Service was the new name of one of the many branches of the former KGB. However, it was a branch known for international espionage and intelligence gathering rather than terrorism and assassination. Bolan filed that fact away for later. They had more-pressing concerns.

"I don't think there's anything we can do about that. They're going to disappear or die in short order." Bolan ran his eyes over the walls of the fortresslike retreat. It no longer seemed very warm or safe. "We should get out of here. This dacha is probably only hours from being compromised, if it hasn't been already."

The doctor nodded. "Yes, very true. We came to fetch you. I'm sorry we made no contact, but after General Ozhimkov's death, we didn't know if we had a secure line over radio or phone. Gather your gear and weapons. We believe the mission remains unchanged, the threat still exists. There are still men loyal to Ozhimkov, and loyal to the motherland. We'll find out who the perpetrators are and annihilate them, or we will die trying. We are willing to assist you in any way possible, and we'll welcome any assistance the United States can give us in this matter.''

Bolan nodded. "Give us five minutes."

"Indeed. There is aircraft fuel in the barn. We'll refuel your helicopter while you get ready."

Bolan turned to go upstairs, and Svarzkova followed him. The lieutenant's eyes fixed into a glare. If looks could have killed, Bolan would have been splattered all over the dacha's walls.

The doctor locked eyes with the big Russian. The lieutenant's face split into a silent snarl and he spun on his heel. The door closed with a slam behind the two Russians.

Bolan spoke low as they mounted the stairs. "What's his problem?"

"He's upset."

"General Ozhimkov was his mentor, as well as yours, wasn't he?"

"Yes. Lieutenant Stepanshuk looked up to General Ozhimkov like a father."

"He blames me for General Ozhimkov's death."

"No. He blames you for spending the night upstairs with me. Senior Lieutenant Igor Stepanshuk is my ex-husband."

12

"Ozhimkov's dead."

"I know," Kurtzman answered. "We've heard. According to the CIA and military intelligence, the shock waves are still rippling out in the GRU and in Russian intelligence circles. Things in Russia haven't been getting any better. The former KGB and the GRU have always hated each other. This could rip things into open war between them in the streets of Moscow."

"It's not making my job any easier, either."

"What's your status?"

Bolan shook his head. "I would say it's way up in the air. We're currently in hiding. Switching from safehouse to safehouse outside Moscow. There's a small cadre of hard-core GRU officers loyal to Ozhimkov who want revenge, and want to finish the mission he started. I think there are others who want to make peace and avoid a war with the former KGB elements. I think even more on both sides are sitting on their hands and hoping everything will blow over."

"What's your assessment?" Kurtzman asked.

"Someone has a very powerful high-frequency laser and is holding the entire American space program hostage. I think we need to stop him. What have you found out on your end?"

"On the Russian front, I can tell you Dr. Gareyev is a good man. He is highly regarded in the world of international physics. He's one of Russia's rising stars, and I think you can count on him. Everything on the CIA dossier on him says he seems to have been very fond of his grandfather-in-law. They often went hunting and fishing together."

"I get the same feeling. See what you can get me on a GRU lieutenant named Igor Stepanshuk."

"What's his angle?"

"He's Svarzkova's ex-husband."

"Oh."

"He may be entertaining thoughts of killing me," Bolan said wryly.

"Well, I can see that."

"Anything else you can give me?"

There was a moment of silence while Kurtzman pondered. "You're still betting this is a Serbian-run operation?"

"That's what my instincts tell me, but geographically it's not stacking up. They would need local support, and that would be hard for a bunch of Serbians to find in equatorial Africa. The closest place they could find any real sympathy and access to Russian support would be Angola, but that's about eight hundred miles shy of where they need to be to be for the laser to get the angle it needs on space objects in equatorial orbit. The logistics are too extreme.

"The other alternative is having the laser mounted on a boat, but I think that one is too dangerous. I wouldn't do it. It would be too easy for the United States to start sweeping the area with observation aircraft, satellites and ships of our own. Ships are slow, and geographically they would have only a fairly narrow strip of either equatorial African coastline to operate in. There's way too much chance that they would be discovered and that we would sink them. I'd want to be in the jungle. Deep in the bush where no one of any significance could find me and my operation, and anyone around would be so insignificant they could be bribed, intimidated or killed into silence without anyone knowing about it."

"Those are excellent points, and I've thought of them, too." Bolan sat up a little straighter. "You've had an idea?"

"I have, but no one likes it very much."

"I'll take wild speculation at this point."

"I'm thinking about Congo," Kurtzman stated.

"What about it?"

"It's a mess."

"I know that," Bolan said.

"Yes, but what a lot of people don't know is that in all the factional fighting down there, there has been a lot of mercenary activity. The ruling government has been utilizing soldiers and aircraft from Zimbabwe and Chad, while the rebels are getting aid and assistance from Rwanda and Uganda. It's a pan-African nightmare down there."

"Yeah, I've been there."

"But here is a little-known fact for you. France is one of the few Western powers down there with any influence. Most of the attempts at peace talks for the region have been conducted in Paris. What hasn't got much press is that some years ago, when the troubles really began, France tried to militarily prop up one of the factions they supported. They didn't want French troops directly involved, so they acted as brokers to bring in Serbian soldiers and paramilitaries fresh from the fighting in Bosnia."

"Jesus."

"Jesus is right. It was one hell of a blunder, politically and militarily. The Serbian mercenaries behaved like savages. They took the ethnic cleansing and terror tactics they had employed in Bosnia against the Croatians and the Bosnian Muslims and put them to good use. They burned villages, slaughtered civilians and engaged in massacres. It caused a very quiet stink internationally, and the French saw to it that the Serbian mercs got pulled ASAP.

"That was some years ago, but our current situation got me thinking about it. The Serbian mercs may have behaved abominably in Congo, but even with all the atrocities they committed, there must have been some local strongmen who were more than happy to have their opponents hammered by outsiders while they kept their own hands clean."

"You're thinking our Serbian friends may have kept some of the pals they made down in the jungle and are calling in their marker now for an equatorial base of operations."

"Your instincts say jungle, Striker. My intelligence says this is the most likely avenue a bunch of Serbs extremists could take to achieve it."

PLAY BANGO!
AND GET THREE FREE GIFTS!

It looks like BINGO, it plays like BINGO but it's FREE

HOW TO PLAY:

1. With a coin, scratch the Caller Card to reveal your 5 lucky numbers and see that they match your Bango Card. Then check the claim chart to discover what we have for you — 2 FREE BOOKS and a FREE GIFT — ALL YOURS, ALL FREE!

2. Send back the Bango card and you'll get two hot-off-the press Gold Eagle® novels. These books have a cover price of $4.50 or more each, but they are yours to keep absolutely free.

3. There's no catch. You're under no obligation to buy anything. We charge nothing — ZERO — for your first shipment. And you don't have to make any minimum number of purchases — not even one!

4. The fact is, thousands of readers enjoy receiving our books by mail from the Gold Eagle Reader Service™ months before they are available in stores. They like the convenience of home delivery and they love our discount prices!

5. We hope that after receiving your free books you'll want to remain a subscriber. But the choice is yours — to continue or cancel, any time at all! So why not take us up on our invitation, with no risk of any kind. You'll be glad you did!

YOURS FREE!
This exciting mystery gift is yours free when you play BANGO!

It's fun, and we're giving away

FREE GIFTS
to all players!

PLAY
BANGO!

SCRATCH →
HERE!

CALLER CARD

YES! Please send me the 2 free books and the gift for which I qualify! I understand that I am under no obligation to purchase any books as explained on the back of this card.

YOUR CARD ↘

B	A	N	G	O
38	9	44	10	38
92	7	5	27	14
2	51	FREE	91	67
75	3	12	20	13
6	15	26	50	31

CLAIM CHART!

Match 5 numbers	2 FREE BOOKS & A MYSTERY GIFT
Match 4 numbers	2 FREE BOOKS
Match 3 numbers	1 FREE BOOK

(MB-OS-09/00)

366 ADL C4H3   **166 ADL C4H2**

| NAME | (PLEASE PRINT CLEARLY) |

| ADDRESS |

| APT.# | CITY |

| STATE/PROV. | ZIP/POSTAL CODE |

Offer limited to one per household and not valid to current Gold Eagle® subscribers.
All orders subject to approval.

© 1999 GOLD EAGLE

DETACH AND MAIL CARD TODAY!

The Gold Eagle Reader Service™ — Here's how it works:

Accepting your 2 free books and gift places you under no obligation to buy anything. You may keep the books and gift and return the shipping statement marked "cancel." If you do not cancel, about a month later we'll send you 6 additional novels and bill you just $26.70* — that's a saving of 15% off the cover price of all 6 books! And there's no extra charge for shipping! You may cancel at any time, but if you choose to continue, every other month we'll send you 6 more books, which you may either purchase at the discount price or return to us and cancel your subscription.

*Terms and prices subject to change without notice. Sales tax applicable in N.Y. Canadian residents will be charged applicable provincial taxes and GST.

If offer card is missing write to: Gold Eagle Reader Service, 3010 Walden Ave., P.O. Box 1867, Buffalo, NY 14240-1867

BUSINESS REPLY MAIL
FIRST-CLASS MAIL   PERMIT NO. 717   BUFFALO, NY

POSTAGE WILL BE PAID BY ADDRESSEE

GOLD EAGLE READER SERVICE
3010 WALDEN AVE
PO BOX 1867
BUFFALO NY 14240-9952

NO POSTAGE
NECESSARY
IF MAILED
IN THE
UNITED STATES

"I'm buying it. Find out everything you can about the Serb mercenary operations in Congo. Call in every marker we have in French intelligence."

"I'm already on it. But like I said, no one is happy about my theory. French intelligence is a tight-lipped organization, and their government is trying very hard to maintain their influence in Africa. Their involvement in introducing Serbian mercs into the civil war in Congo was a major source of embarrassment. They're not going to be pleased with anyone dredging it up and rubbing their noses in it again. Also, keep in mind that the United States doesn't have much influence in equatorial Africa. Most of the consumer goods and weaponry that can't be produced locally are imported from France, Britain, China and Russia. We have no real clout down there, and other than our embassy, we have no real assets to call upon."

"I know, but it's a good start, Bear. It's a real good start."

Kurtzman's voice grew smug. "Well, it's not bad, and I beat the CIA boys to it by about five hours." His voice grew serious again. "What do you intend to do from your angle?"

"I'm not done up here. Ozhimkov died trying to help us. I want to help our associates here, and I wouldn't mind getting a piece of whoever took out the general and gave this technology to Serbian terrorists."

"Avenging Ozhimkov is not our primary mission, Striker. However personally pleasurable that might be."

"I know that. Personal feelings aside, we still need to find out everything I can about our hypothetical laser. What it looks like, how big it is and what kind of care and feeding it needs. See what you can come up with for possible fuel sources it might require and what kind of maintenance it would need. Those kind of chemicals and equipment should be awfully damn rare in Congo, and if we can get any kind of bead on their supply line, we might just get lucky and get a straight shot at them."

"I'm on it," Kurtzman acknowledged.

"Tell Hal to let the President know the situation from here. I know he doesn't want an international situation with the Russians, and I know the politics of having an international incident in Africa are even more precarious.''

"Hal spoke with the President after we learned Ozhimkov had been killed.''

"What does the Man have to say?''

"He says we're still a go on your discretion.''

Bolan smiled thinly. It was rare for the President of the United States to give him complete discretion.

"Tell the President we're a go.''

"OZHIMKOV IS DEAD?''

"Yes. Our KGB friends proved themselves very valuable in this regard. General Ozhimkov had made many enemies over the years. There are even some in the GRU who aren't so sorry to see him gone. His unorthodox methods and special-forces background made him something of a loose cannon—he stepped on many toes. As a whole, the GRU is appalled that one of their own was assassinated, but he isn't one they are willing to go to war over. Things are too unstable already.''

Branko Nemanja nodded. In the modern world it was always the truly capable men who were most feared and loathed by the politicians. It was a phenomenon that the commander had experienced firsthand.

Nemanja allowed a bitter smile to cross his lips. The politicians had loved him well enough when he had fought for them in Bosnia and Croatia. He had done their dirty work, and they had called him a patriot and a hero. When the Bosnian peace accord had been reached, he had become a political pariah and an international war criminal wanted for genocide. The gratitude of the French for the services he had rendered them in the jungle had been little better. Now he was needed again, and he didn't intend to be cast aside once more when their objectives were accomplished.

The commander's smile turned ugly. There was good reason for the politicians to fear a capable man.

"What has become of the prisoners taken during the fighting in Moscow?'' Nemanja queried.

"The former KGB elements took them in custody from the Moscow police before the GRU could get ahold of them."

"Good. What is their situation now?"

"They have been disposed of," Stasny stated. "The men who killed Ozhimkov have been similarly taken care of. I had this done on your authority."

"Good. Very good." Nemanja was pleased. Scum who would shoot their own leader in the head for gold weren't the kind of men who could be trusted to keep their mouths shut. The commander shook his head in wonder. It seemed hard to believe, but even this political toad who was his only link to the civilized world was actually beginning to develop a grasp of tactics. "What is the situation with the American?"

"We don't know his location. Our Russian friends determined that after the firefight, he, Captain Svarzkova and at least two other men they believe to be Americans, took the captured helicopter to a dacha owned by Ozhimkov. Russian paramilitaries assaulted the dacha and burned it, but the American was no longer there. We have the American Embassy, Captain Svarzkova's apartment and most known assets of General Ozhimkov under observation."

"What about families? Does Ozhimkov have anyone we can strike against?"

"General Ozhimkov's immediate family has apparently dropped out of sight. We believe he sent them away as soon as the American presented him with the information."

"What about Captain Svarzkova—does she have anyone we can threaten?" Nemanja pressed.

"An ex-husband. He is a former Spetsnaz officer and was recruited into the GRU by Ozhimkov. He has disappeared."

"How much genuine resistance can we expect in Moscow from the GRU?"

"Little. A small number of officers, field agents and special-forces soldiers have gone missing. The GRU is already beginning to form a cover story that Ozhimkov was involved with the Russian *mafiya* and that this was a criminal matter rather than political assassination. Most will allow that story to stand, however much it galls them. Those who don't can be bribed, intimidated or eliminated,'' Stasny stated.

''Very well. Keep our KGB friends on the alert. The American must show himself sooner or later. Until then, I believe it is time to give the U.S. government a bit more dissuasion.''

''You have a target in mind?''

''I do,'' the commander confirmed.

''The leaders don't wish any more U.S. military satellites engaged while they are moving their military assets out of the Balkans and starting to lift sanctions.''

''We will not strike their precious military space toys. Instead we will give them a mystery. A mystery that they will have a difficult time explaining to the American people.''

13

A map of Russia and the former Soviet republics lay spread out across the coffee table. Bolan rubbed his eyes. If he drank any more coffee, he would burst, and despite that he could barely keep his eyes open. They had been rotating from safehouse to safehouse. Every time they contacted someone in the GRU for information, they risked discovery and death. You could only stay on a high state of alert for so long before you became useless to yourself and everyone else.

Bolan stared at the map. There were top secret military bases in Russia and its former republics beyond counting, and those were just the ones the United States knew about. Top secret protocol had been shattered when they opened a prepositioned satchel of documents that General Ozhimkov had left in case of his demise on this mission. Red dots seemed to cover the map of the continent from the Ukrainian coast on the Black Sea to the peninsula of Kamchatka in the Bering Sea. All of them were heavily guarded. Most of them were deep underground in hardened bunkers, and without General Ozhimkov, they had no access to any of them. There were well over a hundred sites to choose from, and assaulting any of them would be suicide without help from within.

Senior Lieutenant Stepanshuk sighed and shook his head. He leaned back and rubbed his temples. "It's useless. We don't know who in the former KGB to fight. We don't know where to begin to look for a laser or laser facility. It's a needle in a haystack."

Valentina Svarzkova glared at her ex-husband briefly but said nothing. *Give up* wasn't in her vocabulary, but neither did she have any ideas. They were staring at a labyrinth of impossibilities. Their entire assets consisted of the people in the room, one full squad of Spetsnaz special-forces troops loyal to Lieutenant Stepanshuk who had gone AWOL and one GRU general named Torosyan, an old friend of Ozhimkov. With every communication they made with GRU headquarters, they expected to hear that Torosyan had taken a bullet in the brain like his friend. They also had many assets of the American intelligence network at their disposal over satellite link, but here in the outskirts of Moscow they had little to offer. They would receive little or no aid, and any action they took would have to succeed the first time. A failed attempt would mean the enemy would begin striking more United States satellites, many of them vital. They needed to pinpoint the enemy and take them out, and they had to do it soon. At the moment they were paying lip service to the terrorists' demands. Soon they would have to take real action, and that would mean turning over American foreign policy at gunpoint.

The few things they had learned hadn't been good. Both Svarzkova and Stepanshuk had been reported AWOL and were wanted by the military authorities. Dr. Gareyev was wanted by the police on suspicion of a number of charges. All were to be considered armed and dangerous and should be arrested on sight. There was also a bounty on all of their heads of one hundred thousand American dollars. Showing their faces in Moscow would be a death sentence.

Bolan stared at the map again. "Dr. Gareyev."

The doctor rubbed his temples and looked up from the map blearily. "Yes?"

"This is useless. We need an insider. Who do you know in the scientific community who might be of any help?"

"It's hard to say. There are well over thirty scientists I know of personally who would have been involved in such a project. All would be sworn to secrecy. None would answer our questions. Further, if our enemies have any sense at all, they have bought, intimidated or have these scientists under surveillance.

Any attempt on our part to contact them would endanger them and ourselves.''

Bolan had to admit the doctor was right. The others around the table sagged with the weight of Gareyev's words. They were running out of time and options.

Everyone in the room jumped as Bolan's fist crashed down on the tabletop. His finger stabbed down onto a map of Moscow and its outlying areas. The Executioner's finger lay upon a tiny red rectangle representing the University of Moscow. ''Dr. Gareyev, I want you to assume you are a bright young student of physics ten years ago. Your specialty ended up being high-frequency lasers. Who would your instructor have been?''

Gareyev's eyes flew wide. Everyone around the table sat up straight. ''Why, that would be Professor Juris Macs. He was Latvian. A brilliant man, far ahead of his time.''

''Do you know if he is still on staff at the University of Moscow?''

''No, he is no longer there. He returned to Latvia when it declared its independence from Russia. I believe he grew up on the coast outside of the city of Rucava. I was in one of his classes. His family were fishermen—he often told humorous anecdotes about fishing and used many metaphors of his life there in his lectures.''

Grimaldi wore his usual grin. He had never once lost faith that Bolan would come up with something.

Bolan tracked his finger across the map to Latvia and found the city of Rucava on the western edge of Latvia near the Baltic Sea.

''We're going to pay a visit to Professor Macs. I need a four-man team. Dr. Gareyev, you took classes with him, so you're our contact. Captain Svarzkova is the ranking Russian officer, and we may need her to make things official.''

Grimaldi smiled. ''You need a pilot.''

''You're right.'' Bolan looked at Stepanshuk. The big Russian's face had reddened and he sat ramrod stiff. It was clear he didn't like being left behind, and that he liked Bolan giving orders on Russian soil even less. The Executioner met the man's glare without blinking. "Lieutenant, I need you and your men ready for insertion. Possibly in Latvia if the enemy is thinking the same way we are, possibly here in Russia if we get lucky with Professor Macs. You need to be ready to go at a moment's notice." He gestured at Lyons. "He will be your contact with the U.S. Embassy. Anything you need, money, weapons, equipment, he'll requisition it for you."

Stepanshuk nodded slowly. "Yes. I see logic of your plan. My men and I will be ready. We already have parachutes and scuba gear, as well as variety of weapons. Logistics of transportation and insertion I will leave to your man when you tell us where and when to strike. We will await your word."

Bolan turned to Grimaldi. "Get on the horn to the embassy. Arrange us some transportation. I want to be in Latvia before sunrise."

Baltic Coast, Latvia

MACK BOLAN LAY in the sand. There was neither moon nor clouds in the night sky. The ripples of the Baltic's quiet surf were little more than a whisper. The border of Lithuania was a four-mile jog down the beach. The Executioner examined the house through the night-vision sight of the Dragunov sniper rifle the CIA had prepositioned for him in the U.S. Embassy in Latvia.

The house was small but beautifully constructed. There was a porch facing the sea with a hot tub and sauna off to one side. A shiny red Alpha Romeo Spider and a battered-looking Volkswagen van were parked on the gravel by the side of the house. They had observed the house for an hour. Most of the windows were open. There seemed to be only one occupant in the house. Professor Macs had a wife, but she hadn't appeared.

A man came out of the house as Bolan watched. He was short, with hair that fell to his shoulders. His wire-rimmed glasses glinted in the night. The man struggled under the weight of a telescope. Bolan recognized the six-foot cannon-like focal tube as a Newtonian refractor. The man put the telescope into a wooden cradle and pulled off the telescope cover and began collimating his mirrors.

Bolan turned and looked at Svarzkova. She watched the scene through the scope of a rifle that was the twin of Bolan's. "Doesn't appear to be a trap."

Bolan spoke into his throat mike. "Jack, what have you got?"

Grimaldi was positioned a hundred yards down the beach in a stand of grass atop a dune. They had swept the beach after sunset and found no observers. Without being able to sweep the house for bugs, they couldn't afford to contact the professor over the phone or by knocking on his door. This unexpected amateur astronomy session was just about the most best opportunity they could expect.

"All right. Keep us posted on any movement. It will either come from the sea or from the coast road. Keep an eye out," Bolan warned.

"You got it."

"Does Professor Macs speak English?"

Gareyev nodded as he watched through a pair of binoculars. "Yes, he is fluent in seven languages as I recall."

"Good. Use English to greet him."

"All right."

Bolan rose. "Let's go pay the professor a visit."

Svarzkova and Gareyev rose and dusted off the sand. They walked up the beach toward the house. The professor stared raptly up into the sky and then bent to the spotting scope attached to the barrel of his main tube.

They reached the foot of the porch, and Gareyev cleared his throat and spoke. "Professor Macs."

The little Latvian jumped two feet in the air. His telescope swung wildly on its mount. He grabbed his chest and stared wildly at the people on his porch. A stream of shocked words came out of his mouth.

Gareyev spoke uncomfortably. "Professor Macs. It's me, Sergei Gareyev. I took classes from you at Moscow university. You recommended me for a position after I achieved my doctorate."

"Gareyev?" The professor stuttered his English as he beheld

the trio before him. "Gareyev, Sergei. Why are you here? Who are these people?" The professor's eyes widened further as he took in Captain Svarzkova. "Why do they have guns? What's going on? I have done nothing. I have little of value, I—"

"Professor Macs," Bolan spoke quietly but firmly. "I represent the government of the United States."

"If you represent the United States, why do you have a Russian sniper rifle?"

Bolan ignored the question. "This is Captain Valentina Svarzkova of Russian military intelligence. You know Dr. Gareyev. It is very urgent that we speak to you, and it's possible that your life is in danger."

Professor Macs's eyes stayed fixed on the muzzles of the Dragunov rifles. "I can see that."

"Where is your wife?"

The professor stiffened and glared.

"We want to be sure she is safe."

The physicist set his jaw.

Bolan changed tactics. He examined the telescope admiringly. "That has to be at least ten inches of aperture."

The Latvian eyed Bolan warily. "It's twelve."

The Executioner examined the tube. It had been hard to tell through the scope, but up close Bolan could see that it had been painted very crudely with stars, planets and constellations. "You build it yourself?"

"Yes. My granddaughter painted it. She's ten." A grudging look crossed the physicist's face as if he found it hard to believe that anyone who knew telescopes could be a bad person. "My wife is in Finland, visiting her sister."

Bolan nodded. It was one factor they didn't have to worry about. "I see you haven't lost your interest in deep-space phenomenon. How's your interest in more local events in space?"

The professor blinked. "None of the planets are in an optimal phase for observation tonight. I'm not sure I understand your meaning."

Bolan pulled a videotape from the satchel strapped to his side. "Do you have a VCR?"

The professor eyed the tape as if it were a snake. "Yes."

"We've recorded some localized space phenomena that might interest you."

Macs looked long and hard at the rifles in Bolan and Svarzkova's hands.

"The guns are for our protection, and yours, Professor. You are not our prisoner. If you ask us to leave, we will. However, I'll warn you. Your house may have been bugged. If we come inside, it may bring other people to your house. These people won't be anywhere near as nice as we are."

Macs's gaze flicked from Gareyev to the guns to Bolan and then to Svarzkova. Between each glance his eyes were irresistibly drawn to the video in Bolan's outstretched hand. "I'll look at your tape."

"I'll come with you. Put the tape in, watch it, say nothing. Then we will come outside and talk."

Bolan gave him the tape and he followed Macs inside. The professor popped the tape into his VCR and sat on the edge of an overstuffed chair and picked up his remote. He watched in utter fascination as the videotape of space shuttle *Atlantis's* cargo-bay monitor showed the incandescent flash of the main laser and then the fire, smoke and debris of the destroyed satellite hitting the interior of the cargo bay in chilling silence. His jaw dropped as the pale blue beam of the aiming LADAR made its crystal-clear threat to the shuttle itself. The professor began to play parts of the tape forward and back and hit the slow motion and freeze frame repeatedly.

He looked up at Bolan when he was through. The Executioner jerked his thumb back out toward the porch.

As they rejoined Svarzkova and Gareyev, Bolan pulled out a small tape recorder. He played the voices of the shuttle crew as they reacted to the attack. He then pulled out computer-enhanced versions of the three targeting plots Andy Reed had given them. Professor Macs took a red tinted flashlight and examined the diagrams while Bolan spoke.

"The United States lost three top secret satellites before the space-shuttle incident. We're nearly positive that the weapon used was designed in Russia, and is now in the hands of Serbian terrorists.''

''Serbian terrorists?''

''Professor, we believe the weapon has been deployed in equatorial Africa. We believe it's small and highly portable. We're fairly sure it uses LADAR for aiming and the terrorists are using preplotted coordinates from the Internet for tracking. I need to know who in the Russian scientific community would have been in on the development of the weapon and what facility the work would have been done in. I need to know what kind of fuel it would most likely use and what, if any, special maintenance or equipment it would require.''

''This is…inconceivable.''

''It has happened. The Serbians have demonstrated they are willing to use the weapon, and there is nothing to stop them from selling the technology to the highest bidder, either. If they choose to do so, anyone with the money and a grudge will be able to savage or hold the space program of any other nation hostage. We're talking about the militarization of space.''

Bolan emphasized the words. Most astronomers were deeply and morally offended by the idea of space-based weapons systems. The cosmos unfolded in its own perfection, and human hostility had no place in it. The phrase ''militarization of space'' was a rallying call for protests and letter-writing campaigns, and was designed to hit a retired physicist and amateur astronomer whose ten-year-old granddaughter had painted his homemade telescope.

Professor Macs was silent for a very long time. His shoulders sagged as he looked at Gareyev. ''Sergei, tell me, is what the American said true?''

''Yes, Professor. People have already been killed over this. My grandfather-in-law was assassinated trying to investigate the matter. You're just about the only lead we have left. Most of my work has been academic, but you have trained some of Russia's best minds. Many of them went into military development. Any clue you can give us might help us avoid a military and scientific nightmare.''

Macs shook his head sadly and turned to Bolan. "You say my house may have been bugged?"

"We can't be sure, but we have to assume the enemy may have come to the same conclusions we have. You weren't dead when we found you, which is a good sign that they haven't thought of you yet, but that could change at any time. And they may already be lying in wait for us to contact you."

"May I keep these materials for the next twenty-four hours?"

"Yes. Look them over carefully." Bolan reached into his pack again and pulled out a cellular phone. "Take this. The first preset will get ahold of me. If for any reason I don't answer, it means I've been killed, captured or recalled, so use the second preset. A GRU lieutenant named Igor Stepanshuk will give you whatever assistance he can."

Macs took the phone and the packet of materials. "I will think of who I can contact and see what I can come up with. Tomorrow I will go into town and make phone calls. Come back here at this same time tomorrow night. I will have my telescope out again. We'll talk."

14

Dusk was falling, and the red ball of the sun was painting the gray waters black and gold. It was a peaceful sea. Bolan and his team had spent the day in the dunes keeping an eye on Macs's house while he had gone into town. Waiting was the hardest part of any mission, but after a sleepless week of playing hide-and-seek from the KGB in Moscow, all of them had needed the downtime. Grimaldi was a few yards above in the long grass atop the dune on his watch. Dr. Gareyev had dozed off in the sun while watching the surf. Svarzkova lay on the blanket next to Bolan dead to the world.

Her blue eyes snapped open as Bolan's phone rang.

The soldier flicked open the phone. "What's happening, Professor?"

Macs voice sounded anxious. "I believe I'm being followed."

"Are you sure?"

"No, but it's a feeling I have. I believe I've seen the same two men several times, and as far as I can tell they are strangers."

"Are you armed?"

"I have my pistol."

Bolan looked at the side of the house. The battered van was still parked. Professor Macs had taken his sports car. "Are you near your car?"

"I'm sitting in it."

"Come home now. We can protect you here. We'll see anyone coming in behind you. Leave the line open."

Bolan heard the snarl of the little Italian roadster's engine. "I'm on my way."

The Executioner rose and checked the load in his Dragunov.

"Macs is on his way. He may be coming in hot. Grimaldi, get the boat. We're extracting. Now."

Grimaldi rose quickly, and his boots sent sand flying as he ran down the beach. The CIA had positioned a motorboat for them a mile down the beach in a tiny cove.

Bolan reached into one of the gear bags and pulled out an AK-74 rifle and raised an eyebrow at Gareyev. "I'm hoping you didn't get an educational deferment from the draft."

"As one in the top five percentile in scientifics in my secondary school and because of my early acceptance at the Moscow university, I was given the option of an educational deferment from military conscription." Gareyev gave Bolan a bleak smile. "My father wouldn't hear of it. I served two years."

Bolan tossed the weapon to Gareyev along with a bandolier of six magazines. "Get to the boat. We may need covering fire."

Gareyev loped down the beach after Grimaldi. Svarzkova shrugged into her web gear. "Shall we go greet Macs?"

"We're only a few miles from town. The professor should be here any second." Bolan raised the phone. "Professor, where are you?"

"I'm almost there. There is a van perhaps a half kilometer behind me."

Bolan and Svarzkova ran to the house. Bolan threw his rifle to his shoulder and looked through the scope. The red sports car was tearing down the road. He could make out the glint of a vehicle some distance behind it. Bolan swung his scope down the other direction. A van was coming up from the south. The enemy was making a pincer movement.

"Professor, open up that car for all it's worth!" Bolan flicked off his safety and jerked his head down the road. "We have two vehicles coming in. Vans, and I'm assuming they are carrying at least several armed men each. I want to hit them before they can get close to the house."

Svarzkova flicked off the safety of her sniper's rifle. "Very well. I'll take the flank attack. You cover Macs."

"Do it."

Mac's voice rose in urgency over the phone. "They're accelerating after me."

"Just come in. We have you covered."

Svarzkova wrapped her arm securely into the sling of her rifle. "The other van is accelerating."

The Executioner strode out into the middle of the road. He and Svarzkova stood back to back almost like duelists. They both assumed a rifleman's crouch. The professor's convertible came screaming in toward the beach house. It fishtailed and nearly spun out as he stomped on the brakes. Bolan aimed his rifle.

The front windshield of the van filled the scope's reticle. Bolan smoothly squeezed the trigger of the rifle twice. The stock bucked back into his shoulder, and the windshield on the driver's side spiderwebbed with cracks.

The van began to swerve, and Bolan put two more bullets into the passenger side. The besieged windshield shattered inward. Svarzkova's rifle boomed in a long slow cadence of aimed semiautomatic fire.

The Executioner rapidly dumped the last six rounds of his magazine into the van's grille.

When his Dragunov clacked open on a smoking empty chamber, Bolan slid in a fresh magazine and racked the action as the van came to a halt. He looked around behind him. The other van had slammed into a hill by the side of the road, it's windshield shattered.

Bolan turned his gaze back to the other van. The side door of the van shot open, and five men with weapons piled out scrambling.

Both rifles fired. Two of the men went down hard on the pavement. The other two leaped into a drainage ditch. Bolan picked off a third as two more leaped from the back of the van and ran the opposite way. One went down, and Bolan grimaced as the other disappeared down beside the road.

The Executioner slid in a fresh magazine. "I have three hidden beside the road. How many do you have on your side?"

"I eliminated three. Four remain."

"Let's get out of here." Bolan looked over at Macs, who was

crouched beside his car with a small pistol in his hand. "Professor! Get down to the beach. Gareyev will meet you with a boat. We'll cover you."

The professor broke into a lumbering run for the beach. Bolan and Svarzkova faded back toward the house. "Grenades would be good," Bolan suggested.

Svarzkova smiled thinly. "A Hind gunship would be better."

The CIA only had four hours' notice and didn't have the kind of assets on station in Latvia as in Moscow. The boat and the rifles had been a godsend, but heavy weaponry had been too much to ask on such short notice.

The Executioner spoke into his throat mike. "Jack, where are you?"

"Gareyev and I have the boat in the water. We're bringing it up to the beach house. ETA two minutes."

"Get the professor and go. Forget about us. We'll meet you in Lithuania."

"Roger that."

Svarzkova looked up at Bolan. "The enemy will be able to engage the boat and Professor Macs from dunes. There is no cover on the beach."

"I know. We're going to give them something else to shoot at," Bolan responded.

Svarzkova looked over at the red Alpha Romeo. The keys were in the ignition and the engine was still running. "The car?"

"You drive."

They threw their rifles into the back and leaped into the car. Svarzkova pulled her 9 mm CZ-75 pistol and tossed it onto the dashboard. Bolan drew both his Beretta 93-R machine pistol and his .44 Magnum Desert Eagle from their holsters. The little Italian car howled as she revved the engine and ground the gears. The tires screeched on the pavement, ramming Bolan back in his seat as she dropped into first gear. The car shot out onto the road.

The enemy behind them was too far back to make much of a difference, but there were three men ahead of them with weapons. Bolan kept his eye on the side of the road. A man popped up with a weapon in his hands. The Executioner fired a pair of 3-round bursts at him, but he was out of range.

The man answered with a long burst from a submachine gun. Sparks whined off of the front fender, and the side mirror on Bolan's side twisted and broke away from a bullet strike.

He flicked the Beretta's selector lever to semiautomatic. Although he couldn't get a steady bead on the man, Bolan began squeezing the trigger slowly and methodically.

The Alpha's windshield crackled and webbed as three bullets walked up its center. Bolan heard the supersonic crack of the bullets pass overhead as the gunman's long burst continued. Bolan set his jaw and calmly kept returning fire.

The man suddenly jerked, and his weapon fired a long stream up into the air as he fell.

The Alpha screamed down upon the stricken van. Bolan dropped his Beretta and took his big .44 Magnum in both hands. "He was posted to watch the road. The other two may have moved on to the beach. Or they may have been drawn back by the sound of—"

Bolan raised his aim and fired. The other two had indeed come back out of the dunes at the sound of gunfire. Orange fire twinkled directly at Bolan. The Executioner jerked in his seat as sparks shot off the passenger door and two blows, like the jabs of a boxer, hit him in the chest. The Desert Eagle roared in Bolan's hands. The machine gunner fell.

Thunder roared.

The windshield smashed inward. Svarzkova flailed backward and the roadster swerved out of control. Bolan seized the wheel, but Svarzkova sagged forward over his arm. The car spun out of control. The chassis rocked as it left the road and then dropped sickeningly as its left-side wheels left the ground and the car landed in the drainage ditch. Time seemed to compress into slow motion. The car hurtled forward before hitting something solid.

The Desert Eagle flew from Bolan's hand as he was rammed into the dashboard and momentum tried to fold him in half around it. The car bounced on its axles and then settled, and Bolan sagged back into his seat, stunned. His vision was blurred and blood was running into his eyes. What he could see was a dark cloudiness around the edges of his vision and pulsing purple pinpoints lurking in that darkness.

Instinct took over.

He pawed drunkenly with his left hand for the Dragunov rifles behind him. His hands found nothing. The rifles had been thrown clear. The Desert Eagle was gone and he couldn't find his Beretta. His hand closed around the twisted frame of the windshield. Bolan's body obeyed him only grudgingly as he painfully pulled himself up out of the convertible.

His first impulse was to check Svarzkova, but battle instincts prevented him. The shooter would be here in seconds, and her condition would be immaterial.

Bolan wiped the blood out of his eyes as he got himself sitting up on the passenger door. His vision darkened as he reached down and clawed at his ankle holster. The 9 mm Smith & Wesson Centennial snub-nosed revolver came out, and the cold weight in his hand seemed to resolve some of his fuzziness.

The world skewed and his vision nearly went black as he tried to stand up on the hood of the stricken car. He rested a hand against the sharp rock of the ditch wall. A noise above jerked him back into awareness. Bolan stood and punched the muzzle of the Centennial out before him.

A man with a shotgun stood five yards away.

With his blurry vision it seemed like three men. Bolan fired at the one in the middle.

Something like a great fist hit Bolan in his stomach and rammed him off his feet. He sat down hard on the crumpled hood of the Alpha, and his back fell against the other side of the ditch.

The man stood on the edge of the ditch and raised his shotgun.

Bolan brought up the Centennial in both hands.

The killer jerked.

A snapping noise came from Bolan's right. Svarzkova's tiny PSM assassination pistol snapped again. The killer eyes widened and he looked down at two pinpoint stains that had appeared as if by magic on the front of his shirt. Svarzkova's arm swayed like a tree branch in a high wind. The pistol fired again and missed.

The killer opened his mouth and then closed it. He swayed on his feet and slowly brought the shotgun up to his shoulder.

Bolan fired.

The assassin's head jerked back and he fell from sight.

Bolan looked wearily over at Valentina. "Are you all right?" he asked.

Her head lay back on the headrest and her eyes were half-closed as she looked up into the sky. Her voice was a croak as her left hand dragged across her chest. "Shotgun hit me in my chest, but I believe the body armor has held."

Bolan felt his own front. His jacket sported ragged holes in the chest and shoulder. The fabric had been torn like confetti on his stomach. He could feel the ceramic trauma plate of his armor flex where it had cracked against the dashboard. His armor had prevented his rib cage from being shattered. The titanium plate in Svarzkova's armor had been all that had kept her from being impaled on the steering wheel.

"We have to move. There are still three men about a mile back."

"Yes." Svarzkova made no effort to move.

"Come on." Bolan forced his knees beneath him and reached over the windshield. Svarzkova raised a shaky hand. She grunted from the pain as Bolan pulled her up with him as he rose. He staggered a step across the hood of the sports car and put his hands against the side of the ditch. He found a foothold and levered himself up onto the road.

"Come on." It took every ounce of Bolan's strength to pull her up out of the ditch, and the two of them lay gasping on the road. "Did you shoot into the van's grille?"

Svarzkova pondered the question for long moments. "No. I shot out the windshield."

"Good. Come on."

Bolan levered himself up onto his feet. He gave Svarzkova a hand, and the two of them hobbled across the road arm in arm to the van. They covered it with their pistols as they approached.

The sliding door was open, and Bolan helped the woman into it. The Volkswagen's front grille was crunched inward, but the German designers had put the engine in the centerline of the car. There was a chance it would still start.

Two men sat in the front.

The driver's head sagged at an impossible angle, and his chest was awash with blood. The man in the passenger seat was worse. Bolan walked around to the driver's side and pulled the driver out of the seat. The keys were still in the ignition.

"Hey."

Bolan looked back. "What?"

"Someone is coming."

Bolan looked down the road as another van approached. Bolan checked the loads in his Centennial. He had two shots left. A man leaned out the passenger window of the oncoming van. Gunmetal gleamed dully in the afternoon sun. Bolan eased out the driver's side and kept the body between him and the oncoming vehicle.

"I don't suppose there is a rifle back there," he said to Svarzkova.

"No."

"That's too bad."

"There is a rocket launcher," she offered.

Bolan wiped blood out of his eyes. "Really?"

"Yes."

"Hand it to me."

The muzzle of a Russian RPG-18 slid out of the window to him. The RPG-18 was a shameless Russian copy of the American LAW rocket. The light antitank weapon had never been a great success. It had been too light to handle a Russian tank when it had first been designed in the late sixties and it was totally obsolete now. By reputation the Russian copy wasn't much better. There was hardly a front-line armored vehicle in the Western Hemisphere it could handle.

But a 1969 Volkswagen camper van was another matter.

Bolan flipped the release and pulled the telescoping launch tube to full extension. The simple optical sights popped up as the tube locked. Bolan waited until the van came within fifty yards and then stepped out of cover with the launcher over his shoulder.

The rifleman leaning out the window shouted and fired a long burst from his rifle that flew high and wide. The driver panicked and swung the wheel wildly, presenting Bolan with a full broadside angle on the van. The Executioner pressed the RPG-18's trigger button. The rocket sizzled out of the tube trailing a plume of white smoke. The shaped-charge warhead stuck the van dead center and filled it with molten metal and superheated gas.

The windows blew out from the overpressure, and the van shuddered as smoke and flame shot out of it in all directions. It rose up on its chassis as the gas tank ignited and then sagged back down. Black smoke began belching out.

The spent RPG-18 clattered to the road. Bolan walked back around the van and looked in on Svarzkova. "How are you?"

She lay across one of the bench seats and spoke without opening her eyes. "I'm very tired."

"Would you like to go to Lithuania?"

"Yes. I hear it is very nice."

"I'll take you there."

"Thank you."

Bolan climbed inside the van and slid the door shut. He sat in the bloodstained driver's seat and then as an afterthought leaned across and opened the passenger door and shoved out the remaining dead body. With an effort he raised his foot up and kicked out the sagging windshield. The engine started on the first try, and Bolan backed the van out onto the road. He wiped fresh blood out of his eyes as he turned the van south.

He idly wondered if the Lithuanians had a border checkpoint.

15

"This is insane. It's worse than insane. It is intolerable."

Stasny had no good answer. It was indeed an intolerable turn of events. "I don't know what happened, Commander. Our KGB allies had Macs under observation in the town when you gave the order to kill him. He drove out to his beach house where he apparently had heavily armed allies waiting. The Russians were wiped out."

"Do we know where he is now?"

"No. I suspect they fled to Lithuania."

"Does the KGB not have assets in Lithuania?"

"Yes, but Macs was in Latvia. Our friend's assets in Lithuania weren't activated on our behalf until after the shootout on the shore, and by then it was too late. Macs is probably in a safehouse or in the U.S. Embassy. A KGB agent posing as a Latvian lawyer managed to speak with one of the surviving attack team members in hospital. He says reports seeing two of the professor's defenders. One was a large heavily armed Caucasian male who may fit the description we have of the American in Moscow. The other he clearly identified as Svarzkova. They escaped in Macs's sports car. It was a two-seat vehicle, and Macs wasn't seen after he reached his house. The assassin believes the car was a diversionary tactic to draw fire while Macs was extracted by sea."

"Tell me the American and Svarzkova are dead."

"We don't know. We know from KGB intelligence sources that one of the vans the attack team used was disabled by high-power rifle fire. Macs's van was destroyed by an antitank rocket.

The sports car was found crashed in a drainage ditch riddled with bullets. There was a significant amount of blood in both the driver and passenger seats. There were no bodies except for those of the attack team. One of the vans the attack team used is missing. All members of the attack team are accounted for, either in the hospital or in the morgue.''

Nemanja's knuckles creaked as he made a fist. He knew where the missing van was. It was in Lithuania. The American had stolen one of their helicopters when he had needed a way out in Moscow. Stealing one of his attackers' vans was par for the course. This was a source of irritation, but it was immaterial. Macs had been snatched away from under their noses and was now effectively beyond their reach. The American now had a lead. It was a slender lead at best, but the commander didn't like the American to have any lead at all. He preferred the Americans on the run from KGB assassins and his government quietly capitulating.

The Americans had successfully turned the tables too many times.

''Have the leaders accepted my choice of targets?''

Stasny was pleased to change the subject. ''Yes, they think your plan is very clever. They have given it their approval.''

''Good. Tell me, what is being done about the scientists?''

''Well, even with Macs's assistance, there are still over a hundred scientists in Russia who could have been involved in top secret laser research. Over sixty of them studied with Macs. The professor was never involved in the project, directly or indirectly, so any direction he sent the American in would be purely guesswork.''

''The American has displayed a near surreal sense of guesswork up to this point, wouldn't you agree?''

''What is it you propose.''

''Kill the scientists—all of them.''

''Kill them?''

''Yes.''

''You want me to tell the Russians to kill sixty of their own leading physicists?''

"Killing their own citizens is what the KGB has always excelled at."

There was an appalled silence. "I will tell them," Stasny agreed.

"Good," Nemanja said as he checked his watch. "In fifteen minutes I will give the Americans something to think about."

U.S. Embassy, Lithuania

MACK BOLAN WINCED as he forced himself to stretch. His body armor had saved him from being ripped apart from bullets and buckshot, and when the car had crashed it had saved him from broken bones and internal injury. However, while the body armor had kept him in one piece, he still absorbed a massive amount of blunt trauma. Nor had his armor covered his limbs or his head.

Bolan had seven stitches in his head and he looked and felt as if he had been worked over with a baseball bat. Much of his bruising went down nearly to the bone, and it made kinked fists of his muscles that didn't wish to obey him. Bolan focused on his breathing. He filled his lungs to capacity and then let the air out slowly as he forced his body to move. He dropped down low and forced his legs into painfully deep and extended fighting stances. He took his limbs to full extension in slow-motion strikes while he twisted his torso. Sweat broke out across his bruised body. His screaming muscles were given no choice but to obey his will. Slowly, and under great protest, his muscles moved. His motions became more fluid. His body obeyed him.

Svarzkova stood in the doorway. "It hurts me just to watch."

"It was this or spend the next forty-eight hours in bed," Bolan said, taking a drink of water. "How are you?"

"I feel as bad as you look, but the steering column kept me from going through the windshield. The titanium plate in my armor kept the steering column from going through me. The doctor says I will live. I must say I'm surprised. This is the first time I have no major scars from being with you."

"Well, we're not done yet."

"No. Your friend the pilot sent me to fetch you. They are ready for us in the conference room."

Bolan pulled on a shirt. The U.S. Embassy in Lithuania contained only one secure conference room. Macs sat at the table along with the CIA station chief of the Lithuanian station. The man seemed competent if a little overwhelmed by the situation. A satellite link with an intercom hookup sat in front of one seat, which meant Stony Man Farm was part of the conference. Grimaldi and Lyons both looked up as Bolan came in.

The station chief motioned for Bolan and Svarzkova to sit and then spoke to the intercom. "We're all here."

Barbara Price's voice came through from Virginia. "We've had some developments."

"What kind?" Bolan asked.

"Last night half of the eastern United States satellite dish subscribers lost all their basic services."

"Well, it's subtle," Grimaldi stated.

"It is, and at the same time, Western Europe lost their satellite feed of those same services. All the cable services know is that they lost feed and they can't reestablish it. They received almost five hundred thousand angry phone calls on both continents. It overwhelmed their phone systems, and they went down for about an hour, as well."

"I don't suppose we were able to detect anything."

"No. Civilian communication relay satellites don't have attack-warning systems, and no one really has anything actively watching them. All we know is that two satellites are dead in space and a lot of people on two continents can't get their MTV."

"They're warning us to back off."

"We received an anonymous message through our embassy in Croatia that whatever counterintelligence operation we're running is to cease."

"Did they give us an 'or what'?"

"No, just that it was to cease. The Pentagon believes next time they're going to hit something major, probably telephone relays, to really put a scare into us."

Bolan frowned. Nearly every secure conference room had a wall map of the world and his eyes roved over it. "I think it's worse than that. Threatening the shuttle was a good move to put the fear of God into us, but in the long run it's a threat they can't maintain. Sooner or later they know we're going to run another space launch whether they are still threatening us or not. They know we'll have intelligence resources on the ground, in the air and in space watching, and I think they must be at least assuming we've figured the weapon is currently in Africa. Blowing up the shuttle would galvanize the American people. The President could probably get away with tactically nuking whoever did it."

"So what are you saying?"

"I've been thinking there's larger threat to think of. Right now they want the United States and NATO to engage in a pullout and hands-off policy in the former Yugoslavia. They are going to nudge us along until we comply. It's when that's done that we have to really start worrying."

The CIA chief looked at Bolan askance. "I think that's plenty to worry about, much less when they decide to sell it to someone who doesn't like us."

Bolan shook his head. "They won't sell it. It's too good to give away. What they'll do is start selling the capability. The United States keeps an eye on a number of unfriendly powers. What our friends will do is approach everyone with a U.S. intelligence satellite looking down on them and offer themselves like an exterminator service. Libya would be willing to pay a great deal of dinars to have a clear sky over their terrorist-training camps in the desert. God knows how much the Chinese would pay to have no one watching their nuclear-testing facilities.

"But even that is going to earn them our wrath sooner or later. They know we're looking for them. In the end, once they've achieved their objective, it would be a lot safer for them, and easier on us, just to force us to pay them to leave us alone. They stay hidden, our space program stays intact, but the threat is always there. Without significant changes in technology, it's a threat that could go on for decades."

Bolan turned to Macs. "Any help you can give us would be appreciated."

"I thank you for saving my life, and seeing that my wife and granddaughter are being protected in Finland. I went over some old papers I had retained, and made some calls in town before the attack. I couldn't find much. Most of my colleagues who would be in on such developments are sworn to secrecy, and more disturbing, a number of them I simply couldn't get ahold of or even find out their location. I fear for their lives."

"Is there anything you can give us?"

"Yes. Dr. Nikita Teteryatnikov."

"He was one of your students?"

"One of my finest. He's a brilliant astrophysicist."

"Yes, but we are looking for a man who's specialty is high-frequency lasers."

"Teteryatnikov holds multiple degrees. He worked for the military for some time on a number of projects. What I can't believe is that he would be involved in such a thing."

"Why not?"

"He hates the military. He hates war. His brother was a MiG-23 pilot in the Soviet air force. He was shot down in Afghanistan by a rebel armed with a CIA-supplied Stinger anti aircraft missile."

Lyons sat forward in his chair. "That seems like it might be reason enough for him to hate the United States."

"So you might think, but after his brother's death, Teteryatnikov refused to work on any more military projects for the government. He was threatened with imprisonment in a Siberian gulag. However, it was near the end of the war, and the Communist regime was already beginning to fall. He was also a well-respected scientist internationally, and the regime already had too many fires to put out. They revoked his top secret clearance and reassigned him to the astrophysics department at Moscow university, which is really what he wanted anyway."

"This must have been over a decade ago," Bolan stated.

"Yes," Macs said, nodding. "Exactly so. I gave the matter some thought as you asked. The Russian military has undergone extreme financial hardship since the Communists fell. They have had very little money or resources to put into research and development except for absolutely critical projects, like their next generation of fighter planes and other weapons systems they can export for hard currency. Most members of the current Russian government and military know that much of the old Communist doctrine was lies. They know the United States won't launch a nuclear attack on Russia unless it is provoked into it by being struck first. The United States won't invade Russia. Such things are unimaginable in any foreseeable future. Thus, many of the more speculative, high-technology weapons projects were scrapped. Russia still has the largest nuclear arsenal in the world. Most Russian leaders consider it will be deterrent enough until well into this century.''

The professor's words made sense to Bolan. ''You think someone has revived an old weapons project that was scrapped when the Communist regime fell?''

''It's what makes the most sense to me. President Reagan was a nightmare to the Soviets. He increased the size of your armies. He introduced new and highly sophisticated weapons systems from the infantryman level up to the strategic forces. He also pumped untold millions of dollars into your so-called Star Wars defense research. The Soviet military desperately tried to keep up. It failed, and bankrupted itself trying. However, in trying, many desperate and highly ingenious weapon systems were conceived. Most never left the drawing board. Many were sound in design but were simply too complicated or too expensive to field, but during those years, the full might of Soviet science was turned on such projects.''

''You think Dr. Teteryatnikov would have been involved in the development of such a weapon system?''

''He is who I would have chosen to lead my team.''

''Where is he now?''

''I believe he is doing research in California.''

Branko Nemanja was pleased. "The scientists are dead?"

"All who developed the project, who aren't in our pay, have been eliminated. Our Russian friends were appalled at the order, but—"

"But they complied." The commander finished the statement as he relaxed in his chair. The American, however clever he was, was now fresh out of leads.

"Yes, they complied. Your strategy was excellent. However, there is one possible problem," Stasny cautioned.

The commander's muscles tensed. "What is that?"

"There was a scientist who was involved in the project during its inception. A Dr. Nikita Teteryatnikov."

"I assume, for some reason, that this Teteryatnikov is still breathing."

"He's in the United States."

Nemanja had to admit to himself that this was something of a problem. "Why haven't I been told of his existence?"

"As I said, he was one of the developers of the weapon. However, neither the records of the Moscow Design Bureau or those of the GRU credit him with any work."

"Why?"

"He was a political embarrassment. Apparently he became a pacifist and refused to continue work on the project, or any other military project for that matter. The scientists we have in our employ never mentioned him, either. I believe they have taken credit for a great deal of his work. This is why we haven't heard of him."

"He's in the United States?"

"When the Communist regime fell, he emigrated to California. From what I've gathered, he now does research in theoretical physics," Stasny explained.

"What could this man tell the Americans?"

"He could answer most of their technical questions about the weapon system. Other than that, very little."

"You're a fool. Answering their technical questions could generate any number of leads, all of which could lead to me. I have no desire to have a U.S. Stealth fighter dropping laser-guided munitions on my location."

"But, Commander, we—"

"Kill him! Now," Nemanja ordered.

"I believe our KGB friends may have some qualms about having their agents going active on American soil."

"Then have them arrange it through the Russian *mafiya*. I'm sure they have a presence in California."

"That may take time, we need—"

Nemanja's voice rose to a roar. "Do it now!"

Santa Clara Valley, California

BOLAN WATCHED the countryside pass. Rolling hills dotted with occasional immense oak trees filled the landscape. The Santa Cruz mountains rose in the distance. The car rounded a hill dotted with cows, and the sudden great white structure of a radio-telescope dish over a hundred feet in diameter filled his vision. Silicon Valley was an interesting blend of prime farmland and high technology.

"It's beautiful," Svarzkova said as she watched a hillside covered with a small herd of black horses with great interest.

"It's where the computer revolution took place. Apple Computer, IBM, Intel, Sun Microsystems, Hewlett Packard, all started here."

"I like the landscape."

"Before they called it Silicon Valley, it was known as the

Valley of Heart's Delight. Some of the best growing land in the world. The freeway we're on is ranked one of the top ten scenic highways in the U.S.''

"Where are we going?"

"Cupertino. It's coming up."

They turned off the freeway and into a small city that sat at the base of the mountains, and Bolan took the car up into the hills. They had flown to Germany from Lithuania. In Germany they had embarked into three F-15B two-seat trainers and had begun the flight to the United States. They had been met by KC-10 tankers three times for in-flight refueling. It had been a grueling flight that had ended in Moffet field. A team from Stony Man Farm had been scrambled, as well.

Dr. Teteryatnikov hadn't been at his place of work in Palo Alto when Bolan and Svarzkova had arrived. He had gone home early, and he wasn't answering his phone. Bolan feared they might be too late.

Bolan consulted the car's onboard computer-mapping system. They drove past the Steven's Creek dam and wound up into the mountains. Rustic houses and bungalows from before the valley's boom nestled beside gigantic stucco and faux Spanish pastel monstrosities built by the newly rich.

Bolan switched on his tactical radio. "What have you got, Gary?"

Gary Manning was SOG's demolitions expert. "The doctor is in. He came home about fifteen minutes ago," Manning replied.

"What action have you taken?"

"None so far. We have him and the house under observation."

"We tried calling him. Why isn't he answering?"

"He's watering his lawn," Manning explained.

"All right. We're going in. Keep us covered."

"We've got a good position. We can see your car coming up the road now. Consider yourself covered."

Bolan pulled the car into Teteryatnikov's driveway. His house was a bungalow nestled among a sprawl of oak trees. "Where are you, Gary?"

"I'm up the hillside in a thicket. Gadgets and McCarter are with me. The doctor is in the backyard."

"Any dogs?"

"One cat that I've seen."

There was no fence, so Bolan went around the side of the house. Gareyev and Svarzkova followed him. As he came into the backyard he found a stone-paved patio with a green lawn behind it that butted right up against the mountainside and the trees. Teteryatnikov was watering his garden. He was a little man, and he wore khaki shorts, a sleeveless T-shirt, black socks and sandals. With his bald head and thick wire-rimmed glasses, he was a stereotype of what a scientist should look like. He wore a Walkman and hummed as he watered.

He jumped and ripped off the headphones as Bolan came into his peripheral vision. He snarled in heavily accented English. "Who are you? Get the hell off my lawn!"

"Dr. Teteryatnikov?"

"Yes." He took a step backward as Bolan loomed over him. He looked at the bloody bandage covering the stitches in Bolan's brow and the bruises on his face. "What the happened to you?"

"Some people tried to kill me. I would like to prevent the same thing from happening to you."

Teteryatnikov dropped his hose. "What is that supposed to mean?"

Gareyev stepped forward. "Dr. Teteryatnikov, my name is Gareyev. We both studied under Professor Macs in Moscow. I—"

"Gareyev? Sergei Gareyev?"

Gareyev nodded hopefully.

The little man put his hands on his hips. The lines of his face tightened with irritation. "I have read some of your papers on the Internet, Gareyev. Your assertions are pusillanimous and self-serving at best."

Gareyev gaped.

Bolan's head tilted slightly. Dr. Teteryatnikov was one of the more hostile pacifists he had met in recent memory.

Svarzkova cleared her throat. "Dr. Teteryatnikov, I'm Captain Valentina Svarzkova, of Russian military intel—"

"A GRU whore! Here! On my lawn!" The doctor's face went scarlet. "Get your ass off my property."

Svarzkova stared at him coolly. "Are you through?" She drew her CZ-75 pistol from her shoulder holster and leveled it between his eyebrows. "I'm in United States as an official liaison attached to the Russian embassy. My papers are in order. I can shoot you in the head, go to the Russian consulate in San Francisco and claim diplomatic immunity. I can do anything I want." She jerked her head at Bolan. "Only professional courtesy to my American colleague prevents me from pistol-whipping for your unculturaled behavior."

The doctor looked at Svarzkova in horror.

Bolan took a list from his pocket. "Dr. Teteryatnikov, in the last twenty-four hours the CIA has confirmed the assassination of Doctors Ilsa Akulova, Pietor Rybenok, Raisa Zaitsova and Nikita Kovalev. These were all former colleagues of yours. Many more who you may know by name or reputation have disappeared and are presumed dead. We have reason to believe your name is on this list, as well."

Teteryatnikov's eyes bugged. "Ilsa is dead? Ilsa Akulova?"

"The Moscow police found Ilsa Akulova in her bathtub. Someone had shot her in the head with a .22-caliber handgun. An attempt to kill Juris Macs was averted in Latvia less than forty-eight hours ago."

Teteryatnikov was shocked. "Why? What have they done?"

"They had knowledge, Doctor. Knowledge of a weapon system that a terrorist group has managed to deploy with help from branches of the former KGB and traitors within the GRU."

"What weapon system? I don't design weapons. I was almost sent to prison by the Communists for refusing to do so."

"I'm aware of your stance, and I respect it. However, you were involved in top secret weapons design before your brother was shot down over Afghanistan."

"That was decades ago. What kind of project are you talking about?"

"A laser. Ground-based. Highly portable. One capable of taking out orbiting military satellites. It has already been fielded. It's taken out five satellites so far, and been used to threaten the American space shuttle. We have reason to believe you might know something about it."

Teteryatnikov rubbed his head. "No. Impossible. The Skysniper project was a failure."

Bolan's eyebrows rose. "Skysniper?"

"Yes. That is what we called it. It was a boondoggle, as you Americans say."

"Can you describe it?"

"Well, it was brilliant, in conception. It was a high-frequency laser designed to be carried along with the Soviet armored columns. As such, it had to be carried in its own armored vehicle, and be self-contained. It was to have a dual purpose. One was to destroy satellites observing Soviet formations, and a secondary function as an air-defense weapon against NATO war planes and cruise missiles."

"Why was the project a failure?"

"Oh, well, for a number of reasons. A laser that small with so much power was destined to overheat. There were a number of fatal accidents with the power supply in the laboratory. Cooling the weapon was an exercise in cryogenic technology in itself. The system that was developed was found to be too fragile and complicated to be fielded on the ground in a war environment. The laser itself was robust by most scientific standards, but not military ones. It was to be mounted on an armored vehicle, but we simply couldn't stabilize the weapon sufficiently to fire the weapon on the move. This meant the vehicle would have to stop to fire. This left it vulnerable, particularly when the targeting radar was turned on.

"Acquiring satellites in orbit, as well as cruise missiles flying fifty feet off the ground, was another matter entirely. It required two separate radars. The vehicle ended up being an overcomplicated monstrosity. It was vulnerable to antiradar missiles. A single RPG-7 antitank rocket could destroy it. For that matter, one good man with a sniper rifle could disable the target-acquisition radars and destroy the main lenses of the laser itself. This doesn't even consider the fact that if the weapon engaged multiple targets, it was likely to overheat and detonate its fuel source. The chemical fuels themselves were highly volatile and presented their own problems without even turning on the weapon."

The Russian shook his head. "Then there was the matter of cost. Radar-directed cannons and missiles were much cheaper, and such weapons were already in place. In the antisatellite role, it would have been much cheaper to put the weapon system in space, and even then X-ray lasers or nuclear weapons would have been much cheaper in space than the Skysniper."

Bolan considered what Teteryatnikov had told him. "What if you didn't care about any of that?"

Teteryatnikov frowned. "What do you mean?"

"I mean forget about the armored vehicle and moving with tank columns. Forget about the targeting radars, forget about all of that. All I want to do is hold everything in an equatorial orbit hostage."

The Russian shook his head in puzzled irritation. "No, no, no, you would still need a cryogenic cooling system, you—"

"I only need it for one to three shots at a time. I'll use liquid nitrogen, hell, I could pack the damn thing in dry ice between shots."

"But without radars, how would you acquire targets?" Teteryatnikov objected.

"I'd use satellite orbiting paths downloaded from the Internet. I'd use a low-frequency LADAR attached to the main weapon and fire it on the target satellite's predicted path. When it crossed the LADAR's beam, I'd lock on with the main weapon and fire."

The Russian's mouth opened in amazement. "That is...brilliant."

"The question is, Doctor, did you build a working prototype of the laser weapon itself?"

"I... We... That is classified."

Bolan looked at Teteryatnikov long and hard. The Russian flinched under the Executioner's gaze. "Doctor, I need to find and destroy that weapon. We believe it is being deployed in equatorial Africa, probably in Congo, by Serbian terrorists. I need a list of the chemicals the weapon needs for fuel, what it looks like, any diagrams you can give me, as well as any other pertinent information you can recall.''

Teteryatnikov seemed to be undergoing an emotional crisis. He had deliberately walked away from military research to devote his life to peaceful pursuits. He had turned his back on the nation of his birth to devote his intelligence to understanding the universe. Now, a ghost shrouded in the hammer-and-sickle flag of the Soviet Union had come back to haunt him.

The doctor looked as if he might fall over. ''Yes...I'll help you in any way I can.''

The Executioner spoke into his throat mike. ''Gary, get ahold of Jack. Have him find me a plane.'' Bolan looked out across the Santa Cruz mountains and the blue sky of northern California. ''I'm heading for Congo.''

17

"Well now, that's kind of a tall order." The CIA station chief in Congo looked at Bolan and then the map on the desk between them. Darrell Burton was an extremely competent man according to his file. He spoke seven West African dialects like a native and had been a deep-cover field agent until a rifle bullet had shattered his knee. Since then he had proved his ability at high-level intelligence gathering and diplomacy in the region. "Congo is a big place. Finding a hidden firebase in the jungle is going to be extremely difficult."

"I know, but I have some leads," Bolan said, nodding.

"I'd be curious to hear them."

"Our opponents are using a high-frequency laser. It needs some interesting chemicals for fuel. It also burns hot when it fires, so it needs some kind of coolant system. I'm thinking the bad guys have jury-rigged a lot of the setup. They're probably using liquid nitrogen at the very least, so they're going to have to truck or chopper the stuff in."

Burton scratched his short beard. "They could also be boating it in. People in the interior use more rivers than roads for travel, but that's a start. Almost any volatile chemicals or high-tech equipment is going to have to start by being smuggled through the airport here in Kinshasa. What else have you got?"

"Our opponents are Serbians, probably using Russian scientists for tech support, so they aren't going to blend in with the native population very well."

"No, they're going to need local help, and the Serbians didn't exactly ingratiate themselves to the population when they were last here."

"That's right. So I'm figuring a local warlord or local strongman. I'm thinking a real scumbag who doesn't care what's happening or who he's dealing with as long as the money is right, and he's also going to have to have the kind of muscle and connections to pull something like this off. You got anyone like that?"

"Dozens, but you've narrowed things down a bit. We're thinking a jungle base, so deep they want to stay out of the way of government troops and rebels alike. That says to me the northwest. They need constant supplies of all kinds of things, chemicals, rations, equipment, and in this country, people notice choppers going overhead, but no one pays attention to river boats. There are thousands of them."

Burton's finger traced the arc of the Congo River on the map. "A good size riverboat could transport them and their equipment easily up the river. Once you're deep in-country, there are thousands of tributaries that could dump you off into thick jungle. There are lots of hostile natives with no particular political affiliations, and that hostility could be smoothed out with the right combination of cash and intimidation."

"I like it, but let's say I'm a Serbian terrorist. Who do I go to to make it happen?" Bolan probed.

"Well, like I said, there are dozens of possibilities, but you specified a real scumbag." Burton's teeth gleamed out of his dark face. "I suspect the man you want is Colonel Moses Mukantabana."

"WELL, LET ME TELL YOU, my friend. A big white man came into Kinshasa this morning. He went straight to the U.S. Embassy."

Nemanja popped the top off another Belgian beer and looked at Colonel Mukantabana. The colonel was an immense man. Even his grotesque obesity couldn't hide the massive muscles of his arms and chest that strained his tailored khaki uniform. Nemanja considered this information while he speared another piece of water buffalo steak with his fork. Feasting on excellently prepared meat and wild game had been an unexpected fringe benefit of this particular job, and even if Mukantabana was a bloodthirsty, morally corrupt savage, he, like most Africans, had a deeply ingrained sense of hospitality. Nemanja had been stunned by the variety of meat, liquor, drugs and prostitutes that the colonel continually tried to ply him with.

"Did you get a photograph of him?"

"Not a good one. But my operatives suggest he strongly resembles the description you have given me."

"How many men did he have with him?" Nemanja pressed.

"He was alone."

Nemanja smiled thinly and leaned back in his chair. Colonel Mukantabana swirled the single-malt whiskey in his glass. "You think he is trying to tempt you into attacking him."

"It is one way he might make us tip our hand."

Mukantabana tossed back the whiskey and smiled in relish. His eyes flicked to Nemanja. "And are you so tempted?"

"I am. I want him dead."

U.S. Embassy, Kinshasa

"THE MAN IS PLEASED with you," Aaron Kurtzman began.

Bolan smiled. It was always nice when the President of the United States was pleased. It helped with procurement costs at the Farm. "Well, we haven't done much of anything yet really. We just have some possibilities."

"The Pentagon is convinced. There is some other news."

"What's that?"

"We think we have your man," the Bear said.

"Who?"

"I'm faxing him to you now."

The fax attached to the satellite link whirred, and a photograph began to reel up. Bolan took the photo and stared into the eyes of his enemy. The man was relatively short, five foot eight according to the description below the photo. His shoulders were broad in the olive-drab T-shirt he was wearing, and he weighed just under two hundred pounds. He was wearing a shoulder holster, and a Browning Hi-Power rode beneath his left arm. The photo was a casual shot, and the man was smiling. But only his mouth smiled; his eyes looked as if he were casually considering killing the cameraman. Something was wrong with the face and it took Bolan a moment to figure it out. One of the man's eyes was brown, while the other was black. Bolan's own eyes narrowed and a thin smile crossed his face.

There were still parts of Europe where eyes like that were considered the mark of the devil.

"Who is he?"

"Branko Nemanja."

"I've never heard of him," Bolan stated.

"Most people haven't. During the war in Bosnia, the people who got the most press were Slobodan Milosevic, and his flunky, Arkan, who led his paramilitary Tigers on their campaign of ethnic cleansing against the Bosnian Muslims and the Croats. There was another group that got a lot less press. They were never really more than a particularly nasty and unconfirmed rumor. There was supposedly a group engaged in ethnic cleansing, but that was not their main function. They were called Kords."

"The name doesn't mean anything to me."

"The *kord* was a medieval Serbian short sword. The best translation of the name would be the 'Daggers.' Their mission was to prevent peace in former Yugoslavia at any cost. If the Bosnian Muslims tried to engage in any kind of peace talk, the Kords were to assassinate anyone involved and keep up the hostilities. The same with the Croats. If they couldn't assassinate the diplomats involved, then they would engage in particularly heinous atrocities to sabotage the peace process. They also silenced any Serbians who spoke out against the war. Their goal was a united Greater Serbia without any Muslims or Croats in it," Kurtzman elaborated.

"I've read most of the Pentagon's and the CIA's files on

known war criminals in central Europe. I've never heard of Branko Nemanja. How did we get a fix on him?''

"We didn't. The CIA only knew him as a rumor during the war, and even then he was known only as the commander. Your friend Svarzkova is the one who gave him to us.''

Svarzkova hadn't come with him to Africa. She had gone back to Europe. If she was in contact with elements of the GRU, she was setting herself up to be a target again. "How does the GRU know about Nemanja?''

"They trained him.''

Bolan eyes flicked across the map from Serbia to the former Soviet Union. The stakes were going up by the minute. "How much did she get for us?''

"Before the war in Bosnia broke out, Nemanja was already a commando in Yugoslavia's Thirty-sixth Parachute Regiment. He later made several visits to the Soviet Union and received special training in small-unit tactics and unconventional warfare from Spetsnaz. He was on such a training mission when Croatia broke away from Yugoslavia and announced its independence. He returned to Serbia and formed the Kords with a nucleus of men who had undergone Spetsnaz training with him. When the fighting in Bosnia ceased, the Kords did a disappearing act.''

"They disappeared down here to Africa.''

"We can't confirm that, but we think it's a safe bet.''

"What can you give me on a possible location?'' Bolan asked.

"We have three sites. All would give the weapon an unobstructed view of the sky. All three are within the territory controlled by a Colonel Mukantabana.''

"How soon can we get a team here?''

"We're not.''

"What?''

Aaron Kurtzman's voice became somewhat embarrassed. "Your orders are to sit tight. The Air Force is sending in Stealth fighters to take the weapon out.''

"They're just going to indiscriminantly bomb the area?''

"No. Even as we speak, Space Command is having a military observation satellite maneuver into an orbit that passes right over

Mukantabana's area of operations in northern Congo. That should get Nemanja's attention. If that isn't enough, the satellite they're using is equipped with ground-mapping radar. The minute it comes over the horizon, it's going to start pounding the jungle with high-intensity radar beams. They're betting that should put a big enough bug in his britches to make him fire the laser.

"The satellite is a Trojan horse. The LADAR works at the speed of light, but the human operator has to give the main weapon the order to fire. Even if it's set on automatic, there will be several thousandths of a second between the LADAR lock and the firing of the main weapon. That's an incredibly small window to us, but to the battle computers on the satellite, it will be plenty. It will instantly transmit the vector of the LADAR. Then we have them. The F-117 Stealth fighters will be orbiting the area. Once they receive the coordinates, they go in with smart bombs and light the place up."

Bolan steepled his fingers on the table, before replying, "It sounds like an excellent plan."

Kurtzman paused at the tone of the Executioner's voice. "You don't like it."

"No."

"Why?"

"Because I think Nemanja has thought of this already," Bolan declared.

BRANKO NEMANJA STOOD in the command-and-control tent. His Russian technical team leader looked up from his computer unhappily. "Commander, this has to be a trap."

Nemanja nodded as he peered over Kolov's shoulder at the dot that moved across his monitor screen. The satellite had adjusted its orbit and would soon pass directly over them. The information from the Internet described the platform as a "Highly sophisticated, top secret U.S. observation satellite with orbital maneuvering capability. Launched in 1997." It was a very recent satellite, which meant it would indeed be highly sophisticated.

Kolov's face tightened. "If we fire on it, we'll have to move our base of operations at the very least. I believe it's possible they have some form of immediate retaliation prepared."

Nemanja folded his arms across his chest without taking his eyes from the offending dot. "You are almost certainly correct. Prepare to fire the weapon."

Kolov paled.

Nemanja turned his head to look at the weapon.

Skysniper sat on its trailer mount behind a sandbag revetment. The towing wheels had been raised, and four squat, self-leveling hydraulic legs had descended to give the weapon a rock-solid tracking-and-firing position. Skysniper itself looked like a short, fat, amateur astronomer's telescope on steroids. Attached to its ten-inch-aperture cylinder was the much smaller tube of the LADAR housing. However, unlike an astronomical telescope designed to plumb the depths of the night sky, Skysniper's function wasn't to gather light, but to emit it outward in unimaginably destructive frequencies. Skysniper's main housing was wrapped in a thick sheath like a hot-water heater wrapped with insulation. The cooling sleeve was attached to the liquid nitrogen tanks that sat on their own small trailer two yards away.

Nemanja ran his eyes toward the rest of his defense.

Half a mile away he had a truck with quad-mounted SA-8 Gecko antiaircraft missiles. Five hundred yards down the river he had a pair of 23 mm antiaircraft cannons mounted on jeeps. The weapons served the dual purpose of low-level aircraft defense, as well as guarding the river approach to his camp. All four weapons were attached to a pair of small but very powerful Land-Roll H-band radars, each with the latest Russian upgrades.

These weapons would be next to useless against the American attack. The Americans knew whatever air-defense weapons he had would be pitifully inadequate. Their moving their satellite and daring him to fire was proof that they felt themselves invulnerable. This would be their undoing.

Americans placed entirely too much faith in airpower.

"Commander!" Kolov shot upright in his seat.

"What is it?"

"Electronic countermeasures detects extremely powerful radar signals."

"From where?"

"From..." Kolov gaped at a separate monitor that pulsed and glowed across a grid of lines. "From the satellite. They are using ground-mapping radar."

Nemanja smiled thinly. "You had assured me our position couldn't be detected by such means."

"It shouldn't be able to. I can't understand what they are trying to do."

"They are trying to frighten you, Kolov, and they have succeeded. Prepare the weapon."

Kolov stared in disbelief but began typing on his keyboard. Outside, Skysniper began to pivot up and around on its mount with a pneumatic whine. "Satellite should be aligned in... three...two...one...firing LADAR!"

Outside, a pale blue beam flicked on from the LADAR's lens aperture and disappeared in a thin line up into the sky. "Contact, Commander. We have LADAR lock."

Nemanja examined his nails momentarily.

Kolov blanched. Every second contributed toward their suicide. "Commander! We have LADAR lock!"

Nemanja nodded. "You may fire the main weapon."

Kolov punched a key. The commander watched Skysniper fire.

The beam was bright, but far from blinding. Part of what made the laser so devastating was that its light was coherent and focused rather than scattered and refracted in a blinding flash. There was a slight tearing sound as millions of minute airborne particles in the beam's path were destroyed. The beam clicked off a second later. There were mechanical noises as the coolant pumps circulated liquid nitrogen around the laser housing and metal popped and clicked with the immense heat.

"Do you believe we destroyed it?"

"We hit it, and to my knowledge, no satellite launched to date has any armoring capable of withstanding a direct hit from the main laser."

"Good." Nemanja said as he glanced at his watch. "They

undoubtedly got a good fix on us. They will be coming soon.'' He turned to a tall blond man who sat in front of his own array of equipment. ''Dusan, get ready to turn on the antiaircraft radars.''

Dusan's eyebrows shot up in alarm. ''Commander, that would be suicide! If they don't know our position now, they will certainly know it when—''

''I'm quite sure they know our position by now. Prepare to turn on the radars.''

Nemanja looked at his watch again. He patiently watched the second hand crawl around the dial three times. The other men in the tent grew increasingly pale and broke into sweats that had nothing to do with the tropical heat. The commander nodded to himself. ''Turn on the radars.''

Dusan flicked switches and scanned his screen with the eyes of an owl.

''What do you see?''

''I can't be sure, sir. Perhaps some objects, perhaps nothing.''

An unpleasant smile began to crawl across Nemanja's face. ''Nothing the radar can lock on to?''

Dusan grimaced. ''No, Commander. The returns are extremely small. The radar can't lock on to them. I'm not sure if I could lock on to them even if I had a ten-meter Long-Track radar dish, much less the equipment we have here.''

Nemanja grew genuinely smug. ''But, Dusan, from what you can tell, the objects are flying too high to be hit by our cannons?''

''You're correct, sir. They are above engagement by our guns.''

''Fire anyway.''

Dusan looked at his commander as if he were insane but he followed the order. Downriver, the ripping sound of automatic cannons burst out and sent tracers streaming into the sky.

''Our missiles can't lock on to them, can they?''

Nemanja seemed to be answering his own questions, but Dusan answered anyway. ''No. We can't achieve radar lock, even on active scanning. The infrared signature of the objects is nonexistent. Our SA-7 heat-seekers would be totally ineffective against them, even if they were flying low enough to be in range.''

The commander looked at Dusan blandly. "But you're fairly sure you have some objects out there?''

Dusan grew more nervous by the minute. "I'm fairly certain of it.''

"The Americans are using Stealth fighters!''

Dusan already had already grave suspicions in that direction for several minutes.

Nemanja stared up at the roof of the tent. "I remember them well from the air campaign in Kosovo. They were invisible to our missiles. They had no infrared signature, and had a radar cross section so tiny that we could barely detect them much less lock on to them. Even when we knew they are there, they were ghosts that couldn't be touched.''

Kolov was close to panic. Dusan looked to be in little better condition. "Commander! They know where we are! They will be in range to destroy in less than a minute!''

"Exactly so, Kolov. Now, use the radar to aim the LADAR at one of the returns.''

Kolov blinked. Suddenly a grin like enlightenment split his face. "Yes!''

He quickly began punching keys. When Nemanja had told the technicians that he wanted his small antiaircraft radars integrated with the Skysniper fire control, they had thought he was crazy. It was a perfect invitation to have an antiradar missile fly right down the laser's main lens.

Kolov grinned to himself as the LADAR swung, and the main laser swung with it in perfect alignment. Kolov could barely contain himself. "Brilliant! LADAR should be in line with the vector of the approaching object.''

"Fire the LADAR, Kolov.''

"We have LADAR lock. A large object, traveling at six hundred miles per hour at six thousand feet in altitude.''

"You may fire the main weapon.''

Skysniper sizzled into life, and hard blue light reached up into the African night.

Dusan's face was triumphant as he watched his radar screen. "Object eliminated. The other two objects are employing electronic countermeasures."

Nemanja shook his head in mock sympathy. "Probe each return with LADAR. Fire the main weapon when you have a lock."

The pilots of the stealth Fighters were jamming the radio waves, and filling the sky with false images of themselves. It was a useless tactic. The LADAR was a beam of light. It wasn't a radar wave or heat-seeker that could be fooled. The antiaircraft radars might see dozens of false images, but as the LADAR struck each one, the truth would be revealed. The LADAR would only bounce back off of a solid object.

Dusan and Kolov spoke in gleeful tandem. "Ghost...ghost... ghost...solid object. Five thousand feet and diving."

"Firing main weapon."

Skysniper reached out.

"Object destroyed. Continuing search."

Outside a technician shouted. "Commander! The main unit is dangerously hot."

Nemanja grimaced. Even when they had taken out three satellites in one night, there had been minutes of cooling time between shots. Now the weapon was firing in an interval of seconds.

"Lock! Firing main weapon!" Kolov shouted.

Skysniper fired again.

Dusan was ecstatic. "Target destroyed!"

The technician outside was screaming. "Commander! Temperature is at critical!"

Nemanja sliced his hand through the air. "Power down the main weapon!"

Outside the technicians were waving their arms and shouting at one another. Nemanja looked at Dusan. "What do you have on radar?"

Dusan was positively smug. "Nothing, sir. Nothing at all."

"Continue to sweep for one minute and then turn off the radars."

"Yes, sir." Dusan stared unblinkingly at his screen.

Nemanja walked outside. A man named Yuri stood wiping his brow.

"What is the status of the weapon?" Nemanja asked.

Yuri looked at Skysniper. "I believe it will be all right, Commander. The cooling system was at critical. If you fire it again within the next two minutes, however, the main weapon and the chemical fuel cells will blow." Yuri suddenly smiled. "We saw them, sir. We saw the planes explode. It was a magnificent test of the system."

Nemanja stared up into the moonless night. The Americans were helpless. Not all their high satellite technology or military might was proof against one man with a vision. A vision of America on its knees. Nemanja's smile was horrible to behold. Let the Americans taste that.

Let them choke on it.

18

U.S. Embassy, Kinshasa

"Three Stealth fighters and a four-hundred-million-dollar satellite?"

"Total loss," Kurtzman responded, sounding particularly dejected.

"What about the pilots?"

"No word. I don't think they ever saw it coming. There were no tracers or rocket trails. They were sawed in half by the beam, and their fuel tanks detonated in a fraction of a second. We haven't heard any distress calls coming out of the jungle. Word from the Pentagon is that the mission is a total loss."

"How did they do it?" Bolan asked.

"I should have thought of it. Stealth fighters are nearly immune to radar-guided weapons. They fly above cannon range, and heat-seeking and radar-guided missiles just can't lock on to them, but they aren't actually invisible to radar itself. In a radar-cluttered environment like a battlefield, they do literally become invisible, but over Congo they were the only things in the sky. All the Kords needed was just a general idea of where the planes were in the sky and then all they had to do was sweep the LADAR until they got a lock. Our boys never stood a chance. Your instincts were right on the mark. We should have done it your way."

"So I'm assuming I'm a go."

"You are. The satellite was destroyed but it did give us coordinates. We know where the laser is at the moment. The problem is it is in the middle of the jungle in Congo. We have no assets there. Any plane attempting to bomb it or parachute troops on top of it is going to be burned out of the sky.''

"They may be holding all the cards, but Nemanja and Mukantabana won't wait around. They're going to move,'' Bolan said as he looked at a map of Europe. "What have we heard from Valentina?"

"We haven't. The codes we gave her to contact the Farm and you in Kinshasa have been silent since she got us the information naming Nemanja and his Kord assassins.''

Bolan's fist tightened. It was always dangerous to become emotionally involved with your counterparts. It was a dangerous profession. By now, Captain Valentina Svarzkova was either dead or gone to ground. "What about Senior Lieutenant Stepanshuk? Any word?"

"No, and no way of knowing without trying to the contact the GRU through channels. I figure any such attempt could only endanger him if he's still alive.''

"What about our scientist friends?"

"Professor Macs and Dr. Gareyev are currently in safekeeping at the Berlin embassy. Dr. Teteryatnikov is under FBI protection in San Francisco. The Santa Clara County sheriff's SWAT team picked up a carload of men with pistols on the road up to the doctor's house not long after you left. They're in the county lockup and have hardly said a word. The few words they have spoken have been in Russian. Two of them have been identified as local Russian *mafiya*.''

Things had fallen out as Bolan had predicted. The options that lay ahead only grew grimmer by the minute. "Bear, I'm just about the only asset we've got going on around here, and our friends are going to fly the coop. I have to intercept them or hit them before they move.''

"They know you're there, Striker. Nemanja was expecting the attack by Stealth aircraft and he was ready for it. I think he may have something ready for you.''

"You have any better ideas?"

"We're scrambling SEAL Team Six. They can be in Kinshasa in twelve hours."

"That's too long. I have to move now."

"You don't even have a full war load."

"I couldn't realistically carry one up the river anyway," Bolan said as he looked across the table at the CIA station chief. "I'll see what Mr. Burton can dig up for me."

"Striker, they'll have people in Kinshasa watching the embassy and the river. They're going to try and take you out long before you ever get upriver."

"I know."

There was a long pause. "I'm faxing you the coordinates and topo maps of the laser site."

"Thanks, Bear. I'm going to try and find the fastest boat I can and leave within the hour."

The line clicked off. Bolan turned to Burton. "What can you do for me?"

"Well, gun control is very strict in Congo. The only people with military equipment are the government and the rebels. Any citizen caught with an M-16, an AK-47 or an FN is usually shot as a rebel. I hate to say it, but you're white. If you're found on the river with that kind of military hardware by the army or police, you'll probably be shot as a mercenary or a drug runner. The rebels had bad experiences with the Serbian mercs. If they or their sympathizers find you with that kind of equipment, they're likely to put you down in a deep part of the river, as well."

Bolan nodded. He had a lot of ground to cross. As a white man traveling light and fast he would attract attention, and possibly have to get through checkpoints. "Can you get me a hunting rig?"

Burton's face split into a happy grin. "I'm way ahead of you."

The chief rose, and Bolan followed him into the next room. He opened a diplomatic satchel. "These papers identify you as a Canadian citizen, with resident-alien status in Kenya. Occupation hunting guide. There are enough of those kind running around Africa that you should pass. In the money belt there are forty thousand English pounds in case you have to bribe your way through."

The CIA man lifted a long heavy aluminum case and set it on the table. He flipped the latches and opened it with a flourish. Bolan examined the contents.

Inside lay a Lee-Enfield No. 5 Jungle Carbine. The old bolt-action weapon had soldiered through both World Wars in various makes and models, and there were hundreds of thousands floating around Africa. However, this battered weapon had been subtly modified. It's 10-round magazine was squared off rather than sloping, which told Bolan it had been rechambered from the venerable .303 cartridge to the faster and harder-hitting modern .308. A low-power, long-eye relief scope was mounted forward of the action, which allowed the weapon to be fired with both eyes open. A modern folding auxiliary rear peep sight had been added. The sling had three attachments in the dented and weathered stock rather than two. The hard rubber recoil pad and the flash hider of the original weapon had been retained.

"It's a scout rifle."

"It's my personal scout rifle, thank you very much, and I want it back."

Bolan eyed the rest of the weapons. There were an extra six magazines for the Lee-Enfield. Nestled in cut foam below the rifle was a pair of stainless-steel Ruger Redhawk four-inch .44 Magnum revolvers. To one side of them was a .22-caliber Smith & Wesson Model 41 target pistol. Bracketing the handguns with the Lee-Enfield was a beautifully engraved Browning Auto-5 shotgun. The shotgun's barrel had been cut down to sixteen inches. A stag-handled seven-inch Randall hunting knife and a four-inch wickedly curved skinner completed the case.

"You have Congolese police permits in your papers for all of the firearms and ammunition. There's what looks like a spare scope for the carbine, but inside it is a sound suppressor for the .22. I also packed two cameras for you. One has a night-vision scope lens that you can attach to the rifle's scope mount. That's about the best I can do for you unless you want a Marine guard's M-16. If you want grenade launchers and all that kind of stuff, you're just going to have to steal them from the opposition or have them air-dropped to you.''

Bolan nodded to himself. Grenades would be nice, but they would be a death sentence if he was caught with them. "This'll do.''

"It had damn well better do. I have deep sentimental attachments to every one of those guns.''

"Well, I'm going to need all the love I can get on this one.''

Burton grinned. "Give me an hour and I'll get you a boat.''

"BEHOLD, THE CONGO SPECIAL.''

Bolan examined Burton. The man's transformation was almost miraculous. His immaculately tailored tropical-weight suit was gone. He wore a pair of ragged cutoff jeans and a faded orange T-shirt with the neck ripped out. His hair was gone, as were his mustache and beard. His shaved skull gleamed in the sunlight, and every inch of his exposed skin was eight shades darker than it had been an hour before. Most of his front teeth glittered with gold fillings. He noticed Bolan staring and exposed the full facade of gold teeth filling his mouth. "I figured you might need someone who speaks the local dialects.''

"Are you cleared for it?''

"My orders were to render you any and all assistance short of deploying the embassy guards. I figured you also might need someone to drive the boat while you keep watch.''

Bolan looked at the boat critically as it rocked slowly beside the dock. It looked like junk. A tattered canvas awning covered the cockpit. The engine housing was battered but looked somewhat larger than it needed to be. It was a locally made wood-hulled craft about fifteen feet long. It looked as if it might sink any minute.

"I got it from a gunrunner I know. It's much faster than it looks. I had a couple of my men install a satellite transmitter beneath the driver's bench. Unless you know where to look, you'd have to deliberately hack the bench open with a hatchet to find it. Other than that, it's a typical small Congo trader.''

"How soon can it be ready to go?''

"It's ready now. I suggest we get a move on. There are clothes and provisions for both of us in the back."

"Let's do it."

"You're being watched. They're going to wait to hit us when we get farther upriver and there isn't much traffic around."

"That's the way I figure it," Bolan stated as he eased his weapon case down into the boat and looked at the primitive controls beneath the awning. He turned the key in the ignition and was pleased by the throaty snarl of the engine as it belched blue smoke. He suspected the boat was indeed faster than it looked. He saw a second aluminum rifle case among the stores.

"What's that?"

Burton grinned. "Some insurance."

Congo Basin

"THE AMERICAN IS coming for you," Colonel Mukantabana stated. "He has apparently hired himself a boat and is coming up the river in our direction."

Nemanja looked at him in irritation. He had all the problems he needed trying to get his camp ready to move in Congo's totally hostile environment. "I thought you said you were going to kill him for me."

"Oh, I am, but I have to wait for him to come to an open neck of the river without much traffic."

"You have such a place in mind?"

"I do," the colonel said.

"You have the ambush in place?"

"Yes."

"Good. Will it be sufficient?"

"I believe so. I had a patrol boat stop them on the river earlier in the day."

Nemanja sat up in his chair. "Why didn't your friends arrest them?"

Mukantabana shrugged his immense shoulders. "The American's papers were in order. I did tell them to arrest them if they could come up with a reason, and I gave them ten thousand dollars to come up with a reason.''

"And they couldn't come up with one?''

Mukantabana smiled. "The American gave them twenty thousand English pounds not to.'' The commander's face split into a snarl. Mukantabana shrugged nonchalantly. "That is how things are done in Congo.''

Nemanja kept his opinion to himself. Mukantabana poured himself a whiskey. "However, the intelligence they gathered was valuable. The American's boat was thoroughly searched. He is armed with only a pitiful collection of hunting small arms that are legal in Congo. He has no automatic weapons, nor does he have any rockets, grenades or explosives. My men will outnumber him, have faster boats and much heavier firepower.''

Mukantabana sipped his whiskey before continuing. "What I wish to know is the status of the Russian, Svarzkova. She and a squad of Spetsnaz would liquidate my river rats.''

Nemanja waved a dismissing hand. "The blue-eyed bitch has dropped out of sight. Your own spies would tell us if she arrived in any of the airports. Eight or ten Russian special-forces troopers would also be highly noticeable. The only way she can aid the American now is if she can swim up the river.''

Congo River

Bolan sat under the awning and watched the river. The noon sun beat down relentlessly, and there was no breeze to cut the burning heat and suffocating humidity. Only the wind of the boat's passage brought any relief at all, and that wind was considerable. There was more engine beneath the cowling, and beneath the boat itself, than Bolan had bargained for. The engine ran hot as they shot down the river. They stopped only for fuel and coolant. They were making good time, and as they approached their destination, Bolan waited for the ambush that had to come. His eyes scanned the river. Even assuming they broke through the ambush, he wondered what exactly he could do to stop the Kords and their African allies.

Burton smiled as he read Bolan's mind. "You're wondering what we're going to do."

"Yeah."

"Me, too. What are we going to do?"

"Well, I have a vague idea. I have to assume Nemanja and Mukantabana have at least about a platoon of armed men. We can't take them head-on. Somehow we have to sneak in. The only thing I can think of is to get into rifle range of Skysniper."

"You know, if you get within range of Skysniper, it's in range of you."

"Yeah, I was thinking about that. But if I can put a bullet through its main lens, that will put it out of commission long enough to allow the Air Force to come in and bomb the place back to the Stone Age. Failing that, maybe I can put a few rounds into its fuel source or its coolant tanks. Anything that will give the bombers a few hours as a window of opportunity.''

Burton nodded slowly. ''Yeah, that's the way I figured it, too.'' He let out a long breath. ''Well, I guess you're going to need a diversion. Their camp is right on a tributary of the main river. I suppose I can let you off in the trees while I run the boat straight at them.''

''They'll cut you to pieces.''

''Maybe,'' Burton said with a shrug. ''But I really don't see a better way. You're the Special Forces guy. I'm just a CIA spook.''

Bolan eyed the man steadily. He was volunteering to commit suicide. ''We'll talk about it later.''

The CIA station chief met Bolan's gaze. ''I don't want to be a pain in the butt, but maybe we had better talk about it now.''

''How about after the ambush?''

Burton followed Bolan's finger as it pointed upriver. A wedge of small boats was coming at them. Bolan picked up the scout rifle. ''Here they come.''

A submachine gun crackled from the cockpit of the lead boat. The range was still several hundred yards, and the bullets spattered into the river well short and wide of the mark.

Bolan wound his arm into the sling and shouldered the scout rifle. The scope was mounted forward of the receiver so his crosshairs floated six inches in front of his eye. He kept both eyes open. The magnification did little to extend his range. It wasn't a thousand-yard rifle by any stretch of the imagination. What the scout concept allowed for more than anything else was highly accurate shooting at the human eye's own natural limit. Bolan let out half a breath.

With both eyes open, his peripheral vision was ghosted by double images, but through his right eye the crosshairs were crystal clear. Bolan ignored the man with the submachine gun and aimed at the man driving the boat.

The rifle roared and bucked back hard into Bolan's shoulder. The lead boat suddenly swerved as the driver was hammered backward in the cockpit. The boat slammed into the boat nearest as it slid around broadside to Bolan. He took the opportunity to rapidly pump two rounds into its engine.

There were three other boats still coming on. All of them lit up as automatic weapons began to fire. All three surged as the drivers shoved their throttles forward. Wood splinters flew from the boat's rail as a burst walked across the side. Bolan fired again and a windscreen shattered. The boat he hit still came on.

Burton shoved the throttles forward. "Grab the rifles in the other case!"

Bolan knelt and flipped the latches. Inside was a pair of beautifully engraved antique double-barreled Westley Richards elephant rifles. The pair of them would easily fetch eighty thousand dollars at auction.

"Explosive ammo! I had the rounds custom made in South Africa!" Burton shouted.

Bolan shouldered the rifle and put the front sight on the windshield of the approaching speedboat. His finger curled around the trigger and leaned deeply into the rifle as he began to squeeze.

The rifle boomed like thunder. Bolan winced as the massive rifle nearly rammed him off of his feet from the recoil. The windshield of the speedboat detonated in orange fire. The boat yawed wildly and Bolan aimed at the next boat and fired the other barrel. The massive rifle surged against him with brutal power. The windshield vaporized under the impact and driver was flung backward out of the boat.

Bolan dropped the smoking rifle and picked up its twin.

Burton shouted from where he crouched by the controls, "We've got company behind us!"

"We worry about them when we're through!"

The boat surged on. Rifle bullets tore across the prow. The awning sagged as its fabric tore and its aluminum frame buckled from bullet strikes. Bolan rose and fired both barrels in rapid succession. He aimed low beneath the windshield of the new lead boat. The massive bullets punched into the deck just forward of the driver's position. The driver reeled back as his console exploded in his face.

Bolan snatched up the 12-gauge Browning shotgun as the range closed to spitting distances.

The one unscathed speedboat weaved through its careening comrades. A man fired his submachine gun in short bursts as he came, and the driver held the wheel with one hand and fired a handgun with another. A bullet hit Bolan's body armor as he fired. Burton had one of the Redhawk revolvers and squeezed off .44 Magnum rounds as they came broadside. Bolan ignored the gunner and fired at the driver.

The pattern of buckshot smashed him against the side of his boat, and the machine gunner fell back as the boat lurched beneath him. Bolan swiveled his aim and squeezed off his remaining four rounds as fast as he could fire them into the boat's engine.

They were through. Burton whooped as they cleared the crippled speedboats and surged ahead. Bolan knelt and broke open the two elephant rifles ejecting the fired cases. He pulled cartridges the size of Cuban cigars out of the cut foam in the case and reloaded.

Burton scanned backward. "We have a problem."

Bolan looked back.

A boat was coming up the river after them. It wasn't a speedboat. It was about three times the size of their own. Bolan brought up the scout rifle and scanned through the scope. The intruder carried a pair of Russian .30-caliber RPK machine guns on the bow behind a steel shield. The elephant rifle might mangle the shield, but he doubted he could penetrate it, and the rounds themselves didn't carry enough high explosive to do any real damage to the hull of a boat that size. In a few moments they would be in range of the machine guns and they would be ripped into driftwood.

Sparks flew from the steel shield as Bolan fired off a round to keep the gunners down. "Darrell, we're in trouble. You got anything else up your sleeve?"

Burton kept the throttle on full. "No. I don't. I was hoping you might have an idea."

Bolan grimaced. Downriver, two of the speedboats had managed to get themselves back under their own power. They waited for the bigger boat. "There's a chance I can keep their heads down, but there has to be dozen men on the big boat, and their decks are a lot higher. Once they get alongside, they're going to start raking us. That's not even considering that they most likely have some RPGs on board. We can run before them, but I think they have some pretty big diesels. If I were them, I'd use the machine guns to keep us down and then close to rocket range, and then—"

"We're toast," Burton finished.

"Yeah. Unless we beach the boat right now and go into the jungle. Barring that, we need the cavalry to arrive."

Both looked down at the driver's bench as the satellite link peeped at them. Bolan shrugged and kicked the hidden panel. He picked up the receiver and checked the numbers on the LED readout. They were being hailed on the radio frequency he had given the embassy. Bolan clicked on the transmitter. "This is Striker. We are receiving."

Valentina Svarzkova's voice came across the line. "We have detected gunfire. Are you engaged?"

Bolan watched the big river craft bear down on them. "You could say that."

"One moment."

Bolan and Burton waited. The chasing boat fired off an experimental burst at them from its twin RPKs. Green tracers walked across their bow. Bolan whipped up the scout and put a bullet into the machine gunner's shield. They fired another, closer burst in return.

"Striker, we have acquired you visually."

Bolan glanced up at the sky. He silently hoped Svarzkova was somehow calling him from the cockpit of a MiG-29.

"Striker, we have the enemy in sight. Maintain your present heading."

"Jesus Christ!" Burton threw himself down, and so did Bolan. The twin streams of the RPK ripped through the engine housing and sparks shrieked inside the boat. The engine howled as it broke apart and metal ground on metal. Black smoke belched out of the engine housing.

"We're hit! We have lost power! Repeat, we are dead in the water!" More bullets tore in the rear of the boat. Bolan raised one of the elephant rifles and fired both barrels at the machine gunner's shield. Bolan lost his footing from the recoil. Orange fire erupted and the weapon rocked on its mount. The muzzles swung up as the gunner hurled himself down. Bolan picked himself up and brought the second rifle with him.

The steel shield had two smoking dents in it, but the weapons and the gunner were untouched. Bolan picked the receiver up. "We're just about out of options! If you're going to do something, do it now!"

"Affirmative, Striker. Shut off your engine."

Burton pulled back the throttles of the dying engine and killed the ignition. The boat coasted to a stop in the water, and then slowly started moving backward with the current. Burton had taken up the scout rifle and looked at Bolan unhappily. "This isn't good."

Bolan kept his eye on the twin machine guns. The muzzles suddenly swung down, and Bolan fired. Orange fire erupted. The muzzles jerked with the impact against the shield but swung back on target. Bolan fired his other barrel. The gunner's mantlet vibrated on its mount but didn't buckle.

"What the hell?"

Bolan glanced over and followed the CIA man's gaze.

A gray shape shot through the water to starboard. A V-shaped bow wake of bubbles followed it as it streaked down the dark river. Someone on the other boat saw it, too, and the river craft's prow swung as it tried to maneuver. The streaking shape corrected its course slightly to stay in line. The machine gunner desperately yanked his muzzles down and began chopping at the water, but the silver shape just beneath the surface was already under his arc of fire.

The prow of the boat disappeared in a cloud of fire and smoke. Debris scythed through the air as bits of boat flew in all directions. Fountains of water geysered up into the air. The twin RPK mount rose upward like a rocket on a column of orange fire, and then fell smoking back down to the river. The front two-thirds of the boat was gone. The shattered rear keeled backward in smoking ruin and began to slide down beneath the water. The two remaining speedboats whipped around in tight circles and retreated down the river at full speed.

Bolan turned his gaze up river.

The black tube of a periscope peered back at him.

The periscope began to rise and bubbles foamed as a dark hull surfaced. A tiny conning tower half as tall as a man rose from the hull, and the large, single screw was visible where its blades left the water when the sub was fully surfaced. The sides of the midget sub bulged, and Bolan knew from rumor that the flarings housed the sub's tractor tracks for driving on the bottom. Over one of the flarings sat the ugly length of a Russian 406 mm torpedo. On the opposite side, a pair of steel hoops revealed where its brethren had lain.

Burton gasped as a blond head appeared at the top of tiny conning tower. Captain Valentina Svarzkova saluted sharply. Bolan stood in their beleaguered boat and returned the salute. Burton shook his head. "The cavalry has arrived."

"Right on cue."

"Tell me you knew they were there the whole time."

Bolan put down the elephant rifle. His shoulders ached as if he had been beaten with a baseball bat. "No. I pretty much figured we were toast."

20

Congo Basin

"What do you mean they broke the ambush!"

Mukantabana eyed Nemanja. The Serbian certainly spent a great deal of time yelling. "They broke the ambush, apparently."

"How!"

"I'm not sure. The American and whoever he had with them engaged the speedboats in a firefight, at which they seemed to be successful. My man on the scene then sent in the river cutter. The cutter was mounted with twin general-purpose machine guns and had several men armed with RPG-7 antiarmor weapons and 30 mm grenade launchers. The cutter radioed that they had crippled the American's boat and were closing in for the kill."

"So what happened?"

Mukantabana frowned slightly. "I don't know. That was the last communication from the cutter we received. Survivors in the speedboats reported that the cutter blew up in spectacular fashion."

Nemanja considered this. "You said your men who stopped the American on the river found no heavy weapons on the boat."

"That's correct. Only hunting arms. No rocket or grenade launchers were found." Mukantabana shifted his bulk in his rattan chair. "Perhaps they had high explosives disguised to look like something else?"

Nemanja shook his head. "No, even they had fifty pounds of high explosives hidden in their seat cushions, there is no way they could have floated a satchel charge into the cutter if it was still out of RPG-7 range.''

"I see your point. Then it must have been a plane or a helicopter.''

"Did any of the survivors report seeing a plane or a helicopter?''

"No," Mukantabana answered.

"They had help of some kind. Another boat?''

"They were boxed in, front and back. It's hard for me to imagine where they could have hidden a boat armed with weapons heavy enough to blow up the river cutter.''

Nemanja stared out from his tent. Some unidentified creature screamed out in the darkness. Another creature answered it. Under the jungle canopy Congo was a place of incredible darkness. All manner of things lurked within it. Things lurked in the river, as well. The commander smiled coldly. "A submarine.''

Mukantabana snorted. "A submarine?''

"It is the only way they could have done it.''

"That's impossible.''

"Oh?''

Mukantabana laughed. "Listen, my friend. The Congo is one of the largest, and the most shallow rivers in the world. You have seen the boats that traverse it. Most are flat bottomed or of extremely shallow draft. Anything the size of a banana boat or larger must often change course repeatedly in a single journey to avoid the mud and shifting in the sandbars, and then alter their course again many times on the return trip. It would constantly be surfacing. The water itself is so muddy and silt laden that sonar would be next to useless. They wouldn't get ten kilometers up the river without running aground.''

Nemanja nodded. "I hope you're right. I want to be ready to leave within the next twelve hours.''

Congo River

"CONTACT!''

The submerged sub lurched as it hit the sandbar and the gears howled through the hull as its tracks dug in and began to climb.

Bolan sat squeezed between two Spetsnaz troopers who stoically ignored the heat and the stench of twelve bodies in a midget sub that had been built for ten. There was no place to stretch out and no way to stand. A single chemical toilet served the needs of everyone on board. Its chemical odor suppressors had been overwhelmed days ago. The walls and the ceiling of the sub's main compartment were studded with racks carrying weapons that loomed out to slam and jab the occupants with every lurch and shudder of the vehicle. They ran submerged by day and crawled the bottom with the tracks when it got too shallow to swim. They took turns sleeping on the tiny aisle between the benches on three-hour shifts. At night they ran on the surface, and the muggy air of the Congo summer night coming in through the open hatch was all anyone thought about during the day. Standing in the conning tower as they ran at night was a privilege everyone was prepared to kill for. How the Russians had withstood four days of this was beyond Bolan's imagination.

The captain of the sub called back as the vibration in the hull changed and the whine of the screws cranked up. "One hour to target."

"Thank God!" Burton, said, his dark face looked pale even in the poor orange lighting of the hull's interior. The lurching, stinking, claustrophobic ride had forced the CIA man to crawl to the head six times during their journey.

Bolan glanced at his watch. They would be arriving just before dawn.

"How do you wish to attack?" Svarzkova asked.

Bolan had been giving the matter considerable thought. "They will be extracting by boat. I'm betting at least one of the boats will be large enough to house Skysniper, fully assembled with its fuel cells and coolant system attached. They will want it ready to use in case we somehow manage to launch an airstrike against them before they can lose themselves in the river traffic and disappear. With any luck they already have the system mounted on it.

"We have one torpedo left. If Skysniper is installed and we blow up the boat, all of our problems are solved. If not, I want the biggest boat blown up anyway to delay them. If that's the situation, then we're going to have to do it by assault. I want a frontal attack by most of your men right after the boat goes up. I'll take your best rifle shot to flank them and try to knock out the weapon with small arms."

"The frontal-assault team will be slaughtered."

"Most likely."

The Spetsnaz men who spoke English looked at Bolan long and hard but said nothing. It had been a suicide mission from the beginning, and every Russian aboard was a volunteer. Igor Stepanshuk's pale eyes were haggard as he locked gazes with Bolan and then Svarzkova. He sighed heavily. His voice was a dull rumble.

"We have one Dragunov sniper rifle in stores. Valentina is the best marksman among us. She will go with you. Take your CIA friend, as well." The immense Russian ran his eye over the rest of the men in the sub. "I will lead the assault."

Bolan nodded. "We'll disembark at least a hundred yards from the objective. Infiltrate as close as you can to the camp itself. When we radio the captain, he blows up the boat, and you attack. My team will be flanking. If we can't get a bead on the weapon, we'll come in hard. We'll meet you in the middle."

Stepanshuk snorted. "Most likely we will meet in hell, but I will inform my men of the plan."

Congo Basin

BRANKO NEMANJA LOOKED at his watch and then up at a patch in the jungle where a few stars managed to shine. Beneath the multitiered canopy the world was nearly pitch-black. Dawn would be coming soon.

Mukantabana's heavy footfalls announced his presence. "You have halted your move."

"I have," Nemanja answered. He regretted having sent half

his Kords and many of Mukantabana's men downriver earlier to establish their next base. He wanted every man with a rifle he could find at the moment.

Mukantabana's eyes roved the darkness. "You think we're going to be attacked?"

"I do."

"How?"

Nemanja kept his eye up on the night sky. "I don't know. Perhaps they will try to swarm us with Stealth fighters. They have at least a squadron of them in Europe."

"But their Stealth fighters are based in Germany and Italy. You have spies in both locations. They would have informed us of such a massive launch."

"Yes. They would have. I would know if they tried a multiple air-refueling sortie from the United States, as well. I have heard nothing."

Mukantabana's hand rested on the grips of his pistol, and he looked out into the jungle. "Yet, you still believe we'll be attacked."

Nemanja nodded. "I am sure of it."

"Instincts?"

"Yes."

Mukantabana's teeth gleamed in contrast to his dark face. "I have some knowledge of these things myself, and I have learned to trust your instincts. What do you wish to do?"

"I've kept one automatic cannon watching the river, and pulled the other back to guard the weapon and the camp's perimeter. We'll sit tight and wait. We will wait until noon. If nothing has happened by then, we'll embark as planned. I don't fear a daylight extraction. Their Stealth bombers and fighters are invisible by day, and such an attack on their part would risk an incident with Congo's air force. Even if they chose this as acceptable option, we have shown them that we can shoot them out of the air."

"It's the American you fear."

"Yes. He's out there. He won't stop until he has destroyed the weapon or he is dead."

"What will you do?"

The commander checked the loads in his Browning Hi-Power and reholstered it. He unslung his rifle and checked it, as well. The Krinkov carbine was an AK-74 rifle with a barrel that had been brutally shortened to fourteen inches. In the hands of an amateur it was totally uncontrollable. It was a buzz saw in the hands of a man who knew what he was doing. Nemanja generally preferred a sniper rifle, but he had been a jungle fighter in Congo before for the French. In the jungle Nemanja had found no better weapon. He racked the folding metal stock out and it locked in place. "If he comes close enough I'll slaughter him myself."

Nemanja looked back toward camp. In the darkness under the trees, Skysniper sat fueled, cooled and ready. "However, given the opportunity, I'll be quite pleased with burning him in half."

Mukantabana's smiled gleamed in the dark again. "That would be something to see."

21

Congo Basin

The Executioner moved through the trees.

The relief of leaving the cramped and stinking sub had been short-lived. Bolan had been in jungles all over the world, and the jungle of the Congo River Basin was the nastiest in his experience. Thorn foliage, oppressive humidity and wet, sucking ground strove to keep them from their objective. The heat itself wasn't bad. Just before dawn the jungle was cool beneath the canopy, and mist rose off the mighty river and crawled between the trees.

Bolan crouched and used his night-vision scope to see ahead. Mukantabana's camp should be close, but no lights lit up the green-and-gray world revealed by the night scope. The camp was blacked out—they were expecting trouble. They were undoubtedly watching the perimeter with night-vision devices of their own. Only the fog and dense foliage was preventing the adversaries from seeing one another. There was no way Bolan or his team would be able to sit back and take potshots.

The battle was going to be point-blank and personal.

Bolan, Svarzkova and Burton were due west of Mukantabana's jungle encampment. Bolan had the scout rifle, Svarzkova her Dragunov sniper rifle and Burton had his shotgun. Stepanshuk and his team were infiltrating straight up the banks of the tributary that led to the camp. They were the frontal assault, and despite Stepanshuk's protests, Bolan had insisted that the Russians take what heavy weapons they had. It wasn't much. They had one RPG-7 rocket launcher, and two of the Spetsnaz troopers had 30 mm grenade launchers mounted on their rifles.

That was it, and they would need all of it to survive for even a few seconds. The enemy had at least two automatic cannons that the Stealth pilots had reported before they had been slaughtered. There had to be at least a platoon of the enemy, not counting the technicians.

The odds were not good.

Bolan, Svarzkova and Burton had each stuffed their pockets with hand grenades, and both Bolan and Burton each carried one of the Westley Richards elephant rifles slung across their backs. They had split the four remaining .600-caliber high-explosive bullets, as well as the Redhawk revolvers.

Bolan knelt and turned to Svarzkova. "Call the sub."

The woman knelt and spoke quietly into the transmitter of her pack radio. Her blond hair was stuffed beneath a black bandana. Smeared grease from the sub's gears darkened the pale skin of her face. Her conversation was hushed and rapid. She clicked the transmitter off. "Captain Bykova says he is fifty meters from the dock. He is running on the tracks and the conning tower is one meter above water. There are seven flat-bottomed river traders on dock. There is a river barge, as well. He estimates the barge is big enough to hold Skysniper in full assembly and ready for combat. No other boat present is big enough to do so. He's prepared to torpedo the barge on your order."

"Tell him to stand by."

"The midget sub has RPK light machine gun for covering returning swimmers. Bykova has mounted a machine gun to the conning tower. He says after destroying the barge he'll engage river defenses if you wish."

"At least one of their cannons has to be watching the river. If the water is too shallow for him to completely submerge, a 23 mm automatic cannon is going to rip his hull to pieces."

"Bykova is aware of this. He says it will give Stepanshuk's team more time to close in while the enemy is concentrated on the submarine. The destruction of the submarine is unimportant.

Once Skysniper is destroyed and all of the enemy eliminated, he will be happy to pilot a flatboat back to Kinshasa for you."

"All right. Tell Bykova to stand by. Once the barge is blown, tell him to engage any targets of opportunity from his position."

Svarzkova clicked on her transmitter and spoke quickly. She clicked off. "Bykova is ready."

"What's Stepanshuk's situation?"

Another quick conversation ensued. "There is barbed wire strung between trees around the inner encampment. He suspects the wire is rigged with sensors and an alarm will sound once it's cut. There is a second wire perimeter within. He suspects land mines. He'll move on the torpedo's explosion."

Bolan checked his watch and his compass. He flicked off the safety of the scout rifle. "Tell Captain Bykova to fire."

She spoke a single word into her transmitter.

The battle had begun.

"PERHAPS YOU ARE MISTAKEN, Commander. Perhaps the American has— Good God!"

Colonel Mukantabana ripped his .357 Magnum revolver out of its holster at the massive thump. Orange light washed through the trees and threw bizarre shadows in the wake of the explosion. "That came from the dock!"

"Yes," Nemanja said. Secondary explosions and the cook-off of bursting rifle ammunition filled the predawn. "That was the barge. It had explosives and RPG-7s on board." Yellow fire flickered and black smoke created lurid colors as the dock and the shattered remnants of the barge burned. "The American wants us to stay put."

Nemanja flicked off the safety of his Krinkov carbine. Men in the camp began snatching up rifles and running to their pre-assigned positions. Down on the river the snarl of a machine gun ripped into life. Sporadic rifle fire answered.

"That's the sound of an RPK light machine gun. To my knowledge we don't have that particular weapon in camp. They are engaging the remaining men on the docks."

Nemanja picked up his radio. "Milos, what is the situation?"

The commander's man on the river shouted back. "Sir, there is a submarine in the river. It has torpedoed the barge, destroying it. Several of the boats are gone. The dock is burning. The sub is engaging us with machine guns."

"Quickly, Milos, if the submarine has surfaced, use your guns."

"Yes, sir. The cannon is moving into firing position. Cannon engaging."

The rapid-fire hammering of an automatic cannon drowned out the other noises of combat. The 23 mm AZP-23 cannon ripped off staccato bursts. Shrieking and rending metal joined the cacophony as high-explosive incendiaries struck.

Nemanja knew the sounds of war and what he heard made him smile. The gunner was successfully engaging something.

"Commander! The submarine is hit. It's dead in the water and burning above the waterline. We are—"

Rifle fire broke out again and the radio went dead. Nemanja recognized the sound of 30 mm grenade launchers thumping near the river. The cannon ripped into life again, and was met with the hiss of a rocket streaking through the night. There was another explosion, and the cannon made a new and unpleasant sound as it died. Its magazine detonated as the high-explosive antitank round struck it. Plumes of superheated white smoke and streamers of yellow fire spewed up through the trees as the Russian white phosphorus grenades burned.

Nemanja's face was a silent snarl in the dark. The American was here, and he had brought his Russian friends with him. He turned to Mukantabana. "Get everyone inside the perimeter."

BOLAN DROPPED to one knee. A pair of men in khaki shorts and field jackets moved up rapidly from the river. They carried FN assault rifles in their hands. They weren't friendlies. Svarzkova dropped by Bolan's side and the scout and the Dragunov rifles fired nearly as one. Both men twisted and fell. Bolan rose and moved to the two fallen men.

Burton scanned the ebbing darkness as Bolan checked the dead men. "What's up?"

"These two were running parallel to the camp rather than straight for it."

"So?"

Bolan pulled a bloodied piece of paper from an inner pocket of one of the dead men. He unfolded it and pressed a small button on his watch. A small red glow played over the paper. It was a very crude drawing of the camp oriented to the river. There were small *x*s drawn around the perimeter of the camp. Two dotted lines drew paths through the *x*s to the camp inside.

"They were paralleling the camp to get to one of the paths through the land mines." Bolan turned the map in his hands. "There are some kind of markers sketched in, but it doesn't say what they are. Valentina, radio Stepanshuk. Tell him there is a path through the mines within thirty yards of his position. Tell him to look for any kind of parallel markers in the trees. There must be line-of-sight markers visible within the camp's perimeter, as well."

As she spoke rapidly into her radio, Burton pointed. "I've found it."

Bolan followed his finger. Directly ahead was a sapling that appeared to have been broken by some large animal. Paralleling it ahead was a narrow animal path through the trees. A similar broken tree lay a few yards ahead. Bolan brought up his night-vision scope and peered through the dense foliage. There was a path. As rifle fire broke the night, Bolan could make out the flickering fire of an automatic rifle where the camp had to be. The Executioner looked down at the crude map again. The dotted path was a straight line without detours or deviations. "Valentina, tell Stepanshuk to find a deer path. Look for freshly broken saplings. If he finds a path, have him draw a line bisecting the camp and assault."

Bolan rose. "Let's move."

Burton shook his head. "Wait a minute. I have an idea."

COMMANDER NEMANJA LISTENED to the hammering of weapons in the night. The jungle was so thick that enemies could only be seen by the flicker of their muzzle-flashes. The commander was irritated that he had yet to hear the sound of land mines and the screams of wounded and dying men. The American and his Russian friends were being clever. They weren't blundering through the mines in a suicidal charge. It prevented Nemanja from turning his remaining 23 mm cannon on them, but that was all right. The sun would be rising soon. He had a platoon of men. The light was his friend, not the American's.

Nemanja had to admit the Russian midget submarine had been a brilliant move. Nemanja himself had discounted the possibility of submarine insertion and attack. However, the Russian sub was now a torn and shattered hulk, burned to the waterline and stranded on its tracks. The only chance the American had now was to retreat to the docks and take one of the remaining boats back down the river.

But even that was going to be suicide.

Mukantabana had radioed several of his camps. Two of them were less than ten miles away both up and down the river. There were sixty men with automatic rifles coming. They would be converging on the tributary, and then the American and his friends would be trapped. Most of Mukantabana's men were little more than thugs, but he had a picked cadre of men who knew the jungle. The Americans and the Russians knew nothing of the terrain once they were ten yards inland from either shore of the river.

Come the dawn, they were all dead men.

"Commander!"

Nemanja whirled. One of his men pointed off through the trees. Rifle fire had erupted and grenade launchers thumped. The thick foliage and multiple tree canopies destroyed the accuracy of the grenade launchers except at the closest of ranges, but the implication was clear. An attack was coming.

"Sir, there is an assault on the east perimeter."

Nemanja's head snapped up as his mind sifted through the noise of combat. None of the land mines were detonating.

The assault was coming straight down the safe corridor.

"They know our minefield! Swing the cannon around from the river and bring it in line immediately."

Twenty yards away the men in the gun jeep swung the cannon around on its rings and brought it to bear on the eastern quadrant. The muzzle-flash was blinding as it began ripping bursts through the trees toward the mine corridor. Trees smashed and broke apart as the high-explosive rounds detonated.

"Tell the gunners to switch to armor-piercing incendiaries," Nemanja demanded.

There was a pause in the cannon fire. The Kords and Mukantabana's killers poured rifle fire into the trees to keep the Russians down. The AZP-23 suddenly ripped into life again. Nemanja watched through his night-vision goggles. The incendiaries streaked through the jungle. Great holes and flinders of wood and bark erupted as the steel-core penetrators ripped through the wood and tore on. Explosions resumed and Nemanja smiled at the skill of his men. His gunner was using the twin feeds of his cannon to intermix his belts of high-explosive and armor-piercing ammo.

The rifle fire in the trees flickered to a halt. The cannon fire suddenly stopped. His gunner scanned the trees with his night sight.

Nemanja suspected many of the Russians had been killed by the onslaught. The rest were pinned down. The assault had been stalled. Nemanja peered upward from behind his sandbags. Pearly light was beginning to filter down through the canopy. The night was the only friend his enemies had.

Their friend was failing.

"STEPANSHUK IS PINNED down by the cannon. He has lost a third of his men."

Bolan grimaced. Stepanshuk had gone down his corridor with a squad of heavily armed Spetsnaz troopers. The enemy now knew they had discovered the mine lanes. An assault from this side would be suicide with anything short of an armored vehicle.

Bolan and Svarzkova had moved to the edge of the perimeter. The mine corridor was demarcated as he expected. He kept his eye on the camp's inner perimeter and waited on Burton. If the CIA man had a plan, it would have to be brilliant.

The station chief's voice spoke behind them. "It's me. Don't shoot."

Bolan turned.

One of Mukantabana's men stood before him. Burton's ragged cutoff jeans and the orange T-shirt were gone. He wore the khaki shorts and field jacket of one of the men they had taken out. Combat boots shod his feet rather than sandals. A forage cap covered his shaved head. When he smiled, Bolan saw his gold teeth had magically disappeared. He carried a captured enemy FN assault rifle in one hand and his shotgun in the other.

"What kind of grenades do you have?"

"I have two frags and two white phosphorus."

Burton dug into his pockets and pulled out a pair of frags of his own. "I'll trade you. Give me your white phosphorous. I'm going to infiltrate down the mine lane. You two shadow at least thirty yards behind me. If they don't blow me to pieces, I'm going to lob one of these into the cannon emplacement. If I'm still alive after that, I'll see about lighting up that laser. I think some white phosphorus is going to have a bad effect on its chemical fuel cells. If I do the cannon, both you and Stepanshuk assault on both flanks."

"You'll be killed. No Russian soldier would fall for such a trick," Svarzkova said, shaking her head. "Neither will the Kords."

"No, probably not. But I don't have to fool the Kords, just Mukantabana's men. They're not trained soldiers. I only need to fool them for a few seconds. Then it's show time."

Bolan didn't like it any more than Svarzkova did, but it was the only option they had. Bolan took Burton's shotgun and the elephant rifle. "All right. Do it. Valentina, tell Stepanshuk to be ready to move on your go."

Burton began moving from tree to tree down the mine corridor. After ten yards he shouted out in an African dialect.

Rifle fire ripped through the trees.

Burton threw himself down. The gunfire ceased as the enemy scanned for him in the mist and gloom. A voice called out and the agent shouted again. A voice at the camp's perimeter yelled back. Burton rose with his rifle over his head and walked into plain view. He threw the rifle down and began jogging forward with a pronounced limp. He kept his hands held up high.

Bolan moved to the next tree with Svarzkova behind him. "Your friend is very brave," she said.

Bolan agreed. Burton was playing guts ball. He had to have at least half a dozen rifles pointed at him, as well as an automatic cannon.

Burton made it through the minefield and came to the barbed wire strung between the trees around the camp's inner perimeter. Bolan could see a sandbag revetment at the camp entrance to the minefield. He could no longer make out Burton's voice but he saw him stumble slightly. A rifleman rose from the revetment and grabbed Burton's arm and helped him walk.

Burton disappeared into the enemy camp.

Bolan moved forward to the next tree, and Svarzkova shadowed him.

The unmistakable roar of a .44 Magnum revolver split the night. It fired three times in rapid succession. Bolan tracked the sound with his night scope. A man was running inside the camp from tree to tree toward the south. A huge stainless-steel revolver gleamed in his hand. Bolan tracked with his scope. A man rose from a foxhole in Burton's path. Bolan had the shot and took it.

The scout rifle shoved back against his shoulder in recoil, and the killer fell.

Burton ran on. He disappeared from Bolan's scope for a moment as the trees were too thick to see through.

The night suddenly lit up in a flash of burning white phosphorus. Freakish shadows lit up the jungle in the intense glare, and then orange fire strobed as the cannon's high-explosive rounds cooked off in the intense heat. Tracer rounds burst and streaked in all directions.

Svarzkova shouted into her radio in Russian. "Go!"

Russian weapons opened up on the east perimeter.

Bolan charged.

"We've lost the cannon! They are approaching the inner perimeter!"

Nemanja was already aware of this. The problem was that he didn't have a proper firebase. A real firebase would have had the trees cleared in at least a hundred-yard perimeter with interlocking lanes of machine-gun fire to create kill zones. But such a firebase would also have stuck out like a sore thumb to anyone using surveillance satellites. What had made a perfect hiding place for Skysniper wasn't making such an effective fortification. There were too many trees for the enemy to hide behind, and the foliage was too dense to get any proper rifle fire. Grenade launchers thumped to the east, and grenades detonated against the trees along the inner perimeter. That was one thing they had going for them. The enemy had to get close to come to grips with them. They held the defensive ground, and they outnumbered their attackers.

Nemanja's cannon was burning. Its twin belts of 23 mm ammo had cooked off, and white phosphorus clung to it and burned. That irked him. His inner perimeter had been penetrated. Someone was loose in the camp posing as one of Mukantabana's men. Something would have to be done about that.

Nemanja leaned close to his one of his Kords and spoke in Slavic. "Kill any African who comes within twenty meters of Skysniper."

The man's eyes widened momentarily and then he nodded. He drew his bayonet and clicked it into place over the muzzle of his rifle. He motioned two more Kords to him, and they moved out toward the laser emplacement.

Mukantabana approached with an FN rifle clutched in his massive hands. One of his men was with him. Nemanja kept his eyes just above his sandbags and scanned the jungle. Occasional tracers licked out of the darkness, and his men and Mukantabana's fired back. The enemy was probing him, trying to get close enough so that they could effectively use their grenades and RPG-7 rocket launcher.

Rifle fire broke out on the western perimeter. Nemanja knew the sound of a Dragunov sniper rifle. One was firing to the west in slow, careful semiautomatic fire. There were screams within the perimeter as men were hit. Someone out there had to have a night-vision scope attached to his weapon, but was still firing too fast to be acquiring a target for each shot.

It was covering fire.

"Get men on the western perimeter! Now!" Nemanja shouted in Slavic.

The spiteful crack of a fragmentation grenade answered his orders. More men screamed on the perimeter, and the crack of the first grenade was followed by a second. The Dragunov began hammering again in rapid semiautomatic fire. To the east the Russians opened up with every rifle that was still firing. Mukantabana's men were close to panic. Two men were falling back from their positions on the perimeter and retreating to the main camp.

Nemanja glared at Mukantabana. "What the hell is wrong with your men!"

The colonel raised his rifle and shot one of the men down. The other stared up in amazement. The colonel's bodyguard shot the second man and sent him twisting to the soft earth. Mukantabana lowered his rifle and shrugged. "They are cowards."

Nemanja saw another man creeping back toward the main camp. The coward must have thrown away his rifle.

Mukantabana roared at him, "Get back into position!"

A massive glittering handgun appeared in the man's hands like a magic trick. Flame roared from its muzzle, which seemed to point straight at Nemanja.

Mukantabana's bodyguard reeled as the bullet struck him and he fell backward into the soft earth. A second bullet tore into the sandbag by Nemanja's head and sprayed sand into his face. Nemanja's Krinkov carbine fired. The gunman jerked and fell behind a tree. Bark tore as Nemanja dumped the rest of his magazine into the tree. He dropped behind his sandbags.

Mukantabana's man was a mess. A bullet had torn out the big man's throat and taken out most of the back of his neck, as well. Nemanja had never heard a handgun with such a powerful firing signature, but its effect was as devastating as its sound.

Mukantanbana pulled a hand grenade from his belt. He pulled the pin and the cotter lever pinged away. He lobbed it past the tree the gunman was hiding behind. The grenade cracked and spit yellow fire. Jagged metal fragments hissed through the foliage like tiny saw blades traveling at just under the speed of sound.

Mukantabana studied the grenade's effect judiciously. "I believe that is the man who blew up our second 23 mm cannon."

Nemanja peered over the revetment. "I believe you're right." He kept the front sight of his Krinkov on the battered tree trunk. The man had infiltrated the camp and destroyed the remaining cannon. Nemanja suspected he was an American. The bastard would not stop. Nemanja would have to rip out the Yankee's lungs.

Mukantabana gripped his rifle and shook his head. "The situation is becoming untenable. We're fighting Russian Spetsnaz troopers and American Special Forces. They're reaping my men like wheat, and too many of your Kords went downriver to secure the next laser site. All they have to do is destroy the laser. Once they have accomplished that, their Stealth fighters will bomb us at will."

"I agree with you, but look, already the jungle is lightening. The men you radioed for can't be far away. The Russian sub they came on couldn't have delivered more than one squad. They have taken casualties and they can have little more than the ammunition they carried in on their backs. All we must do is guard the laser and hold out until our reinforcements arrive. Then it's our turn to hunt.''

"You're right, my friend, but how are we to do that? Our opponents are ghosts in the mist. We have no high ground to hold. Our heavy weapons have been destroyed."

Nemanja grinned at Mukantabana. "There is one thing you are forgetting."

"Oh? What's that?"

"The laser is fueled and ready."

"Ah." Mukantabana's face lit up in the predawn.

"I think we have spent too much time defending Skysniper. I think it is time for Skysniper to start defending us."

BOLAN FIRED the scout rifle and a man fell. He flicked his rifle's bolt, put the crosshairs on another man and fired. FN assault rifles hammered back as Bolan faded behind some foliage and hugged a fold in the wet ground. Mukantabana's men didn't have night-vision devices, and picking them out with the night-vision scope was easy. However, the scout was a full-power .308 rifle with a nineteen-inch barrel. Its muzzle-flash announced Bolan's presence every time he fired. Swarms of automatic rifle fire sought him out.

Svarzkova was crouched some yards behind, and her Dragunov fired off several rapid 7.62 mm rounds. Every time the killers answered one of Bolan's shots, she made them pay for it. They still had not figured out the cycle and they kept dying. Bolan had watched one man rise and throw away his rifle only to be shot down from behind. If there wasn't a minefield, Bolan suspected most of Mukantabana's men would have fled already.

The Kords, however, were different; they were likely to fight to the death.

That was another problem. The Kords Bolan had killed had been carrying Russian weapons. The Executioner could detect few extra AK-74 firing signatures excluding the Spetsnaz team. That told him that the Kords had pulled back to the center of camp. They were using Mukantabana's men as cannon fodder.

It was an excellent strategy. Bolan patted down his web gear. He was running critically low on ammunition. The Russians had to be in the same shape or worse. However, at least they had the option of cannibalizing the equipment of their dead and wounded.

Bolan craned his neck around and spoke very quietly. "Valentina, radio Stepanshuk. I want to know his situation."

There was a momentary pause as she checked. "Stepanshuk is down to five men including himself. Ammunition is critical."

The Spetsnaz team had received fifty percent casualties. Bolan stuffed more shells into the action of his rifle. They didn't have enough men to take the camp.

Burton's voice spoke in Bolan's earpiece. "Hey, I've got an idea."

"I thought you might be dead. You weren't answering."

"I've taken a bullet, and there were some shooters too close to allow me to talk. They've moved."

"Are you all right?"

"I'll live. Listen, Mukantabana's men are close to panic. I'm going to yell out that we don't give a damn about them or Mukantabana. I'm going to tell them all we care about is destroying the laser, and that we'll pay a bounty to the men that destroy it and another bounty to the men that bring us Nemanja's head. I'm also going to tell them that if they throw down their rifles, we'll let them pass down the mine corridors unmolested and let them take boats from the docks to get out of here."

"Well, it can't hurt anything, except you. You start shouting in camp and someone is likely to drop a grenade on you."

"They've already tried that," Burton declared.

"Well, then, what the hell, go for it."

Deep within the camp Darrell Burton started shouting out in a rapid West African dialect.

NEMANJA RIPPED off a burst in the direction of the voice. He shouted in Slavic to his Kords. "Goddamn it! Michael! Paulus! I want that man flanked and killed."

Paulus and Michael moved out like ghosts through the underbrush in a pincer movement to flank the infiltrator.

The voice in the trees shouted out again. The gunfire on the perimeter almost ceased altogether. Nemanja had no idea what the man was shouting, but his trained ear told him the man was repeating himself.

Nemanja squeezed off another burst and then turned to the colonel. "Do you understand what he is saying?"

Mukantabana's eyes were slits. "Yes."

"Well?"

The colonel cocked his head a moment as he listened. His finger slid soundlessly around the trigger of his Belgian battle rifle.

"What is he saying?" Nemanja shouted. He could see the wheels turning in Mukantabana's mind. Nemanja's carbine was the shorter and quicker weapon. He deliberately relaxed his shoulders to whip his carbine around and fill Mukantabana full of lead if necessary.

The colonel slowly smiled. "The man says they don't care about me or my men. They say we can throw down our rifles and go down the mine corridors unimpeded. All they want is Skysniper, and you." Mukantabana's grin widened. "They say they will give a million American dollars to whoever destroys Skysniper, and a similar sum to the men who bring them your head."

Nemanja kept his shoulders relaxed. "And?"

"And I don't believe them. They will let my men pass, but I'm an indicted war criminal wanted by the Hague, and a drug runner wanted by Interpol. We will sit tight. Men from my other camps will be arriving very soon to help my men hold the perimeter and—"

Rifle fire tore the sandbag emplacement. The rifles were FN assault rifles. Nemanja whirled and killed one of Mukantabana's men who was charging their position firing from the hip. Mukantabana's own weapon hammered out rapid semiauto rounds as he cut two of his own men down. Russian gunfire erupted from the east. The man in the trees fired his massive handgun. The Kords around Skysniper began firing in all directions.

Hell had broken loose.

Nemanja's voice tore from his throat in a mocking snarl. "This is how things are done in Congo!"

Mukantabana shot down another of his men. "Indeed, it is."

"I'm going to kill the American. I'm going to kill the Russians. I'm going to kill all of your men."

Mukantabana kept his eyes on the perimeter. "The river is full of such scum. I can get more."

Nemanja roared at the top of his lungs in Slavic. "Kords! Down! Hit the dirt!" He switched to Russian in the same stentorian voice of command. "Kolov! Fire Skysniper! Ground-defense mode! Three seconds! Three hundred and sixty degree arc!"

He turned to Mukantabana. "You'd better get down."

BOLAN CHARGED down the path through the mines. He saw three bodies as he approached. Burton had cleared the path, and the camp was a bedlam of gunfire. Whatever Burton had said was working. Mukantabana's men on the perimeter and the Kords in the inner camp were engaged in a desperate firefight. Valentina Svarzkova charged a few yards behind him.

Bolan's eyes flared as he charged in. The FN rifles on the perimeter were still firing. The Russian weapons of the Kords had ceased. Bolan slowed slightly at the sound of a hideous scream, followed by a second, then a third. Bolan heard strange bursting sounds, superseded by a sound like a scuba tank rupturing. Men were suddenly running and screaming in all directions. Bolan saw a hard blue light moving swiftly through the trees. The trees were blowing outward, smoking and shattering.

Bolan skidded to a halt and grabbed Svarzkova. He dragged her down with him as he threw himself to the ground.

They were firing Skysniper.

A man ran screaming from the laser in blind panic, but it planed around faster than he could run. The blue beam sliced across him.

The man burst like a water balloon.

The laser continued its arc, burning everything in its path. Anything wet in the jungle hissed and shrieked into exploding steam. Anything dry instantly burst into flame before the scything beam of supercoherent light.

The laser beam whipped over Bolan and Svarzkova and then winked out as quickly as it had appeared. The deadly light had shown for only a matter of heartbeats. The devastation was total. Huge old-growth trees sagged and cracked with big chunks of their trunks missing. Other hardwoods were going up like dry kindling. Anything that had stood more than four feet in the air had been mowed down.

Inside the camp nothing moved.

Shafts of pearly light were beginning to filter down through the shattered canopy as dawn broke. The light made ghostly rays and tenuous rainbows in the burning smoke and rising steam.

"Valentina, see if Stepanshuk is still alive."

Svarzkova whispered into her radio at the same time as Bolan spoke into his throat mike. "Burton, you alive?"

The CIA man's voice was shaky. "Yeah."

"What's the situation in the camp."

"The Kords are positioned in and around the laser. They have something of a strong point built up around it with some foxholes."

"What about Mukantabana's men?"

"Jesus, I've never seen anything like it. Most of them had stood up to fire on the Kords or were charging. The laser just...they're gone. They just exploded when the laser hit them. If there are any survivors, they're hugging the ground."

"All right, sit tight."

Svarzkova leaned close to Bolan's ear. "Stepanshuk is down to two men. They have consolidated weapons and ammunition. The grenade launchers are gone, the RPG-7 is still functional, but they have one rocket. A man carrying the spares was cut in half and the rockets he was carrying detonated."

Bolan squinted around the stump they were hiding behind. "Ask him if he has a line of fire on Skysniper's revetment now that half the jungle has been burned down."

"Stepanshuk says he has line of sight, but he doesn't believe the RPG rocket will penetrate the revetment."

Bolan scowled and spoke into his mike. "Burton, how thick is that barricade?"

"I didn't get a good look at it, but I think at least three bags thick. The laser rose and then went down again. It's on some kind of hydraulic mount."

Bolan took a long slow breath. He put down his scout rifle and pulled the Westley Richards rifle around on its makeshift sling. He checked the .600-caliber high-explosive loads. They were going to have to make the laser rise again. To do that, they were going to have to draw its fire.

"Valentina, tell Stepanshuk I want him to fire the RPG at the revetment and then charge. When the laser rises, tell them to find cover if they can. I'm going to move in and try to put one of these bullets into the firing assembly when the laser exposes itself."

"You will all be cut down in milliseconds," Svarzkova stated.

Bolan nodded and shoved the second elephant rifle at her. "Probably. You're going to stay down. The minute the laser stops firing, I want you to pop up and see if you can hit the weapon with this. It's going to kick like a mule and I doubt you will have time for a second shot. So take an extra second to aim and make your first shot a good one. You won't have to hit the main lens. Aim at the biggest point you can put your sight on. There's enough high explosive in the round to knock the weapon's optics out of alignment even if you don't hit anything vital. After that, send a burst transmission to Kinshasa. A B-2 bomber is orbiting out over the Atlantic with a tanker. It will be here in less than an hour to clean house from high altitude."

"This is suicide."

"Just do it."

Svarzkova's arctic-blue eyes stared into Bolan's own. The morning was getting brighter by the moment. "Very well." She relayed the message to Stepanshuk.

Bolan gave Burton the news. The CIA man didn't seem surprised. "What would you like me to do?"

"I don't know, whatever comes natural."

Svarzkova leaned close again. "Stepanshuk is ready. He says

the last firing of Skysniper was a three-second burn. He suspects the laser is dangerously hot.''

Bolan slung the scout rifle and hefted the massive double-barreled elephant gun. ''Tell Stepanshuk he is a go.''

''Go!'' Svarzkova shouted.

A pair of AK-74s snarled into life from the Russian position. The Kord riflemen fired back. A Russian suddenly rose with the RPG-7 across his shoulder. The rocket hissed from its launch tube. He was cut down a second later.

The rocket flew through the steaming and burning tree trunks and struck the revetment. Orange fire blossomed and fragments flew through the jungle. Rifle fire arced back and forth. Bolan moved forward at a crouch.

Nemanja didn't know that was their only rocket, and he couldn't afford to let the Russians pound away at his position. An ugly black tube rose over the edge of the barricade faster than Bolan would have thought possible. It didn't immediately aim at the Russians on the perimeter of the camp. Bolan snarled as he shouldered his weapon and sighted down the twin barrels. Nemanja had figured out their strategy. Skysniper stared straight at Bolan and burst into blue life.

Bolan squeezed his trigger and threw himself down.

Foliage hissed and burned as besieged trees burst outward and burned anew. Bolan hugged the dirt and heard the tearing noise of the laser destroying steam, dust and flying particles in the air. Heat seared the back of Bolan's neck as the beam cleared him by inches. The laser whipped about its arc and burned at the Russians.

Bolan jumped up and brought the rifle to bear.

Burton had risen. One arm hung limp at his side. The other was cocked back with a white-phosphorus grenade in hand. The laser whipped back instantly. Burton desperately hurled himself up into the air in an attempt to leap over the beam as it scythed toward him.

Burton's knee exploded and his lower leg flew away from his knee. The CIA man fell twisting to the ground back behind the tree trunk he had been using for cover.

Bolan dropped without being able to get off a shot. Svarzkova hadn't had enough time, either. The beam sizzled over Bolan's body by a foot.

He was below the arc of the weapon as long as he stayed flat on his belly. Bolan rolled behind a thick burning stump as rifle fire reached for him. "Burton!"

The CIA man's voice trembled with shock. "I'm okay. I think...I mean, my leg's gone. Jesus, my leg...it's cauterized, but it's...gone."

"Sit tight! If you lay low, below the beam, I'll get to you!"

"Jesus, my leg is gone."

"Sit tight! I'll get you!" Bolan said as he tried to figure out just how he was going to do that.

The Dragunov fired behind Bolan on rapid semiauto. Kords around the laser fell. Svarzkova shouted above the gunfire as she charged. "That was another three-second burst! Laser must be overheating! Attack!"

Bolan rose to one knee. It was as good a plan as any. Getting the Kords to blow up their own laser was as good a plan as any.

The two surviving Russians rose and threw hand grenades as they came. Bolan fired his remaining high-explosive round and rose with the Redhawk revolver in his hand. A Kord was firing his weapon. A bullet smashed into Bolan's armor and he put the front sight of the Ruger revolver into the offending muzzle-flash and fired. He clawed a grenade from his belt.

Bolan charged straight at the revetment.

23

"Fire the laser!"

"Commander!" Kolov's voice rose to a hysterical scream. "Laser temperature is critical!"

Nemanja looked back. Even in the wan light he could see ripples of heat rising through the air off the laser's lens assembly. The weapon itself ticked and popped like the hood of an over-heating car.

A sandbag on the lip of the revetment burst as an explosive projectile hit it. Sand sprayed in all directions. The Russians outside fired their weapons continuously. Smoke and fog was no defense against their night-vision equipment. Every time one of Nemanja's men fired, he was shot down. They weaved their way in, killing as they came.

Nemanja flinched as a grenade skidded and detonated on the edge of the barricade. Fragments whizzed through the air but most were diverted upward. Skysniper stood miraculously untouched, but the invaders were within hand-grenade range.

Nemanja seized Kolov by his shirtfront. "Fire the laser!"

The technician was wide-eyed with terror. "You'll kill us all!"

Nemanja rammed Kolov against the sandbags. Inspiration suddenly struck the commander. "Fire the LADAR! Maximum intensity! Strobe it at maximum speed! Three-hundred-and-sixty-degree arcs!"

Kolov blinked. "Yes."

Nemanja hurled the scientist at the control panel. Kolov's fingers flicked across the key pad. The laser's optical sight clicked on and fed the information to the computer. A window in Kolov's display lit up with a real-time view of what the optical sight saw. The hydraulic legs of the weapon mount whined, and Skysniper rose smoothly over the edge of the revetment. It still clicked and popped and heat washed off of it, but the weapon smoothly rose to the fight. Nemanja grinned to himself. He had been fairly sure he had committed every known war crime. He was about to be the first man to commit a fairly recent one.

The screen on the display showed the devastation of the camp. It showed people firing rifles at the revetment. A woman ran forward with her arm drawn back to throw a grenade.

"LADAR is ready!" Kolov shouted.

"Fire!"

BOLAN CHARGED IN.

The ruptured bodies of Mukantabana's men littered the battlefield. None had survived having their insides blown out and boiled. Svarzkova dropped to one knee and fired her Dragunov. Her nightscope cut through the mist and smoke, and she killed the Kords who still fought from outside the revetment.

The Executioner tossed his grenade and snarled as it hit the edge of the stronghold and detonated upward. Bolan whipped Burton's shotgun around on its sling. A rifle fired out of a foxhole at the Russians, and Bolan fired a pattern of buckshot into it. The Russians started hurling grenades. They were almost within the lethal range of their own weapons but they charged onward heedlessly. Bolan yanked his shotgun upward.

The lethal eye of Skysniper rose over the revetment. The main lens glinted as morning light reflected off of it. It glared straight at Bolan. The Executioner put the gold bead of the shotgun's front sight on the weapon's lens.

Rifle fire erupted almost right in front Bolan.

A long burst of fire from a battle rifle walked up Bolan's chest. Heavy bullets hammered him and his boots slid in mud as he was knocked off his feet. A pale blue beam passed only inches from his face as he fell.

Svarzkova screamed in agony behind him.

A rifleman rose from his hiding place. He was swiftly ejecting the spent magazine from his FN rifle and stuffing in a new one. Bolan raised the Browning Auto-5 in one hand and fired. The shotgun twisted and recoiled out of his grip. The rifleman shuddered and mud flew off of him as he took the full pattern of buckshot in the chest.

The battlefield was suddenly deafeningly quiet.

Bolan ran a hand over his chest. He felt like he had been beaten with a sledgehammer. Wetness covered his chest but he couldn't tell if it was mud or blood. Bolan deliberately took a long deep breath. His lungs burned as his aching ribs expanded. His armor had held.

Bolan looked backward. From his angle he could see Svarzkova lying in the dirt between the bodies of two of Mukantabana's men. A fold in the ground and a fallen tree hid her from the men behind the revetment. Bolan reached out for the fallen shotgun and pulled it to him.

"Valentina!"

The GRU captain lay curled clutching her face and shuddering in pain.

"Val!"

Rifle bullets struck the stump Bolan was using for cover. Svarzkova looked up. She cupped her left eye with one hand. Tears streamed from the right, but her cobalt-blue gaze met Bolan's. Except for grease and mud, her face looked unscathed. The look on her face was terrible, but she nodded at him that she was all right. Bolan's face twisted as he realized what had happened.

Nemanja had fired the LADAR.

The LADAR was Skysniper's aiming laser. It was a tiny fraction as powerful as the main weapon, but it was still an incredibly focused beam of coherent light, capable of tracking satellites orbiting miles above the earth. The LADAR wasn't powerful enough to burn a man in half. It wasn't even powerful enough to set a piece of paper on fire.

But the beam was bright enough to burn out the light receptors of any human eye that looked into it.

Svarzkova pulled a field dressing out of her web gear and

began winding it around her head in an eye patch. She tied it off and pulled her Dragunov rifle to her.

Bolan tapped his earpiece and spoke into his mike. "Burton, you still with us?"

"Yeah." The CIA man's voice was weak but steady. "Have we won yet?"

"No. Not yet."

"God...damn it..."

"Nemanja is aiming LADAR as a blinding weapon. Valentina's down. I don't know about the Russians."

"I left my sunglasses on the sub."

Bolan smiled tiredly. "Yeah, me too."

"Well, what do you want to do?"

"What kind of shape are you in?"

"Well, I'm kind of a mess. The laser cauterized the leg and I've tied it off. Everything below the knee is laying in the dirt about a yard away. I got a hole through my left shoulder, so I can't raise my arm over my head. I've still got one frag grenade and one of the white phosphorous you gave me. I managed to reload my revolver. I suppose I can flop over this stump and take a few potshots at the revetment. After that it's just me and my machete."

"That may be enough," Bolan stated. "Val, can you shoot?"

Svarzkova had her left eye covered with her field dressing. Her right eye was red and still streamed tears. She shook her head. "I can't use the optical sight."

Bolan reared up and threw her the shotgun. "Trade me!"

The Dragunov sailed end over end at Bolan and bounced off a body. Bolan snagged the sling with his boot as bullets tore the ground around the rifle stump.

"Give me the elephant gun, too!"

Burton fired off to the left. Bullets whined back in response. Two spare magazines for the Dragunov slapped down in the mud near Bolan seconds later. The Executioner checked the Russian rifle and shoved the spare magazines into his web gear.

"How many smoke grenades do you have?"

"One."

Bolan only had one himself. "Pop smoke. Then toss the white phosphorus."

"You sure want me to waste it as a screen? It's the last we have."

"Yeah, I do."

"You got it."

Bolan pulled his pin and tossed his grenade. It bounced near the revetment and began belching out green marking smoke. Burton's smoke grenade joined it a few yards away. The white phosphorus followed and the jungle dawn erupted in streamers of yellow fire and white smoke.

Svarzkova nodded as she saw what was happening. She threw her own smoke grenade farther off. Marking smoke, white phosphorus, the smoke of burning trees and fog mixed together to make a hellish landscape in the twisted and burning jungle.

Bolan rose and ran wide. He yanked the brim of his forage cap low over his face and kept his eyes on the ground.

Bolan ran for his life. His shoulders tensed as the LADAR played over him. Bolan plunged into a bank of green marking smoke, and the coherent light broke as it struck millions of smoke particles. Bolan held his breath as he ran around to flank the revetment. The shotgun roared and Burton's Ruger boomed twice. Russian AK-74s opened up off to the east. Svarzkova must have gotten them on the radio. Even blinded, they still fired their weapons.

The Executioner ran in with the elephant rifle in his hands. He hurdled a dead Kord and his boots hit the sandbags. Bolan ran up them like stairs. He could see the muzzle-flashes of riflemen firing on the other side of the revetment. A man lurched up with a rifle in his hand, his eyes flaring as Bolan suddenly towered over him.

The elephant rifle boomed.

The barricade was partitioned with beams and sandbags. Mukantabana and three riflemen swung their weapons around. Skysniper was on the other side of the partition. On that side was a pair of metal cylinders with attached hoses that sat in a trailer bed.

Bolan fired his other barrel into a cylinder and dropped.

A high-explosive bullet hit the metal cylinder. The cylinder tore apart and ripped into its twin. Two hundred gallons of pressurized liquid nitrogen flew in all directions. Bolan slid back down the face of the revetment as the mist and fog above instantly turned to ice crystals and rained down on him. Something wet splattered against the barrels of his elephant rifle, and Bolan winced as more wetness splashed against his back.

The Executioner waited a full second for the sensation of cold, but the horrible burning didn't come. Bolan pressed upward off of the sandbags and then began climbing again. The Dragunov rifle slung across his back cracked in half and fell in two pieces behind him. Bolan heard the back of his body armor crack and break where it had frozen. He tossed the elephant rifle away. The last six inches of blue barrels had turned gray. They shattered off as the rifle clattered to the ground.

Bolan drew his .44 Magnum revolver and moved to the edge of the revetment. Everything inside was sheeted in ice. Fog and mist over the barricade still turned to tiny snow crystals and fluttered down through the jungle, and thick white fog rose as the spilled liquid nitrogen began reacting with the air.

Moses Mukantabana stood with a .357 Magnum pistol in his hand, pointed at Bolan. Mukantabana stood absolutely motionless. His huge form had taken on a bluish-white sheen. The ice beneath his boots cracked with his unbalanced weight. Mukantabana fell backward in his pose as stiff as a statue.

The big man cracked in half like glass as he hit the corner of the trailer bed.

His arms snapped off and the crystallized corner of the trailer broke away from his weight hitting it. The rest of his body cracked and fractured inward as it hit the ground. His boots still stood where his body had cracked off at the ankles. The liquid nitrogen had plunged his body to 250 degrees below zero. He had been instantly crystallized.

Suddenly Skysniper rose over the partition.

The weapon steamed and clicked as heat distorted the air around it. It stared at Bolan like death itself.

Bolan punched the Ruger Redhawk forward in both hands. He

ignored the main laser and squared his sights into the smaller lens of the LADAR. The .44 Magnum roared and the 240-grain lead hollowpoint shattered the LADAR's lens inward and ripped outward from the base of its shaft. Bolan whipped his sights onto the main laser and squeezed the trigger.

The big pistol bucked in his hand.

A black hole the size of a quarter appeared in the main lens. The rest of the lens went opaque as the thick glass spiderwebbed. Bolan pulled his last frag grenade and threw it.

The grenade detonated as Bolan ran through the choking smoke. A hissing filled the air, followed by a loud pop. Bolan threw himself behind a smoking stump.

Skysniper's breached fuel cells detonated.

Fire ripped up into the air as if the sandbag revetment were some colossal model of a volcano. Much of Skysniper and its peripheral gear flew up into the sky with it. Burning sheets of chemical fire rained back down like ribbons of liquid flame. The barricade had contained and shaped the explosion to send the fire shooting straight up.

Bolan rose and ran as fast as his legs could carry him. He ran to where Svarzkova crouched and dived in behind her.

"I think we got it."

Svarzkova sighed wearily. "Good."

Bolan glanced over their cover. Clouds of burning black smoke, green marking smoke and white phosphorus crawled through the ruined jungle. Trees burned everywhere, reflecting off the smoke in lurid oranges and reds.

Outside the circle of hellish devastation, the morning sun's light pierced the jungle with golden-yellow shafts.

Bodies lay everywhere.

Bolan opened the Ruger's cylinder and dropped in six fresh rounds. He rose and walked over to Burton. The CIA man leaned against his cover with his own revolver on his lap.

"Did we win yet?"

"Yeah, I think we did."

"Good."

Bolan reached out his arm. "I'll carry you."

Bolan took Burton's arm and bent to sling him across his shoulders in a fireman's carry. Svarzkova walked past them to the eastern side of the camp. Bolan followed her slowly with his burden. He kept his eyes open for stray Kords.

Svarzkova called out, "Igor!"

"I'm here." The senior lieutenant rose awkwardly. Both his eyes were covered by a field dressing.

"Igor! No!" Svarzkova screamed.

She ran to her ex-husband and clutched his face. They murmured to one another, and then she turned to Bolan. "Will it be permanent?"

Bolan shook his head. "I don't know. I don't know the wattage of the LADAR. Only time will tell."

Stepanshuk ran a hand over her face. "You have lost an eye."

She smiled beneath his hand. "One will have to do for both of us."

"What happened to Stepanshuk's other man?"

Svarzkova spoke quietly to her ex-husband and then turned. "He fought as long as he could. Then he bled to death."

"Get on the radio. Tell Kinshasa that the mission is accomplished."

Svarzkova gave her call sign to the American Embassy and spoke in English. "Skysniper is destroyed. Kords are destroyed. We have taken heavy casualties and have wounded. We're extracting."

Burton wheezed tiredly over Bolan's shoulder. "Can we get the hell out of here now?"

"No."

Burton raised his eyebrows. "No?"

Bolan considered the carnage he'd seen at the revetment, and the carnage he hadn't. "There's one last thing that needs taking care of."

Burton sagged. "Nemanja isn't dead yet."

"I haven't seen his body."

"So what are you going to do?"

"I'm going to hunt him down."

"He knows the territory. You don't," the CIA man argued.

"I'm going to use bait."

"Jesus!" Burton was appalled. "You're going to offer yourself up to the bastard as bait!"

Bolan shook his head as he picked his scout rifle out of the mud. "No, actually, I'm going to use you," Bolan said as he held out his loaded revolver.

Burton took the Ruger in his good hand and stared at the big man. "You're a real peach, you know that."

BRANKO NEMANJA HID behind a charred stump and watched his enemies. His left hand had deep chemical burns. It throbbed constantly. His right hand itched for a weapon. His Krinkov was back in the revetment, and his pistol lay on the ground covered with the same volatile chemicals that had burned his hand. There were rifles scattered around, but he would have to scout the battlefield to find them, and with only one hand he couldn't manage a full-size FN battle rifle. Nemanja yearned for a weapon. The Serb's lips split back into an ugly smile.

He examined his enemies again with the eyes of a trained killer.

The giant Russian was blind, and the woman who supported him was half-blind. The black man was crippled, and the big American carried him like a sack of potatoes over his shoulder.

They were ripe for the taking.

And he had a weapon.

Murder moved behind Nemanja's smoke-reddened eyes. He was a Kord. he had formed the Kords, and he had murdered more men than he could count. His hand moved to his web belt and closed around the horn grips of his dagger. It was the ancient weapon of the Serbs. In the olden days every man who counted himself a warrior had carried a *kord*. The seventeen-inch blade was more a short sword than a dagger.

The gleaming dagger slid silently from its sheath.

Nemanja held the blade low along his leg as he broke into a loping run through the burning trees. He lost sight of his enemies for a moment as he moved through a fog of white phosphorus and green marking smoke.

He snarled and came to a halt.

The giant Russian carried the black man. The woman led the two of them toward the path through the minefield.

The American had disappeared.

MACK BOLAN MOVED through the smoke and fog. He had taken Burton's web gear but left the wounded party the remaining handguns. Bolan squinted against the heat as he stepped around a great hardwood tree that burned like a torch. Everything was smoke and fire. The stink of burned bodies, rocket propellant and the burning chemicals that had fueled Skysniper's wrath was almost unendurable. Everywhere the ground was littered with bullet-riddled bodies and the Executioner checked each one he came across. Those that hadn't been shot had been instantly boiled and burst by the laser in a death too horrible to contemplate. The few wounded and dying moaned and howled their torment up into the smoke-darkened dawn.

The man who had created this killing field was still out there.

Suddenly Bolan's every instinct told him he was being hunted.

The Executioner whirled at a slight sound.

An object skidded into the mud at his feet.

It was the squat beer-bottle shape of a Russian RGD-5 anti-personnel grenade.

Bolan hurled himself through a thicket of burning foliage. Fire rose around him, and then he was clear. There was nothing beneath him and he kept falling. His head struck the edge of the foxhole and his arms and legs shot out instinctively to slow his fall. A dead body broke his fall six feet below. Behind him the grenade detonated with a sound like a whip cracking.

Bolan shook the pulsing purple lights from his eyes. Blood was coursing down his face. He seized his rifle and vaulted upward despite his dizziness. The foxhole had saved his life, but he was a fish in a barrel to anyone who had a gun or another grenade.

Bolan led with his weapon as he came out of the hole.

To his right a great glittering blade blurred down at him.

Bolan raised his rifle.

The short sword sheared through the floorplate of the scout's magazine and bit into the steel of its body. The rifle bucked and recoiled in Bolan's hands as it fired. He ripped the rifle free, and the Serb sliced at him again.

Nemanja didn't cut at Bolan's body or head. His dagger sliced at Bolan's fingers where they held his rifle.

The scout rifle spun in Bolan's hands with precision.

Nemanja jerked his hand away as the rifle barrel whipped at his wrist. The glittering blade in his hand rang like a bell as the scout rifle's barrel connected with it. Bolan spun the rifle back up and thrust. He had no bayonet, but the nineteen-inch barrel rammed into Nemanja's midriff.

Bolan snarled as his muzzle met body armor.

The force of the blow shoved Nemanja back, and Bolan took the split second to work the rifle's bolt. It barely moved a quarter of an inch. The magazine had been nearly sheared in half down the middle. The magazine spring had been cut and the cartridges were stacked out of alignment. The rifle was hopelessly jammed.

Bolan flung the rifle in Nemanja's face.

The Serb blocked the rifle with his left arm, and it spun away into the burning underbrush. Nemanja grinned at the feebleness of the attack.

Nemanja's smile faded. Throwing the rifle hadn't been an act of desperation.

It had been a diversion.

Bolan reached over his shoulder.

Burton's machete slid free of its sheath with a rasp. Bolan's own fighting knife came out his web gear with the ring of stainless steel.

The two men glared at one another with smoke-reddened eyes. Cold steel filled their hands.

Nemanja screamed and lunged.

Bolan held his ground. Nemanja stopped short, and his neck muscles bulged. Bolan snapped his head downward, and the spittle meant for his eyes splattered the bill of his forage cap. He slapped his machete out to cover Nemanja's blade and moved the tanto knife sideways to cut across the top of Nemanja's wrist.

The two men leaped away simultaneously as they cut at each other's hands. Their blades rang as they parried. Nemanja twisted his wrist and his blade slid across Bolan's like a serpent. The fabric of Bolan's blacksuit parted and he felt the burn of steel. The blow was weak, but the *kord* was almost supernaturally sharp as it sliced.

Blood welled up out of Bolan's forearm from a cut that would take twenty stitches to close.

Nemanja danced back from Bolan's return blow smiling. The dagger glittered and twisted in his hand as he began to circle for the kill. They were both wearing body armor and any body blow would be chancy at best. The head and the limbs were the primary targets, and Nemanja had struck first and well. He was the better knife fighter of the two of them, and they both knew it. Both also knew it was a matter of scant seconds before Bolan could no longer wield the machete.

Bolan raised his tanto between them in his left hand.

Nemanja smiled like a shark as blood poured down Bolan's right arm and the machete sagged.

Bolan whipped the machete up for a wild blow with the last of his right arm's strength. Nemanja jumped back and raised his dagger defensively.

Bolan flung the machete with all of his might.

There was no room for the blade to revolve. It flew point first at Nemanja's throat.

Steel rang as the commander blocked the flying blade.

Bolan bore into the Serb in a flying tackle.

Bolan had the weight advantage, and he drove Nemanja back. The two men rammed into a tree trunk with a bone-jarring impact. The *kord* was pinned between them. Nemanja ripped it upward. Bolan's chin and cheek split, and the blade passed millimeters from his eyes and he wedged his face against the Serb's neck.

Nemanja's mistake was fatal. He had raised his right arm to cut Bolan.

Bolan rammed his tanto blade into the Serb's unarmored armpit.

The razor-sharp seven-inch blade sank in to the hilt.

Nemanja gasped and his body locked as the steel invaded it. Bolan reared his injured face back and snapped his forehead between the Serb's eyes. Nemanja's head flew back from the blow.

Bolan pulled the tanto free and thrust again. The armor-piercing point punched through Branko Nemanja's right eye socket and entered his brain.

The Serb commander's left eye crossed to stare at the intruding object. His body sagged. Bolan released the hilt of his bone-wedged fighting knife and shoved the commander away from him.

The Serb's dead body crumpled to the floor of the jungle.

Bolan shakily pulled a field dressing from his web gear and began wrapping it around his arm. He grimaced and tried to move his hand. The wound burned and his fingers ached with the pain of damaged muscles and tendons, but his digits wiggled to his will. The nerves hadn't been cut.

Bolan bent to pick up his scout rifle and slung it around his shoulders. A few yards away he found an FN rifle and crooked it in his left arm. The battle was won.

But he wasn't free from the hellgound—yet.

The

24

Congo River

"Well, ain't life a bitch," Burton said, shaking his head tiredly.

The current was with them and the boat they had commandeered was making good time down the river. Now six boats the size of their own or larger were coming up the Congo at them. Each was filled with men carrying rifles.

"What is it?" Stepanshuk asked.

Bolan flicked off the scout rifle's safety. He had removed its damaged magazine and loaded his spare. He pulled the FN assault rifle he had picked up on his way out of camp. "We've got about sixty of Mukantabana's men coming upriver at us."

Senior Lieutenant Stepanshuk grinned beneath the field dressing covering his eyes. "The Popsicle's revenge."

Burton burst out laughing.

Svarzkova's one eye narrowed. "What is a Popsicle?"

Stepanshuk explained it to her and she giggled. The gallows humor was flying thick. The four of them knew they were about to die.

Stepanshuk held out his hands. "Give me a rifle and point me in the correct direction."

Burton took an AK-74 from a bench and handed it to the Russian. "Just stick next to me. I'll shove your muzzle where it needs to be."

"Thank you," he said, taking the rifle with pleasure. He

seemed just as pleased to die fighting as live blind. Burton drew his .44 Magnum from his belt.

"I wish I had my Dragunov," Svarzkova said as she took up a rifle.

Bolan brought the scout to his left shoulder awkwardly. He had dismounted the night-vision scope and reattached the two-power scope once the boat had gotten under way. He wrapped the sling around his wounded arm and took aim at the lead boat. "Valentina, take the wheel."

She took the wheel and laid her rifle across the lip of the wooden cockpit. "Which way? Forward or back?"

"Forward," Stepanshuk's voice rumbled determinedly.

Bolan nodded. "Forward. There's nothing behind us but more of Mukantabana's camps." He jerked his head downriver. "Kinshasa is that way."

Svarzkova shoved the throttles forward. Bolan steadied himself in the surging boat and took careful aim.

Svarzkova's field radio crackled. A voice spoke in Russian. The captain's one eye opened wide as she snatched up the transmitter. She spoke rapidly and then clicked off. She grinned up at Bolan as she cut the engine.

"We have fish in the water?"

"Yes. It isn't good for us to make engine noises at this moment."

One of the boats ahead blew up in spectacular fashion. Bodies and chunks of boat flew up into the air. A second and third boat blew up, and then the remaining river craft hit their throttles and began weaving in all directions. Men dived out of the boats and into the water as another boat was blown to splinters. The fifth boat blew and the sixth turned about to charge back the way it had come.

Three long black shapes rode low in the water before it. All three opened up with the RPK machine guns mounted on their conning towers. Men behind the machine gunners fired their 30 mm grenade launchers.

The last boat's engine died and smoke rose from its riddled ruins.

Bolan watched a dark shape flash by underneath the water. It traveled another fifty yards upriver, and then water erupted upward in a geyser as it exploded.

The radio crackled again and more words were spoken in Russian. Svarzkova started the engine again. "All torpedoes have now detonated. We are safe to move ahead."

The boat pulled up slowly to the Russian midget subs. The machine gunner on the lead boat waved and then awkwardly crawled back down into the hold. Bolan was startled as a man rose to take his place. Svarzkova shouted with joy.

General Ozhimkov stood in the conning tower.

The boat pulled to a halt. Svarzkova yelled at Stepanshuk, and both of the Russians saluted.

Bolan set down his rifle. "I had been led to believe you were dead, General."

Ozhimkov squinted against the bright African sun. "It was useful for me to appear that way. I have an opposite number, formerly of KGB internal security, who is roughly of my build. He made his reputation killing Soviet citizens for the Communist Party during the cold war. I decided it was time for him to serve his country."

"They said you had been shot in the face with a shotgun and had been identified by your dental records."

The lines on Ozhimkov's face threatened to fracture as they rearranged themselves in an uncharacteristic smile. "The KGB scum wore false teeth." He tapped his incisors. "So do I."

"I'm glad to see you alive, General."

Ozhimkov nodded. "It was quite liberating being dead, and allowed me to move unseen. I had myself flown to the Kirov in the Atlantic and then to a submarine off of Africa. There are few better places to hide than in a nuclear attack submarine."

Bolan knew all about being dead. He had been pronounced dead or captured more times than he could count. "You were the cleanup crew in case we didn't succeed."

"We didn't have time to join up with you once you and Captain Svarzkova were already on the river, and we thought it inadvisable to try to contact you. It might have warned our enemies.'' The grin broke out on the old man's face again. ''I'm glad you have succeeded.''

The general looked about and his smile faded. ''You are all that is left?''

Svarzkova nodded. ''Casualties were ninety percent, General.''

''We have a medic on board. I'll have him embark on your boat and see to the wounded.''

The Russians began awkwardly getting men up and down the conning towers. Svarzkova's hand crept into Bolan's and gave it a squeeze. Bolan squeezed back. The two of them looked back the way they had come. Plumes of smoke rose out of the jungle into the blue African sky a few miles behind them.

The new millenium wasn't proving to be any easier than the one just past.

**A journey through the dangerous frontier
known as the future...**

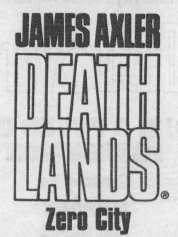

JAMES AXLER

DEATH LANDS ®

Zero City

Hungry and exhausted, Ryan and his band emerge from
a redoubt into an untouched predark city, and uncover a
cache of weapons and food. Among other interlopers,
huge winged creatures guard the city. Holed up inside
an old government building, where Ryan's son, Dean,
lies near death, Ryan and Krysty must raid where a local
baron uses human flesh as fertilizer....

On sale December 2000 at your favorite retail outlet. Or order your copy now by
sending your name, address, zip or postal code, along with a check or money order
(please do not send cash) for $5.99 for each book ordered ($6.99 in Canada),
plus 75¢ postage and handling ($1.00 in Canada), payable to Gold Eagle Books, to:

In the U.S.	In Canada
Gold Eagle Books	Gold Eagle Books
3010 Walden Ave.	P.O. Box 636
P.O. Box 9077	Fort Erie, Ontario
Buffalo, NY 14269-9077	L2A 5X3

Please specify book title with order.
Canadian residents add applicable federal and provincial taxes.

GDL52

Gold Eagle brings you high-tech action and mystic adventure!

THE Destroyer™

#121 A POUND OF PREVENTION

Created by
MURPHY
and SAPIR

Organized crime lords are converging in the East African nation of Luzuland, for what looks like an underworld summit. Remo—with his own problems—is just not in the mood to be killing his way up the chain of command in East Africa. Chiun has gone AWOL, and unless he can beat some sense into his pupil's skull, Remo's bent on nuking a mob-infested Third World city to deliver a pound of prevention to wipe out a generation of predators....

Available in October 2000 at your favorite retail outlet.

Or order your copy now by sending your name, address, zip or postal code, along with a check or money order (please do not send cash) for $5.99 for each book ordered ($6.99 in Canada), plus 75¢ postage and handling ($1.00 in Canada), payable to Gold Eagle Books, to:

In the U.S.	In Canada
Gold Eagle Books	Gold Eagle Books
3010 Walden Ave.	P.O. Box 636
P.O. Box 9077	Fort Erie, Ontario
Buffalo, NY 14269-9077	L2A 5X3

Please specify book title with your order.
Canadian residents add applicable federal and provincial taxes.

GOLD EAGLE®

GDEST121

James Axler

OUTLANDERS®

DOOM DYNASTY

Kane, once a keeper of law and order in the new America, is part of the driving machine to return power to the true inheritors of the earth. California is the opening salvo in one baron's savage quest for immortality—and a fateful act of defiance against earth's dangerous oppressors. Yet their sanctity is grimly uncertain as an unseen force arrives for a final confrontation with those who seek to rule, or reclaim, planet Earth.

On sale November 2000 at your favorite retail outlet. Or order your copy now by sending your name, address, zip or postal code, along with a check or money order (please do not send cash) for $5.99 for each book ordered ($6.99 in Canada), plus 75¢ postage and handling ($1.00 in Canada), payable to Gold Eagle Books, to:

In the U.S.	In Canada
Gold Eagle Books	Gold Eagle Books
3010 Walden Ave.	P.O. Box 636
P.O. Box 9077	Fort Erie, Ontario
Buffalo, NY 14269-9077	L2A 5X3

Please specify book title with order.
Canadian residents add applicable federal and provincial taxes.

GOLD EAGLE®

GOUT15

DON PENDLETON'S

STONY

AMERICA'S ULTRA-COVERT INTELLIGENCE AGENCY

MAN*

DRAGON FIRE

The President orders Stony Man to place its combat teams on full alert when top-secret data for U.S. missile technology is stolen. Tracing the leads to Chinese agents, Phoenix Force goes undercover deep in Chinese territory, racing against time to stop China from taking over all of Asia!

Available in November 2000 at your favorite retail outlet.

Or order your copy now by sending your name, address, zip or postal code, along with a check or money order (please do not send cash) for $5.99 for each book ordered ($6.99 in Canada), plus 75¢ postage and handling ($1.00 in Canada), payable to Gold Eagle Books, to:

In the U.S.

Gold Eagle Books
3010 Walden Avenue
P.O. Box 9077
Buffalo, NY 14269-9077

In Canada

Gold Eagle Books
P.O. Box 636
Fort Erie, Ontario
L2A 5X3

Please specify book title with your order.
Canadian residents add applicable federal and provincial taxes.

GSM49